NO LONGER
PROPERTY OF PPLD

D1006076

RAGTIME COWBOYS

BOOKS BY LOREN D. ESTLEMAN

*A Forge Book

RAGTIME

COWBOYS

LOREN D. ESTLEMAN

A TOM DOHERTY ASSOCIATES BOOK
NEW YORK

This is a work of fiction. All of the characters, organizations, and events
portrayed in this novel are either products of the author's imagination
or are used fictitiously.

RAGTIME COWBOYS

Copyright © 2014 by Loren D. Estleman

All rights reserved.

A Forge Book
Published by Tom Doherty Associates, LLC
175 Fifth Avenue
New York, NY 10010

www.tor-forge.com

Forge® is a registered trademark of Tom Doherty Associates, LLC.

The Library of Congress Cataloging–in–Publication Data
is available upon request.

ISBN 978-0-7653-3454-1 (hardcover)
ISBN 978-1-4668-1338-0 (e-book)

Forge books may be purchased for educational, business, or promotional
use. For information on bulk purchases, please contact Macmillan
Corporate and Premium Sales Department at 1-800-221-7945,
extension 5442, or write specialmarkets@macmillan.com.

First Edition: May 2014

Printed in the United States of America

0 9 8 7 6 5 4 3 2 1

This book is dedicated to Dale L. Walker:
friend, Jack London scholar, and
consummate professional historian,
and to the memories of Russ and Winnie Kingman
and Becky London, whom it was my privilege
to know and love.

The Bible says he who makes two blades of grass to grow where only one grew before has benefited mankind. And that hits Yours Truly.

—Charlie Siringo, *A Cowboy Detective*

"I hope you're satisfied with the way your work got done."
"It got done."

—Dashiell Hammett, *The Dain Curse*

They started gobbling everything in sight like a lot of swine, and while they gobbled democracy went to smash.

—Jack London, *The Valley of the Moon*

PART ONE

FORGOTTEN BUT NOT GONE

Buffalo Bill's defunct.

—e. e. cummings

1

There was nothing wrong with his eyes.

He watched a coyote lift its leg against the base of the HOLLY-WOODLAND sign a quarter-mile away from his window. Men half his age would need binoculars just to identify the animal. And he was watching through stripes the rain made in the chalky dust from the gypsum refinery down the street. It was like trying to make out his reflection in a mirror streaked with toothpaste.

No, there was nothing wrong with his eyes; but he'd trade one for a new set of joints and one good piss.

Just then the roof sprang a new leak. The water broke through in a sudden trickle—just the way his pizzle worked, when it worked—and splattered one of the few dry spots of floor left. Other holes, some as big as a man's fist, had rusted their way through the galvanized iron, letting the water pour into pots, pans, and a Hog Heaven lard bucket. He was running out of containers. Casting about, he spotted the blue enamel camp coffeepot on the woodstove. He'd been using it to heat water since his electricity was turned off, but his wash-up could wait till the sun came out. He took off the lid, dumped the water into the sink, and placed the pot under the new leak.

He went ahead and emptied all the containers, then pulled

his chair up to the Smith-Premier typewriter that looked like a toy piano, right down to the black and white keys, and listened to the water bing-bonging against metal, like slugs hitting the stove and Dutch oven and soup tins in the line shack in New Mexico where they said Billy Bonney had come to roost in '80. He and the other members of the P.C. had clobbered the place with long rounds and buckshot for three quarters of an hour before somebody got the bright idea to go down and check the place out. All he found was a lot of ruined gear and a dead armadillo that had chosen the wrong day to crawl in out of the heat.

When an animal expert told him armadillos were unknown north of Mexico before 1900, he'd said, "Well, maybe that critter we cooked and ate was a possum with a bad case of shingles."

He stuffed his pipe to smoke out the mildew stink. His pouch leaked tobacco. Buffalo scrotum wore like iron, but nothing lasted forever, including the beast itself. He raised the chimney from the lamp and held the bowl bottom-side up over the flame, drawing on the stem. Once it got going, there was no excuse for delay. He cranked the platen and read what he'd written; sat back, folding his arms and puffing up gales of smoke, then tore loose the sheet and threw it in a tight ball into the Hello Sunshine crate he used for a trash bin. The oranges on the label went on smiling their asses off. They didn't give a shit.

He wore his daily uniform of blue flannel shirt—the roomy pockets were good for tobacco and extra cartridges—whipcords, and Arapaho moccasins: dependable range wear he preferred to any suit of clothes made to his measure in St. Louis. The creature comforts were all a man cared about at the finish.

He tried again, rolling in a new sheet and stabbing the keys with two fingers:

"Kid" Curry had a cross-eye and you never knew whether he was shooting at you or someone else until the slug hit home.

He shook his head again and sent that page after the last. There wasn't anything wrong with what he wrote, just with the subject. He was plumb written out on the Wild Bunch. Once he put a memory on paper it ceased to be real, as if it was a story someone else had told him. Considering how many books he'd written, he was on the point of rubbing out his entire life. Maybe that was what happened when a fellow got old and forgetful, not remembering if he'd eaten and disgracing himself in his pants. Maybe they were all memoirists.

The only time things came back to him, really came back like he was watching them from the front row of a picture house, was when he dreamed, or when something familiar brought them bearing down on him like the *Sunset Limited*, which was dreaming too, he decided. But when he reached for them on purpose, they were as dead as Old Man Pinkerton, the only person in history ornery enough to have bitten himself to death.

He sat back again, puffing tobacco and scraping his gaze along the shelf of his books for inspiration. Water stained, every one. Could've been worse; he'd just gotten them out from under the last new leak before they soaked up enough to swell up like a dead steer.

No help there. They were headstones erected over the graves of murdered memories.

He wondered what Ince was up to.

The man had been a pest in the old days, sending him weekly wires pleading for permission to make a picture play out of one of his titles. But he'd been proud then, not wanting to see some jasper with painted lips and false eyelashes prancing around in front of a camera pretending to be him, and eventually Ince had gotten tired of being turned down and stopped writing. A year ago, that was: He couldn't believe it was 1921. Now he'd sell him the whole bunch for the cash to fix the roof. Tomorrow he'd run down to the library and see if he was listed in the directory.

Then all he'd need was a nickel for the phone.

He disregarded the knock at first, thinking it was a new note courtesy of the rain; as the receptacles filled, the pitch changed. If he were musically inclined, he'd have experimented by moving them around, raising or lowering the levels of the water, reaching for some tune he recognized. It was no more a waste of time than trying to coax a story out of his worn-out brain, and might have gotten him a job in vaudeville.

When it came again, he got up, threw a rubberized cover over the typewriter in case another leak opened up above it, and went to the door, scooping up his old brown Colt on the way. Los Angeles was filled with Mexicans fleeing the failure of the revolution, and the elderly were the favorite prey of banditti looking for grubstakes.

"Who's there?" He had to shout to be heard through the thick panels. The rain had stepped up, clanging on the iron roof and striking the drip-catchers hard enough to slap water off the surfaces onto the floor.

"Oh, let me in, Charlie. I'm wet through."

He couldn't tell if the voice was familiar, but at least it came without a Spanish accent. He slid back the heavy bolt and opened the door three inches, thumbing back the Colt hammer in the same motion.

The face was leaner than he remembered, gaunt, the handlebars white, the strong jowls loose now and wobbly. A pair of brows still dark but growing wild drew together over faded gray eyes. "Don't you know me, Charlie? It's Earp."

"I can see that. Which one are you?" They'd looked alike, that whole pack of brothers, and not even a trained detective could tell them apart at a glance. That was one of the reasons there had been so much confusion among the witnesses as to who did what in that mess in Tombstone.

"The one that's left. You going to let me in or cut loose with that dog's hind leg? It gets me out of my misery either way you choose."

"I guess it's the Christian thing to do." He took the revolver off cock and stepped out of the way.

Wyatt Earp—he knew which one it was now, the irritable one nobody liked—stepped inside, took off his drooping slouch hat, and shook water off it onto the foot mat. He looked around the room. "I can't tell if it's wetter inside or out. I'm glad I didn't come to borrow money."

"I chopped them holes myself. I slept under the stars so long I can't get used to any other way."

When Earp bent his head to sweep water off his lapels, the light from the lamp glistened on pink scalp. He'd been vain of his hair when it was yellow, slicking it down with pomade and letting it curl over his collar, but it had quit the field, leaving behind a few pale strands on the crown for seed. "I never could figure what the hell you were talking about half the time. That's one thing hasn't changed."

A humorless man, Siringo recalled now. He'd met a few like him, and had always felt sorry for them, like someone born without arms. But an armless man could train his feet to act as hands. A man who couldn't appreciate how flat-out ridiculous the world was lived every day out of step with existence.

He had trouble feeling sorry for Earp, though. He'd been

meaner than a shithouse rat when he was young, and now that he was old and his looks were gone he was no company.

"I wouldn't turn down a drink."

"I thought you didn't."

"That was before Alaska got into my bones. I keep a fire most days even in summer."

Charlie opened the icebox—doing cabinet duty until he absolutely needed to pop for ice—and hoisted out a demijohn.

"Moonshine?" Earp's handlebars drew down severely.

"It's all moonshine now."

"Just because it's illegal don't mean you have to go blind drinking it."

"I soak my biscuits in it, and I can still pick the eye off a potato at fifty yards. Fellow I arrested in Virginia retired to Barstow a few years back. He drops off a couple of jugs whenever he's in town and we shoot the breeze. It's just a hobby now, so he don't cut it with lye-ball like in the old days." He blew the gypsum dust out of a pair of mismatched tumblers and filled them a third of the way, drawing the cork with his teeth and shouldering the jug.

"You get on with folks you put in jail?"

"He didn't know I wasn't one of him till I slapped on the irons. By then we liked each other too much to turn."

Putting his hat back on—he was still vain, no surprise there—the tall man sat on the edge of Charlie's bed, the springs braying like a donkey, and sniffed at the clear liquid in the glass. "What made a runt like you turn detective, anyway?"

"Head bumps." Charlie grinned at his reaction. He leaned forward in his writing chair and touched his scalp through the fine strands covering it. "Phrenologist in Kansas. He gave my skull the once-over, found a bump of caution and a bump of intelligence, said I'd do all right as a stock raiser or a newspaper editor or a detective. Well, I'd worked with cows all I cared to and I can't spell, so there was just the one thing left."

"You have to spell to write books."

"You'd think so, but no."

"I wouldn't let a stranger grope my head for a double eagle."

"He had nice hands, like a barber's. Oh, he also said I had a stubborn bump big as a mule's."

"That part I believe."

They drank in glum silence.

Siringo wondered what the hell this was all about, but he knew from past experience his guest never answered questions, only barked orders or expressed opinions. The two adventurers had taken a dislike to each other from the first. Siringo, the affable type, had made a specialty of ingratiating himself with outlaws, worming his way into their confidence with tales of shared experiences, cowboy ballads, and the latest jokes from the burly-Q's in St. Louis and San Francisco. Earp, on the other hand, got through to them with the butt end of a Smith & Wesson. And he was half-outlaw himself, with rumors of a horse theft in his past and more recent stories of claim-jumping in the Klondike.

The former detective and the on-again, off-again lawman might have settled their differences with lead long ago, if only their immediate interests had come into conflict.

Earp looked at the shrouded typewriter. "Still scribbling, I see. I gave it a dally myself; I'd rather grade track. Fellow named Lake's been sniffing around asking to write me up. What's the pay like?"

"Oh, I'm rich as Midas. Got a bigger house on the beach with twice as many holes in the roof."

"No good?"

Siringo shifted the conversation away from his poverty. "How's the horse-raising business?"

"I thought it was a gentleman's game, but it's just stable work without regular wages." Earp swirled the liquid in his glass, lifted it to his lips. His Adam's apple worked twice. He shook his shoulders like a bull swarmed by gnats. "Jesus. Sure there's no lye in this?"

"You can't ever tell by the taste. Your gut can, but by that time it's too late."

Earp wasn't listening. He seldom did unless the conversation was about him. "The ranch is what I'm here about, Charlie. I got me a hoss thief."

Poetic, thought Siringo, finishing his own drink. It went down like water.

2

"Where you got this thief?"

"That was just a way of speaking. I don't have him. That's the problem." Earp took a deep breath and let it out. "It's Spirit Dancer."

"That the thief?"

"Hell no, it's a horse. What kind of a name is that for a person?"

"I thought maybe it was an injun or a belly dancer, like Little Egypt." He'd spent most of what he made in Tombstone on dinners and liquor to get to that, and when he did it was a disappointment, as just about everything was after weeks of anticipation. She'd left all her best maneuvers on the stage of the Birdcage Theater. "What's the thief's name?"

"If I knew that, I'd know where the horse is. Will you stop asking about the thief till I tell you what happened?"

"Sorry. Asking questions is a hard habit to get shut of."

"Spirit Dancer's the prettiest filly you ever saw, and lightning on the hoof. I've been three years raising and training her: She's by Gold Dollar out of Treys-Over-Deuces."

Siringo shrugged. "I've rode more horses than I can count. I couldn't tell you any of their names offhand. I always held it a waste of time. They don't come when you call."

"I'm not here for the conversation, Charlie. You never used to chew the rag so much."

"It comes from living alone. Go ahead on."

"Dollar and Deuces are solid winners, trust me on that. I mortgaged the ranch to buy Dancer. I had her all primed for Louisville, and then some son of a bitch stole her right out from under my stable boy's nose. Which is one nose I won't have to look at anymore."

"You fired him?"

"No, I gave him a raise and an oyster dinner at the Ambassador Hotel. Sure I fired him."

"You should of kept him on."

"What in Christ's name for? Shovel shit and keep an eye on the best horse in the string, that was the extent of his responsibilities. All he did was shovel shit, and he wasn't even good at that. He kept tracking it onto the back porch."

"Did you think to ask him who paid him to look south when the filly was going north?"

Earp's face got angriest when he realized he'd made a mistake. Siringo reckoned that admitting it would bring foam to his mouth.

"He didn't have that kind of brains. When you recruit a shit-shoveler, you don't exactly go down the dean's list. This one didn't have sense enough to smoke a cigar by the cold end."

"I spent twenty years of my life tracking train robbers and murderers, and I paid attention. It don't take brains to be a thief."

"I tracked my share."

And shot the wrong ones when you caught up with them; but there was no percentage in dragging up his guest's pitiful record as a lawman.

"Keeping the peace is one thing, finding out who broke it's

another. I don't reckon you know where he went after you let him go."

"I got a wire from a ranch up in Sonoma County yesterday asking about his fitness. The son of a bitch used my name for a reference."

"What did you say?"

"I haven't answered it yet. Josie says I should cool down before I say anything I might regret. She treats me like a horse; I'm surprised she doesn't rub me down with a piece of burlap before she puts me to bed."

Siringo always thought Josephine was too smart for her husband.

"If I was you, I'd paint a pretty picture of the boy, get 'em to hire him on. Then you'll know where he is so you can pump him."

Earp chewed the ends of his handlebars. Finally he nodded.

"It sticks in my craw, but sure. Only if it's me doing the pumping, I might just kill him."

"You're too hotheaded for the job. Fists are no good in detective work. If they're tough it just makes 'em stick down deeper and if they ain't all you get is lies to make it stop. You got to oil a saddle to bring out the grain."

"Well, I'm no hand at that sort of thing. That's why I'm here instead of out beating the brush for my horse."

Siringo pulled on his pipe, found it had gone out. He placed it next to the typewriter to cool.

"I'm out to pasture," he said. "Hire a Pinkerton. I'm down on the outfit since they let me go, but I guess they can still handle horse stealing."

"You quit, the way I heard it. Seems to me I read it in that *Isms* thing you wrote, or as far as I got into it. A gentleman rancher such as myself hasn't a great deal to do but sit around and read, but that one lost me in the tall grass."

He knew the "gentleman rancher" lived off his wife's money, but he wasn't one to judge a man for making his way however he could. Siringo had sniffed around some well-set-up widows after Mamie died, but he'd lost considerable of the looks and charm that had gotten him so far in the past. All he'd been able to throw a loop around was Lillie. That had not ended well; certainly not in riches.

"*Two Evil Isms: Pinkertonism and Anarchism*," he said. "The Agency confiscated every copy. Anyhow, there wasn't much to do after I was fired but go ahead and quit."

"Well, I tried the Pinks in Frisco. They wanted too much up front, with no guarantee they could even turn anything, but a secretary there told me on the Q.T. about this young fellow who sure enough quit them over principles. He had some."

Siringo was prepared to like the man, but he couldn't see Earp being impressed. The next thing he said cleared up the confusion.

"I saw when I met him that was just an excuse. He's a lunger, like old Doc was, rest his soul in hell. The work got too strenuous on a steady basis. He's in the way of being a writer, like you, only the publishers can't see it. He's got a gal who's expecting and he intends to marry her, so he accepted my offer."

"You're all set up, then."

"Hold on. He's got the smarts and experience, but I suspect he's distracted." Earp, who had set down his glass, fashioned an imaginary one from his fist and flipped it toward his mouth. "Just like Doc."

Who was no great loss to posterity. Siringo had hung around killers, but that was all in a day's work. He found them a filthy lot, and too dumb to see they were no better off than if they'd kept the Sixth Commandment. The man sitting on his bed had always seemed to prefer their company over decent men's.

Siringo took a swig from his own glass, which was real enough.

"It happens to the best of us. Last time I got so distracted I woke up in Chihuahua three days later with my ears pierced."

"I know you're just fooling about. You've been at it long enough to know how to walk a straight line under a load." Earp pointed at his drink on the floor at his feet, with one sip gone. "This is as much guzzling as I've done since I landed in jail in '71; I'm a danger when I'm drunk, as much to myself as to anybody, which is why I can't ever go back to Arkansas. But I've seen you drink a party of teamsters under the table and order another round for the trail."

"I was younger then, and the liquor wouldn't strip the hide off a buffalo. I don't know the bootleggers in San Francisco. I'm sixty-five, Earp. I haven't sat a horse in years. The last time I fired that Colt was at a biscuit tin. I missed."

"Who said anything about riding and shooting? All I'm asking you to do is take the train to Frisco and see what he's got. I gave him everything he needed to start. While you're there maybe you can drop in on that ranch and talk to the stable boy. I'll go straightaway from here to Western Union and give 'em such a glowing report they'll want to run him for governor."

"Don't overdo it. They might think he's too good for the job."

"Rain's letting up, Charlie. I can't sit here all day. I got stock to feed, and I'm short-handed one man."

"I gave you my answer."

"I'm asking again."

Siringo squinted up through a hole in the roof. The clouds were sure enough breaking apart; the percussion section inside had slowed to a desultory tinkle, the sound a saloon maestro made killing time until the last drunk was swept out. "When did this horse go missing?"

"Be two weeks tomorrow."

"That's cold tracking."

"I tried it when it was fresh, then lost it in the creek."

"I'm even less interested now than I was the first time."

"If you were always this picky, it's no wonder the Pinks threw you out."

"Your horse is gone, Earp. Sold for breeding stock up in Canada or pickup races down in Mexico."

"There hasn't been any money in Mexico since before the Alamo. You want to profit off that situation, you run her as a ringer under a fresh name back East somewhere and clean up from race to race in hick county fairs. It's a sinful waste of the best three-year-old anyone's seen this century. Next year she'll be over the hill as far as all the big gates are concerned; but without papers it's the only way."

"Well, I don't figure to go from track to track like a tout, getting fresh with strange horses and getting bit doing it."

"You got anything better to do, other than scratch your ass and wait for your house to fall down around your ears?"

"I just started a book."

His guest had never been the type to pursue an argument, not to press a point or even for sport: It was his way or none. He produced a leather folder from the inside breast pocket of his damp suit coat, scribbled in it with a gravity pen, tore loose a sheet, and stuck it at Siringo.

It was a bank draft drawn upon the Marcus family account—his wife's people—in the amount of five hundred dollars.

Siringo took it, waved the ink dry. His heart did a happy little two-step. There was a new roof there, Consolidated Edison made happy, and three months' worth of grub besides. He folded the draft and put it in his shirt pocket behind the scrotum pouch.

"I don't figure it'll hurt to take a look. I'll go to the station in the morning. What's this lunger call himself?"

"Hammett. Dashiell Hammett. It's a nancy sort of a name, but growing up Wyatt didn't hurt me any in the man department."

3

After Earp left, the sun came out, bright as a double eagle. It was as if the man traveled under his own portable overcast. Siringo decided it must be hell to be Wyatt Earp.

He got up, looked out the window, at the wet glisten on the big wooden letters spread across the hills. A dash of water had made startling bursts of color in the shriveled brown bushes that surrounded them; ephemeral things, doomed at birth by the desert, but gay for the moment. It was on such days the developers behind Hollywoodland chose to photograph the scene for their brochures: Salting the mines.

From under the bed his guest had sat on, Charles A. Siringo dragged an old wooden footlocker bound with iron, the name penciled on the lid belonging to a horse soldier long since dead in Nebraska. Dust bunnies stirred awake and rolled off the top.

From the dry-rotted interior he drew a bedroll wrapped in a canvas cover, which when he unbuckled the straps and spread on the bed exhaled a gust of cedar. That smell never failed to catapult him back to Matagorda County, Texas—place of his birth—with the restless cattle bawling all about, the sun lying like a hot flat rock on the back of his neck, dust drifting fine as flour and settling on his sweat, turning his skin to sandpaper.

And with the cedar came the stench of scorched hair and singed flesh as the iron burned the Rancho Grande brand onto yet another bovine haunch.

———

"Oh, there you are, Charlie," said his boss, eyes peering down at him from a tangle of beard like a tumbleweed stuck to his face. "You ought to wear a bell. I near stepped on you."

"No need, Mr. Pierce. I heard them clod-busters coming the second you stepped off the front porch."

Abel Head Pierce—"Shanghai" to his intimates, ever since one of them had compared his six-foot-five-inch frame in Spanish dress and huge Mexican rowels to a Shanghai rooster—threw back his head and roared with laughter.

———

Siringo smiled sourly at the memory. Built on the slight side, with narrow hands and a way of appearing neat in his clothes even after six weeks trailing herds to Kansas, he'd always suspected the rancher kept him on just to serve as his personal court jester. Never mind that he worked as hard as any man in the outfit, and rode up right alongside when Pierce led a party after a gang of rustlers—sometimes straight into an ambush in his rage and eagerness for a fight.

The rancher liked the ruckus so much he'd charge in, pistols blazing, when the easiest thing to do was surround the thieves while they were busy changing the brands and round them up without firing a shot. The lazy bastards always stopped at the first level place and built a fire whose smoke could be seen as far as Houston. There was no detecting in the work, not back then.

Fortunately, Pierce was too big to sit a mustang, and when rich living made him a burden even to his big studs and he took to a buggy, he'd come to see finally that things managed themselves best when he stayed behind, confining his battles to his wife and Mexican servants, who picked fights with him knowing he'd fire them, then hire them back at double wages when he sobered up. It wasn't long after Siringo took charge that the night riders shifted their operations to outfits less likely to dangle them from their own lariats.

People had been underestimating Siringo his whole life. It stung a man's pride, but he acknowledged it had seen him through the fire into old age, when others who stood a head taller and lived twice as loud had been fertilizing the earth for fifty years.

He opened the blanket, its black-and-red checks faded to gray and pink and raddled with moth holes, exposing first his other Colt, a showpiece with gold plate and nacre grips, the mother-of-pearl rubbed by handling to a high finish. He set it aside, to return to its place after he got out what he wanted. The revolver had been presented to him by James McParland, the legendary superintendent of the Pinkerton office in Denver, for his first five years of loyal service, and while Siringo appreciated what it represented, it was only good for the Independence Day parade. Out in the open it caught the sun from every angle and attracted unfriendly fire.

Next he came to his Winchester carbine in its leather scabbard, its brass painted black to cut down on reflection and walnut stock shiny as an outhouse wall where everybody leaned his hand when he pissed. This he propped up in a corner for cleaning, oiling, and loading.

He placed the cleaning kit in its rosewood case and the cardboard box of cartridges on the nightstand, drew the bowie from its chamois sheath, inspected the twelve-inch blade for rust, resheathed it, and laid it on his pillow. The folding spyglass, brass compass, and his lucky rabbit's foot, attached by a cinch ring to his little Forehand & Wadsworth hideout pistol, he laid next to the knife. Then he folded the circus revolver back into the blanket, stowed it and the footlocker back under the bed, locked up, and went to the bank.

The hollow-cheeked clerk behind the wooden cage peered through his spectacles at the draft, holding them like a magnifying lens. He asked him to wait and went through a pebbled-glass door behind the counter marked PRIVATE. Siringo didn't begrudge him for seeking a second opinion; he'd bounced a couple of drafts drawn on the bank in the past.

Waiting, he turned and rested his elbows on the counter, overhearing murmured conversations among customers and employees; memorizing noses, ears, moles, visible scars, and postures; noting the time on the big Regulator clock and even the date on the calendar with its steel-point engraving of the bank's Chicago headquarters, corner foremost like the prow of a big solid dependable ship—he'd known an open-and-shut case to fail in court because the detective on the stand got confused and gave a date that didn't match the day of the week. He did all this without thought, and when he realized he was doing it, it annoyed him, like a retired farmer waking up automatically at four a.m. when there were no cows to milk and no hogs to slop.

"Once a detective, always a detective." Jimmy McParland smiled. "You know, one day last month I jumped out of bed and was half-dressed when it came to me the breakfast appointment I was dressing for belonged to a Molly Maguire who died in prison five years ago."

Jimmy Mac. He wondered what he was up to. Dead, most like, and no wire column to announce it to readers not yet born when he was saving the lives of their grandparents, and who wouldn't recognize the name. It seemed to him most of the addresses he'd written among the floor plans and pornographic doodles in his dilapidated memorandum book should be forwarded to the cemetery. Who was left to lug his own coffin from the parlor to the planting ground?

Then again, wasn't that the idea?

"Thank you for your patience, Mr. Siringo."

The clerk's spectacles were back on his nose where they belonged and his tone had gone up a hitch or two in the cordial department: A single telephone call to Earp's bank had wiped out all past transgressions. If the last century had been built on determination and individual initiative, this one was constructing itself on net worth. Siringo, watching the sickly little man deal notes onto the counter, was not inclined at the moment to question the system.

He kept out a hundred for expenses and deposited the rest. Folding the notes into a shirt pocket, he remembered the streetcar. "Dollar in change, please."

The man obliged. "Please come again."

"I hope to." He touched the brim of his Stetson and caught the car out front just as it was starting away from the curb.

The motorman scowled at him from his tractor seat. "Don't be so impatient, old-timer. Next time you might leave a grease trail clear to the Valley."

Siringo said nothing, dropping his nickel into the slot and unconsciously committing the man's lobeless ears and turnip-shaped nose to memory.

———

Back home, he unscrewed the socket from an electric lamp that needed rewiring, stuffed the banknotes into the cavity, and replaced the socket. Then he traded his moccasins for a pair of calf-length Kip boots, thrust his Colt under his belt, hung the Winchester in its stiff scabbard on his shoulder by the strap, and went out the back door with a handful of .44 shells in each pocket next to his pipe, matches, and tobacco. He brought along his canteen and bean sandwiches wrapped in waxed paper and stashed inside his shirt.

The scrubby brush was still wet, and by the time he reached the base of the HOLLYWOODLAND sign his boots were soaked, but the thick lumberman's socks he wore underneath kept his feet warm and dry. He'd learned from experience to take especial care of his feet. The cowboys he'd ridden with in early days had been contemptuous of their lower extremities, considering them no fit transportation for a man broken to the saddle; but horses gave out, often before men, and a fellow who bore up under conditions of thirst and hunger and heat and cold and exhaustion folded like a canvas bucket at the first blister.

His bad knee grieved him worse as he climbed. He limped under the best of conditions, but he was usually able to dissemble it with his rolling prairie walk. He stopped from time to time and stood like a crane with the leg bent a little until the throbbing flattened out, more or less.

He pulled himself up the last few yards to the top by grasping fistfuls of grass and the trunks of firs, then unslung the scabbard, took off his hat, and mopped the leather sweatband with his bandanna, chugging like a locomotive and listening to his heart walloping in his chest. It skipped every fourth beat; but it had been doing that since he was a yonker. The sawbones who plastered his splintered knee in Texas had told him his "unpunctual heart" would do for him before he was forty. He drew the same bad hand from the doctor who stitched him up after he got bucked into barbed wire at Longmont. According to medical science he'd been dead a quarter-century.

He sat in the grass, dry now where the sun beat down on it, unwrapped his lunch, and ate beans between thick slices of coarse bread, washing them down with water from the canteen. Then he smoked his pipe, gazing down at the back of the eyesore sign and *Ciudad de Los Angeles* creeping out in every direction from its dusty little start, the good homely adobe missions blending into stucco and red tile, concrete and macadam poured over ancient bones. The swimming pools of the picture players looked like turquoise chips scattered by a careless jeweler. Trust a New York City cowboy like Bill Hart to come to the desert for a swim.

The sun was still high above the ships moored off Santa Monica, but when it slipped this side of the hills he would be making his way back down in the dark. The bones were too brittle for that. He knocked out his pipe, got up, opened his fly, and let water onto the glowing ash, then buttoned up and thumbed fresh loads into the revolver and carbine.

He spent a pleasant hour plugging trunks and branches, a clod of earth and grass flung high, which made a satisfying burst when he connected, like Bill Cody's blown-glass balls in the arena, not as pretty but just as easy to mark your progress. He'd hoped to spot a coyote or a rabbit, some moving target to measure his skills against, but they weren't cooperating that day. He speared the sheet of waxed paper from the sandwiches on the end of a ponderosa branch where it caught the breeze, paced off a hundred yards, turned, fired at it first with the Winchester, then with the Colt, standing with that weapon sideways to the target with the barrel parallel to his arm and shoulder, until he'd exhausted his rounds. His ears rang and his hand throbbed.

When he went back to inspect the result, he was dissatisfied. It was possible he'd put a few rounds through the tears he'd opened earlier, but as many as he'd spent, the piece of paper should have been obliterated. Raw yellow wounds showed in branches above and below where he'd fired wide.

Well, there wasn't likely to be shooting in the thing. Horse thieves were cowardly types, ready to leave a man on foot in hostile country, but not so quick to trade fire when there was a hole big enough to crawl into handy. Which was why you hung them when taking them into custody was inconvenient. He didn't reckon turning the century had made any modern improvements in their *cojones*. Siringo himself had never made much use of his ordnance other than the ornamental. He'd shot to cover himself and others, hurling swarms of lead more hazardous to the indigenous wildlife than the opposing parties, and when there wasn't a less valuable bludgeon within reach he'd made use of the handle end, but an assumed name and a good line of gab had always been his weapons of choice.

Jesus Mary, though, a man was reluctant to acknowledge he'd lost ground.

It wasn't his eyes, just rust. Rust and the old-man shakes and too much thinking. You could scrape off the first through practice and conquer the second with determination, but when the bump of intelligence grew so big it got in the way of your target, there wasn't much you could do about it except drink, and that would put a big dent in the travel expenses.

4

He stuck his ticket inside his sweatband and smoked his pipe on the bench in the station waiting. On one side of him sat a couple with a little girl dressed all in yellow with an enormous bow on top of her head and on the other a thickset Mexican in overalls holding a fat hen on his lap. Siringo wondered if he'd had to buy a ticket for the chicken.

His train arrived on time, and he rode to San Francisco reading the *Los Angeles Express*, watching the scenery, and eating a bean sandwich he'd packed to save the expense of the dining car. The Mexican with the hen got off in Santa Barbara, where an even thicker-set woman greeted him on the platform with four children in tow and a rooster under one arm. Siringo reckoned he'd witnessed the beginning of a poultry empire.

In San Francisco he made his way to the post office and found a telegram waiting for him in care of General Delivery. He'd sent a wire that morning to an address Earp had given him, and here was the reply:

LOOKING FORWARD TO OUR COLLABORATION
STOP ADMIRED TWO EVIL ISMS

HAMMETT

His relationship with automobiles was tenuous, and he rode the high old Daimler taxi with both hands on the blanket rail. The driver spat tobacco out the side of the car and kept up a running commentary on how far San Francisco had gone to pot during his residency.

"You can't buy a Chinese girl off the street corner anymore, that's for sure." Siringo slid to the middle of the seat to avoid the backsplash.

He got useful information finally when he asked if there was a hotel near his destination. The driver said the St. Francis was two blocks from it. "The bellhops know some good bootleggers."

They came to the hotel first. He had the cab wait while he checked in and carried his valise and scabbarded carbine up to his room. Before going back down he unstrapped the valise and swigged from one of the jars of moonshine he'd packed. Then he took out the Colt, grabbed a pillow from the bed, stuck the revolver inside the slip, and put pillow and weapon on top of the walnut wardrobe: an inadequate precaution, but better than none.

The address Earp had given him, 120 Ellis Street, belonged to a narrow frame house that looked as if it had been there since before the earthquake; so did the landlady, who directed him to Hammett's room. He climbed two flights of outside stairs and knocked. From inside he heard the familiar chopping sounds of a typewriter. A bell rang and then a board creaked on the other side of the door. A tall, narrow-gauged man opened it.

"Mr. Siringo. You're a foot shy of your reputation."

"I'm short, but I don't cost much to feed." Siringo took the hand offered. The grip was firm and dry. "You're older than I thought."

"Don't let the white hair fool you. I'm twenty-six, going on a hundred."

He saw the truth of the statement then. Hammett's sandy

moustache was a shade darker than his hair, very thick and swept back from a high forehead. The hair, and his sunken cheeks, were not the result of age, but chronic illness. He remembered that Earp had said he suffered from consumption. The young ex-Pinkerton wore shirtsleeves and slacks, held up by a pair of suspenders, and silk socks without shoes. He smelled strongly of whiskey—in the middle of the afternoon—but the whites of his eyes were clear.

"Sorry you had to wait. I spent the morning tracking down a word and I didn't want to spend the rest of the day looking for it all over again."

"They will give you the slip. I've run down mail robbers that were easier to catch."

"Me, too." Humor glinted in the young ex-Pinkerton's eyes, falling short of his mouth. He stepped aside to let his visitor in and closed the door behind him.

Hammett seemed to live the way he dressed, orderly and simple. There was no rug on the polished oak floor, and a worn leather armchair and rocker comprised the leisure appointments. A straight-back chair stood before a small table with a Remington typewriter on it, beside a stack of yellow paper and a bottle of Old Log Cabin. An electric hotplate took the place of a kitchen and a twin bed on a painted iron frame showed beyond a half-open door. Books and newspaper sections scattered the floor.

"Snort?" Hammett lifted the bottle.

"Little early for me, thanks." He didn't like to confess to weakness in the presence of a stranger.

"It's later where I stand." Hammett coughed and topped off a smeared glass with amber liquid.

"It's none of my business, but you know that's no good for you."

"You're right, and this isn't your business either." Hammett built a cigarette from scratch and lit it with a match he struck off a thumbnail.

"Oh, hell. Give me a glass."

Something like a smile touched the young man's lips. "Better. I don't trust a man who drinks by the clock." He got a coffee cup out of a cupboard. "Hope this is okay. I live alone and a fellow only needs one glass at a time."

"When I'm alone I drink from the bottle." Siringo stepped forward and filled the cup. "I was hoping you'd be better company than Wyatt Earp."

"He didn't have anything good to say about you, either. What's the story there?"

"I caught him in a lie once and it got into print."

"That'll do it. He's a sour old cob. If I ever had a horse I'd be grateful I had it for as long as I did instead of bitching about it when I didn't. You can't pack a horse in a suitcase."

Siringo nodded. "The Pinks will move you around."

"Anywhere's jake with me, so long as it isn't Butte, Montana."

"Make it Gem, Colorado, and I'm with you." Siringo lifted the cup and drank. It was smoother whiskey than he was used to; he made a mental note to go easy on it.

"Forget that crack about advice," Hammett said. "Everybody you meet's a doctor when you're sick."

"That, or whatever they had was worse." He made a dismissive gesture with his glass. "I talk too much. It happens when you spend all your time with just your own company."

"Not me. I never learned anything talking to myself."

"Well, you won't be alone much longer. I hear you're getting set to put on hobbles."

"Jose is a good old gal. I don't suppose she'll put up with me for long, but when a man sets out to follow his dick he has to do it all the way."

"That sounds like a rule wrote by a woman."

Hammett laughed, a sound made almost entirely through his nose. He was cynical for his age; for any age. Siringo put it down to his disease. "With my luck, it'll be a girl. I'll be surrounded."

"I've had both. One sasses you and the other smells."

"Where are they now?"

"The girl married and went back East. The boy's mother took him when she left. I ain't seen him since."

Hammett changed the subject. "I never heard of Gem."

"You're a lucky man. It's not there no more and the world's better for it. I had to saw a hole in a floor and drop down through to keep from getting massacred. That was during the Coeur d'Alene strike."

"The old-timers were still talking about Coeur d'Alene when I hired on." Hammett drank off half his glass in one jolt. "The Agency had me strikebreaking in Butte. That's where I found out I was on the wrong side."

"Any side's better than the anarchists'."

"I heard it was Marxists in Coeur d'Alene."

"Marxists, socialists, anarchists, revolutionists: If it's got an 'ist' on the end it's no place for a decent man."

"I got that impression from your book. I didn't get the impression it was Marxists you were talking about. I read *The Communist Manifesto* back to front and couldn't find anything in it that didn't make sense."

"Not if you don't mind sharing your paycheck with John D. Rockefeller."

"Rockefeller'd be sharing his with me, don't forget."

"I seen men blowed up by men who thought like that. It's a yellow-belly way to make a point. You and I might not get along, Mr. Hammett. And here I thought we had something in common."

"We do, Mr. Siringo. We're both fed up with the Pinkerton National Detective Agency."

"Hope it's enough."

"Two horses don't have to like each other to pull the wagon one direction."

"Well, it's good we're talking about horses. I lit out of Chicago first chance I got to avoid long meetings."

Hammett nodded. "Three men go into a room and come out an hour later with three different ways to go about the same thing. It's one of the reasons I chose writing."

The young man's drinking had slowed down. That first taste seemed to have been medicinal, and his guest relaxed a little. He thumped a jug with the best of them, but he worried about partners who couldn't control their thirst. They got jumpy staking out places and made all the wrong decisions when the ball started.

Siringo pointed at the stack of yellow sheets. The one on top was typewritten, with addenda penciled in the margins. "You can't plow a straight furrow when you're writing your memoirs. I kept remembering things that happened in Salt Lake City when I was writing about Prescott."

"I wouldn't know how to go about writing my memoirs. I'd rather fold them into a good yarn, where everything makes sense."

"Publish yet?"

"Hell, no. They all want that bird Galsworthy or a fair copy."

"With me it was Ned Buntline. Bill Cody kilt more injuns in one chapter than he ever saw in life. You ever kill a man?"

"I came close when I turned over an ambulance full of our own wounded during the war; haven't driven a car since the Armistice. You?"

"I don't even like riding in one."

"I meant did you ever kill a man."

"Maybe, though not my own. I throwed some lead in my time, but others was throwing it too. You don't stop to sort it out after. I like to think I didn't. Look what it did to Earp."

Hammett refilled his glass, tilted the neck of the bottle Siringo's way. He shook his head. Hammett twisted the cap back on. "Well, we're burning his money. Might as well earn some of it."

When they were both seated, Siringo in the leather armchair at his host's insistence, the other in the rocker, Siringo filled his pipe and lit it. "Earp says his stable boy come to rest up in Sonoma County."

"That's new. When I asked him why he didn't pump him, he said he didn't know where he wound up."

"I asked him the same thing. No wonder he got so irritable. He got a wire from the ranch day before yesterday asking for a reference."

Hammett's ghost of a smile returned. "I bet that got his back up."

"He was born with it up."

"Of course you told him to give the boy a good write-up."

"What else?"

"What's the name of the spread?"

Siringo drew out his memorandum book. "Beauty Ranch, in a place called *The Valley of the Moon*, if you can feature it. Know it?"

"I sure as hell do. I'm surprised you don't. I drew the conclusion from your books you're a well-read man."

"What the hell's reading got to do with horse-stealing, I'd like to know?"

"Something, in this case. Beauty Ranch in *The Valley of the Moon* is Jack London's old spread."

"The writer?"

"Just about the most famous since Dickens. Earp's dictating his own life story, you wrote yours, I'm eating up more paper than a goat. If this stable hand is guilty, between us three he's got to be the most literary horse thief in history."

5

Hammett, leaning a little on the banister—not because of the liquor in his system, Siringo thought, so much as because of his illness—led the way to the ground floor, where he gave the landlady a coin and used the wall telephone in the foyer to place a call through the long-distance operator. Once the connection was made, he stuck his finger in his ear and raised his voice. Ellis was a busy street and the neighborhood liked its chain drives and Klaxons.

"Mrs. Shepard, is it? My name is Walter Noble Burns."

After that, Siringo heard only snatches of the conversation and couldn't make head nor tail of it.

Hammett pegged the earpiece. "That was Eliza Shepard, London's stepsister. She's managed the ranch since before London died. She hired the boy—Abner Butterfield, his name is—on Earp's recommendation. She says we can come see him tomorrow."

"He'll bolt for sure when she tells him."

"I asked her not to, so he wouldn't form any preconceived notions before I talked to him."

"Who's this fellow Burns?"

"Historian of some sort. I did some snooping for him just before I left the Agency, tracking a couple of saddle tramps he wanted to talk to. He was writing a history of the Old West, he said; personally I think he was trying to dig up blackmail. I don't know what ever came of it, but he was keen on the Earp brothers."

"She ever hear of him?"

"No. I didn't expect her to, but a lie gets off the ground quicker when there's some truth under it. She thinks I'm writing Earp's biography and I want a worm's-eye view from a former hand."

Siringo felt himself grinning. "Promise her a footnote?"

"Her name in the acknowledgments. And a signed copy of the book, of course. You approve?"

"It'll serve. If I was your age I'd turn on the manly charm. A woman's heart is a fine soft place to look for sign."

"My experience is different. All women are dark to me."

A strange observation.

"This place reachable by taxi?"

"That'd be dear, but I'd rather not hire a car."

"What about a livery? You ride?"

"Not since I broke up the Wobblies in Butte. I don't guess they've gotten any easier on the ass."

"It's been a spell for me too. I never could feature how sitting on something stuffed with hay raises blisters."

"Alcohol's best. Applied internally."

"I got to line my belly first. Where's a good place for chow?"

"John's Grill. I'll get my hat and coat and join you. John's particular about dress, if not about who he serves."

John's, across from a fleabag called the Golden State Hotel, advertised steaks and seafood on an electric sign. Inside, it was pleasant enough, cedar-paneled like the inside of a humidor, with waiters in ankle-length aprons serving the predominately male clientele seated at linen-covered tables. It was noisy as a Dodge

City saloon, but instead of a tin-tack piano and random gunfire the racket came from clattering crockery.

"Two setups, Gus." Hammett hung his hat and topcoat on a clothes tree next to a booth upholstered in worn leather.

The waiter, who looked as if he'd slammed face-first into the caboose of a train he was running to catch, nodded and went away. Moments later he returned and set two glasses on the table with ice cubes inside. He waited, looking bored, while Hammett slid a large pewter flask from inside his suit coat and floated the cubes in whiskey.

Hammett looked up from his leather-bound menu. "How are the chops today?"

"I wouldn't know. I'm a vegetarian, remember?"

The young detective smirked at Siringo. "Gus gave up eating meat after he killed Sailor Dumphrey in the sixth round in El Paso."

"Juarez," corrected Gus. "Governor Culberson banned prize-fighting in Texas, so we took it across the river. It was the fifth, not the sixth. How was I to know he had a bad appendix, I ask you?"

Siringo said, "I was at that fight."

The waiter's scarred face was unimpressed.

"You and half the forty-six. If everybody that says he was there was there, the gate would have been millions."

"I didn't pay. I was posted at the back door to sing out if there was a raid. I got paid twice that day, once by the promoter and the second time by the Pinkertons, who were going to be the ones raiding the place, only Chicago backed out at the last minute. The Agency decided it didn't want to start a war with Mexico just yet."

The ex-fighter stroked a badly sewn lower lip. "If this joint's going to be a hangout for dicks, I'm off to the States Hof Brau."

Hammett said, "Bring me a couple of chops, Gus. Plenty of onions in the fried potatoes."

"I'll have the same." Siringo handed his menu to Hammett, who stacked it with his and gave them to the waiter.

"You take chances," he told Siringo. "There was a revolution on. Either side might have blundered on the side of caution and shot you for a spy."

"There's been a revolution on down there since Sam Grant was a shavetail. Anyway, I like to keep an eye on my investments. I had fifty bucks on Dumphrey. I'd of broke even if the promoter didn't stiff me on my pay."

"Well, you were working the double-cross."

"He didn't know that."

The meals came, and they ate for a while without speaking. Siringo chased his drink with water, shook his head when Hammett offered to pour again from the flask. The young man's water stood untouched while he drank more whiskey.

"What's my part in this historian story?" Siringo asked.

"You're my publisher. You said yourself you're a man who looks after his investments."

"No wonder you ain't in print. If you knew anything about publishers you'd know they never get up from their desks. Make me your researcher."

"It's copacetic with me, if you don't mind the demotion."

Siringo ordered coffee. When it came, he blew on it, set down the cup untasted, scratched his left eyebrow.

Hammett caught the gesture; that much about the Agency hadn't changed. He glanced over his right shoulder, as if looking for the waiter. The man Siringo had spotted was loitering by the narrow paneled hallway leading to the toilets, reading a copy of the *Chronicle* with yesterday's date. He wore an out-of-season white linen suit, severely wrinkled, a Panama hat with the brim turned down all around, and had a dead cigarette hanging from a corner of his mouth. His face was even thinner than Hammett's and sallow to the point of jaundice.

"It ain't that big of a newspaper," said the older man. "It shouldn't take you two days to get through it."

"He's a cheap crook any way you look at it. Why spend a nickel when you can scoop it out of a trash bin for free?"

"You know him?"

Hammett nodded. "Mike Feeney. Runs errands for Paddy Clanahan. The kind that's hard to muck up."

"Bootlegger?"

"Boss politician. Eight years ago he was just a ward heeler, but when T.R. split the ballot with Taft and Wilson got in, the Democrats back East took notice. Everybody who got the vote out moved up a notch."

"Ancient history. Harding's Republicans are in now."

"Everything comes back around. There's an oil scandal heating up in Sacramento, with cabinet officials involved. Clanahan's on it with both feet. If his timing's right, he could be postmaster general."

"For an anarchist you know a lot about government."

"Marxist. When the wind shifts from the capital, you don't have to be close to the governor to smell the stink."

Siringo frowned. "You think this fellow Feeney's trailing you around to find out how much you know?"

"All I know is what everyone does who's got ears. But if Clanahan's put Feeney on the job, it means I'm supposed to spot him: All you need to tell him is don't get seen, and he'll do the rest. That way I won't look at who's really trailing me."

"Who's that?"

"We'll ask Feeney."

"Good luck with that. These fellows run like rabbits when you go to brace them."

"Why would I do that? He goes where I go; in this case the gents' room."

"I never knew a case to draw fire this early. What else you working on?"

"A story for *Smart Set*, but I doubt that's the attraction. You?"

"Not even that. Maybe it's Earp they're after. He's sold gold bricks and town lots he had no claim to. This oil mess sounds like just his meat."

"If all he wanted was to scare somebody off, why bother with the horse-theft dodge?"

"He knows I don't do that kind of work."

"Me neither."

"Could be it's an old complaint. Earp makes enemies the way Will Rogers makes friends."

"If Clanahan was ever to confide in people, he wouldn't start with Feeney. But his invisible friend might know something."

Siringo borrowed Hammett's flask, sweetened his coffee, and gave it back. He took a bracing sip. "What do you need from me?"

"Nothing right now. Two of us might spook Feeney. Go back to my place and wait for me. I never lock up. What's to steal?"

"I reckon I'll offer you my hospitality at the St. Francis instead."

"Got a bottle?"

"How you feel about shine?"

Hammett grinned wide.

Siringo glanced Feeney's way. He seemed to be reading the women's page. "Don't lean too hard. He looks brittle."

"These reedy ones can surprise you. They just bend where Sandow the Magnificent would break in two."

Hammett paid his half of the check, put on his hat and coat, and strode down the hallway, passing within inches of the skinny man in the wrinkled suit, who suddenly became interested in an article and pulled the newspaper up in front of his face. Siringo lingered over his coffee, looking at nothing in particular.

After five minutes or so, Feeney began to fidget. He checked his strap watch twice, tore his paper snapping it open to the sports section, kept glancing down the hall toward the toilets. Siringo rose then, put a banknote on the table, and went out.

He turned two corners, window-shopping, paying attention to the sights of the city, which had changed demonstrably since he used to report to the Agency office there. There was Telegraph Hill trailing its strings of cable cars like circus streamers, and down below the wharves, with more smokestacks than sails straining at the hawsers; but where were the opium dens, the almost-respectable gambling hells, the saloons built from wrecked ships, the girls working balconies wearing nothing but what God gave them? It didn't seem possible that a little quake and some vigilante raids could have destroyed the Barbary Coast after fifty years of loyal service. Likely it had just gone underground, where a detective never knew where to start looking for what he needed to know. You had to leave a good source of villainy for seed; that was something the crusaders never understood.

He stopped to light his pipe, turning into the doorway of a haberdashery to shield the match from the wind. He kept his back to the street and saw Feeney's scrawny figure reflected in the glass of the door, hurrying along now in the direction Siringo had been heading with the day-old newspaper tucked under one arm. He was following Siringo, not Hammett.

6

"What do you make of it?" Hammett asked.

The young man had come along a few yards behind Feeney, as Siringo knew he would; trailing him after he didn't show up in the toilet, trailing Hammett. They remained inside the deep doorway.

"It don't signify. I ain't been in town since before it shook itself to pieces. This fellow Clanahan don't know me from Mrs. Bloomer."

"I don't know who that is."

"You ought to wear knickers or something so I don't forget you're still wet behind the ears. What's his interest in me is the point I'm making."

"Well, we'll get what we can when Feeney backtracks." Hammett glanced up at the building, one of the newer ones designed without gimcracks to fall on pedestrians' heads when the ground got restless. "I've got an idea. Keep him busy till I get back." He opened the door and went inside.

Siringo knew better than to waste time asking himself questions. He stayed in the doorway, smoking, until the thin man in the white suit came hurrying back the way he'd come, swiveling his head from side to side looking for his quarry. Siringo stepped out in front of him suddenly. Feeney had to backpedal to avoid collision.

The old detective asked him for a match.

Feeney's face flushed a deeper shade of yellow. He patted his pockets, then saw the smoke rising from the other's pipe.

"Well, what do you know?" Siringo stared at the bowl. "That last one caught finally."

The other made a sickly smile and started to step around him. He countered that with a step to the right.

"Didn't I see you on the train?"

"Must've been somebody else, old-timer. I ain't been out of Frisco all year."

"I don't think so. I never forget a face."

"Look, you made a mistake." He tried to circle around him again.

This time Siringo flattened a palm against the man's chest. He could feel his ribs through two layers of cloth. "We bumped into each other in the club car. I missed my wallet right after."

Feeney swept the hand away, reaching under his coat on the follow-through. He brought out a Colt Army semiautomatic that bent his wrist under its weight.

"Say that again and you'll be chewing lead."

"The smaller the fry, the bigger the talk," said Hammett, coming up behind him. "Come back to my dump and help me patch up my dialogue."

The man jumped, started to turn the big pistol his way. Siringo drew the little Forehand & Wadsworth from under his belt and thrust it into Feeney's stomach, where it nearly met his backbone. He cocked it in the same motion.

Feeney hesitated just long enough for Hammett to reach over his shoulder, grasp the .45, and twist it out of his skeletal grip.

"Like snatching a quarter from a blind newsie," he said.

"I'll get you guys," Feeney said. "You won't always be twins."

"That ain't bad." Siringo grinned at Hammett. "Can I have it, or do you want it?"

"Help yourself. I'm still working on that chewing-lead line. It needs a little something. Nice belly gun. I never spotted it."

"I got a little more belly than I used to. Where'd you drop from?"

"Wrong direction. After the quake they rebuilt the neighborhood on top of a series of connecting cellars where the hopheads used to chase the dragon in old Chinatown. Some of the floors are original, trapdoors and all." He jerked his thumb back over his shoulder, toward a Christian Science reading room on the corner. "I may have turned a couple of readers into Methodists when I came up through the floor."

"I like them cellars. Used 'em yet?"

"In a story? Not yet. Dibs."

"It's yours anyway. I clerked in a store once and that was as close as I ever want to get to being buried alive."

"When you girls are through gabbing I got a bus to catch."

Hammett was still holding Feeney's weapon. He shifted his grip to the barrel and tapped him behind the ear with the butt. Siringo caught him as he fell.

"Now we get to lug him all the way back to your place," he said.

"I got bored. Feeney's the original Johnny One-Note. We'll go to your hotel; it's closer. Just a second." The young man stuck the .45 under his belt, took out his flask, opened it, hesitated. "The St. Francis has room service, right?"

Siringo saw where he was heading. "No need to worry. I never travel dry."

"Swell." Hammett removed the unconscious man's Panama and dumped what was left in the flask over his head, soaking his white coat dark. He moaned a little but didn't come around. Hammett stuck his hat back on him and took him by one arm. Siringo took the other.

On the way to the St. Francis they passed another couple. The woman, wearing a cloche hat and a dead fox around her neck, waved a gloved hand in front of her nose. "I thought Prohibition was going to put an end to all that."

The man, built square in a striped suit and gray homburg, changed positions with her, placing himself between her and the two men carrying their reeking companion. "I'll write a letter to the *Examiner* tomorrow."

The clerk in the paneled and potted-palmed lobby halted in the midst of sorting mail to watch the pair bearing a limp stranger toward the elevator.

"I'm glad it's you, Mr. Hammett," he said. "Management has a strict policy about guests rolling drunks."

"Don't count on that, Floyd. I'm one rejection slip away from picking pockets."

"Should I send up coffee?"

"Pitcher of water," Hammett said.

"A big one," said Siringo.

"Glasses?"

Hammett said, "Just two. And ice."

The elevator operator, trussed in a uniform two sizes too small, with dundreary whiskers and a little round hat like a Maxwell House coffee tin perched on his crown, glared from his milking stool at the unconscious man. "He gets sick, I won't clean it up."

"Sure you will, Sol," Hammett said. "You'll do anything they tell you to stay out of San Quentin. You're forgetting who got you this job."

"How can a man do that, when you keep reminding him?"

Sol jerked the lever and the car started up with a jolt Siringo felt in his bad molar.

"Is there anyone in this town you don't know?" he asked Hammett in the hallway on his floor. The toes of Feeney's shoes made tracks in the nap on the carpet as they dragged him along.

"Only the respectable ones. They're no use to me."

The room had a steel radiator that shuddered when the furnace kicked in, scraping the chill off spring in San Francisco. The particles of rust and dirt rattling in the pipes sounded exactly like an old Pinkerton clearing his throat.

Which reminded him. His valise was still on the bed. He handed Hammett a Mason jar from inside.

"What is it, blasting oil?" The clear contents distorted his features like a magnifying lens when he held it up to the light.

"It's the barrel aging adds color. My friend in Barstow's clients won't wait that long."

Hammett unscrewed the top, sniffed, shrugged, took a sip. He shook himself. "I was right the first time. You could blow a safe with a jigger of this stuff."

"That Canadian blend spoilt you." Siringo took back the jar and helped himself. "What do we do with this?" He kicked an ankle belonging to the man they'd dumped in the room's only chair, upholstered in green tufted leather. It made his suit look all the worse for lack of pressing. His hat had slid down over his eyes and he was breathing evenly.

"We'll let him rest a while. He's an angel when he sleeps."

Just then Feeney's mouth dumped open, exposing teeth like yellow tumbledown tombstones and taking in air with a rattling snort.

A bellman came to the door, carrying a tray with two glasses, a brass ice bucket, and a pitcher that belonged with a washbowl.

Hammett gave him a quarter and poured moonshine into the glasses, adding water and cubes to cut the bark off it.

"Tell me about this Clanahan." Siringo stretched out on the bed with his glass.

Hammett leaned in a corner, pushing his hat to the back of his head and holding his glass. He looked down at it dubiously, like a diver judging his chances.

"He came in on the boat, like all the rest of us. A little later than most, and they say he left a wife and three kids behind in Limerick. Sometimes it's five, but it's always just the one wife. As if that weren't reason enough to leave, they say he got into some trouble with the authorities. He couldn't come through Ellis Island with that on his back, so he shoveled coal in a tramp steamer all the way through Panama and swam ashore off Santa Barbara to avoid Immigration. A few years ago he bought citizenship, which comes dear, but it was worth it to him not to get deported. There's a rope waiting for him in Ireland, not to mention an angry woman saddled with three kids. Maybe five."

"I'd take my chances with the rope."

"Who wouldn't? There's no appeal from a butcher knife. He's got himself a place on Nob Hill that looks and smells like a museum. Before that he did business in a packing-case parlor on a wharf, peddling whores. After a little it got to be the place where the money men and the board of supervisors rubbed shoulders, and that's where he got his toe in.

"They tried him out first as a messenger boy, carrying cash in a little black satchel between Ed Doheny and Sacramento, then had him knocking on doors, trading free coal for votes. I told you about his big break when Washington changed hands. Now Clanahan's the one sends out the messengers. Our boy Feeney, for one."

"Who's Doheny?"

"Pan-American Oil."

"Never heard of it."

"You would if you owned an automobile. Doheny invented the drive-in filling station. Before that, you needed gas, you had to buy it by the jar in a drugstore. Now he's got them all over the country. And you're likely to hear more about it soon. Pan-American's merging with Mammoth Oil. Harry Sinclair?"

Siringo drank, frowned, shook his head.

"Well, it seems even the rich aren't rich enough to have everything they want. They're pooling their resources to buy leases on oil fields here in California—which is where Clanahan comes in, smack-dab in the middle—and in Wyoming."

"Where in Wyoming? I know every inch of that place."

"This one's after your time, I think. Place called Teapot Dome."

7

Siringo shook his head. "I don't know it. It don't even sound like Wyoming."

"It's there, or everybody wouldn't be scrambling all over it. The navy took over the oil reserves about fifteen years ago, when it started converting from coal. The talk is President Harding's considering transferring them to the Department of the Interior."

"Interior of what? All I know about Washington is to stay clear of it."

"It's run by a bird named Fall. Maybe you crossed trails sometime. He was a cowboy before he got into politics."

"So was Tom Mix—though not politics—but we never met either. What's it signify?"

"Maybe nothing. But it's a sure thing he knows a lot more about the country west of the Mississippi than a president from Ohio."

"What this all has to do with a stolen horse is what I'd like to know."

A groan from the direction of the armchair drew Hammett's attention. "Welcome back, Feeney. We were just talking about you."

But Feeney's eyes remained closed.

"Last time a little buffaloing put a man out this long, he had a bad brain leak," Siringo said.

"Well, he can't afford it." Hammett scooped up the big pitcher and splashed him head to foot.

Feeney sat up straight, spluttering like a horse. A hand went automatically inside his coat. Hammett showed him the .45. The thin man glared, water dripping off the end of his long nose. "Everybody's a tough gee with a rod in his hand," he said.

"Everybody except you. Who's your partner?"

"Flo Ziegfeld."

Feeney's long legs were stretched out in front of the chair, his buttocks perched on the edge of the cushion. Hammett hooked a foot behind his ankle and jerked. The thin man skidded forward and fell hard on his tailbone on the floor. Vile insults followed.

Hammett started coughing from the exertion, his hacking mingled with cursing from the man on the floor. Siringo, concerned about the neighbors, set his glass on the table, got off the bed, and kicked Feeney on the side of the knee, hitting the knob of bone that sent pain rocketing in all directions. Feeney howled.

"Stop disgracing yourself and get back up in the chair. I don't believe you know what Mr. Hammett's ma did for a living. That was just idle speculation on your part."

"You wrinkle-ass old piece of—"

Siringo drew back his foot for another kick. Feeney's slash of mouth snapped shut like a trap and he levered himself up off the floor, supporting his throbbing knee with one hand as he climbed back onto the chair.

"You okay?" The old detective looked at Hammett.

"Yeah. Just swallowed another piece of lung." He studied the white lawn handkerchief folded in his hand, then stuck it into an inside pocket. "Who's your partner, Feeney? Don't say Fanny Brice. She's too picky for the likes of you."

"Go fuck yourself."

Hammett scooped up the pitcher to give him another douse. Siringo touched his arm.

"Don't waste it. I got a better idea."

As the young man watched, Siringo unplugged the electric lamp on the table next to the bed, picked up the lamp, and broke the cord near the base with a yank. He put the lamp back down and took his bowie from the valise. He stripped two inches of fabric insulation from the two strands of wire, one copper, one silver, put them on the bed, then laid the wires aside while he opened the room's only window and used the knife to slash the screen free of its frame. It peeled away with a shower of rust.

At a nod from him, Hammett held the prisoner at bay with the big pistol while Siringo snatched up each of his feet and stripped it of shoe and sock. Then he lifted them again to slide the screen under his bare soles. There was black dirt between his toes and his nails were as thick and yellow as old isinglass. Finally Siringo connected the strands of electrical wire to the edges of the metal screen and got up, holding the plug out for Hammett to take.

The young detective had caught on by this time. He belted the automatic, took the plug, and knelt by the baseboard outlet, waiting for his cue.

Feeney grasped the arms of his chair, prepared to spring to his feet, but was restrained by Siringo's stubby revolver trained on his sternum. When Siringo picked up the pitcher of water, he knew what was going to happen, but before he could cry out, he was soaked once again from head to feet. Hammett, grinning, lined up the prongs of the electric plug with the slots in the outlet.

"Jesus!" It was a shriek. "You'll fry me alive!"

"Why are you trailing me?" Siringo asked.

"I don't know!"

"Plug it in," Siringo told Hammett.

"Just follow you wherever you go and report back, that's all I was told! Nobody ever tells me nothing. Oh, God, don't kill me!"

Siringo looked at the other detective. "You know him. He that good a liar?"

Hammett remained kneeling, poised with the plug a quarter-inch from its connection. "Take a whiff. You tell me."

The stink of corruption rose to Siringo's nostrils. He lowered the pitcher. "We had a saying: 'If he shits—'"

"'—he ain't shittin'.' It was still around when I came on. But I told you Clanahan doesn't confide in a mutt like Feeney."

"I believed you. I just wanted his measure. Your turn."

Hammett blew on the end of the plug, brushed an imaginary piece of lint from a prong, bent again to his task. "Who's your partner? Say George M. Cohan. It isn't every small fry can say he blew out all the fuses in a ritzy joint like the St. Francis."

Feeney hyperventilated.

Siringo thought. "What was the name of that first fellow they electrocuted, back in '89?"

Hammett touched the prongs to his lip, thinking. "Kemmler: killed his girl. Something went wrong with one of the electrodes. He crackled for ten minutes. They said it smelled like a barbecue in a shithouse. Nobody consulted Kemmler on his point of view. He was black enough there was some discussion about burying him in the colored section of the Auburn Prison cemetery."

"That was a fluke. They used too big a jolt, that being the first electrocution and they wanted to make sure, and they didn't wet him down properly. That won't be a problem here. Feeney looks like he just came in from a swim around Alcatraz. Fire him up."

Hammett spat on the plug, aimed it at the outlet.

"The eel!"

Hammett stopped, shook his head.

"Horseshit. The eel only works Mexico, everyone knows that. It's the chair for him the minute he shows his face this side of the border. Stand back, Charlie." He leaned forward on his knees.

"It's the eel! Oh, Christ on the Cross! It's the eel! The eel!"

Hammett sat back on his heels, nodded at Siringo.

Siringo kicked the screen out from under Feeney's feet. The thin man's belly filled with air, becoming almost a paunch, then let out. He found a cracked yellow handkerchief in a pocket and mopped his face.

"How skinny do these fellows get?" Siringo asked. "Feeney looks plenty eel-ly to me."

Hammett stood, twirling the plug by its cord. "I think they call him that because he slips in and out without so much as a fish fart. I can't think of a soul who knows what he looks like, except Clanahan. The eel's a top-notch shadow, but his real specialty is filling graveyards."

Siringo looked at Feeney. "Who's Wyatt Earp?"

"What's that, a cure for hiccups?"

"What do we do with him?" he asked Hammett.

"Kick him loose. Feeney wouldn't swat a fly, on account of it might swat him back."

"G'wan, shamus, talk big. Forest Lawn needs daisies."

"I sort of hate to see him go," Siringo said. "I made a lot of friends singing cowboy songs. He and I could write one together."

"Feeney can't read or write. It's a great loss to literature. Maybe we should put out his eyes and send him on the road like Homer."

"Try it, peeper; just try it, and bring your pal Homer along, whoever he is. You two and the old bird'll wind up swimming across the bay with a coal wagon tied to your backs."

"You call it," Hammett said.

"You're right. He wears thin on close acquaintance."

Hammett unlocked the hall door and swung it wide. "Fly, flea."

Feeney fumbled into his shoes and socks, stood, swept a hand under his nose, and looked down at the result on his knuckles. *Cocaine-dipper*, Siringo thought. He'd worked with some, against others; it was the character of a man that affected the outcome. "What about my gat?"

"What's a gat?"

"Hogleg," Hammett told Siringo. He unshipped the heavy automatic, kicked the magazine out of the handle, and offered it butt-first to Feeney; keeping a finger inside the trigger guard. Siringo knew what was coming.

"Smart guy." Feeney reached for it.

Hammett executed a neat border-shift, twirling the pistol on his finger until the butt rested in his palm and the muzzle pointed at Feeney. "One in the chamber, Young Wild West. No charge for the lesson." He worked the slide, springing a glittering brass cartridge out of the chamber onto the rug, and turned the weapon over to its owner.

"Smart guy. Smart guy." Feeney tried twirling the weapon, nearly dropped it, flushed, and socked it under his belt.

Hammett hoisted his brows nearly to his white hairline. "History in the making, Charlie. Aloysius McGonigle Feeney ran out of patter."

"Go fuck yourself." The thin man left, his feet squishing in his shoes.

Siringo and Hammett gave him the respect of a minute to the elevator, then began to chuckle.

"You don't know Mrs. Bloomer, but you remember Kemmler."

Hammett stirred the half-melted cubes in his glass with his

forefinger. "I know my criminals down to the ground. I'm working on the rest of my education from the noose on up."

"We'll attend to it."

"That was a swell trick with the lamp. I don't know why I didn't think of it myself."

"You yonkers take electricity for granted. All part of your education. How much do you know about phrenology?"

"I learned just enough to break up a fortune-telling ring in Sausalito."

"It's science, not palmistry. I wouldn't have been a detective without it."

"It was just a paycheck to me."

"How'd that work out?"

Then, for no reason worth examination, both men broke into bunkhouse guffaws, ending in three minutes of coughing on Hammett's part. While he was catching his breath, Siringo did the honors, emptying a Mason jar into their glasses, just enough to float the ice.

"How's your head?"

"My bump of regret's pounding fit to bend my hat," Siringo said. "How's yours?"

"No complaints. The thing I don't get about drys is how can a man wake up knowing that's as good as he's going to feel all day long. Did you remember to pack some hair-of-the-dog?"

Siringo patted the new bedroll strapped behind the cantle of his hired saddle. Hammett grinned, excavated the flask from inside his whipcord coat, and helped himself to a swig. His companion shook his head when he offered it. "I'd go slow, too. No sense making things easier for this eel character."

"I think we're safe this trip. I never heard where he had any equestrian leanings."

The proprietor of the livery, an elderly Chinese in traditional dress garnished with yellow rubber boots to his knees, had placed the money they gave him under his mandarin's cap and brought out a dappled mare and a blue roan gelding for their inspection. Siringo checked both from teeth to fetlocks, pronounced them sound, and selected the mare for himself. The two detectives rode them to the Golden Gate ferry, paid the fare, and loaded them aboard. Leaning on the railing, they smoked and watched a luxury liner steaming north where the Pacific met the sky, pouring black smoke into the latter. Siringo had thought the *Titanic* would have put an end to all that, but folks were restless.

"They say they're going to build a bridge across the bay," Hammett said. "The bill's in the legislature. That'll make a cozy retirement for Clanahan and every other tinhorn politician in town."

"Ain't interested. Talk about something else."

"That'll be a challenge. I don't go to church and I gave up baseball when Chicago threw the Series. I can't impress you with my detective stories. Politics is all that's left."

"I ain't voted since Taft. When I saw what we got I figured I didn't qualify to make that decision." Siringo shifted his weight from one foot to the other. They'd only ridden a few blocks and already his backside was as sore as his head.

"I cast my ballot for Debs."

"There was a vote wasted. You can't go from the hoosegow to the White House."

"If Doheny gets his way it may go the other way around."

"Better a crook than a radical, I say."

"They jailed Debs for speaking out against the Espionage Act. Wilson was using it to open his opponents' mail. If that makes Debs a radical, what was Thomas Jefferson?"

"Change the subject before we end up drawing down on each other."

Hammett coughed and spat over the railing. "What's this lie you called Earp out on?"

"Ancient history."

"Oh. A gentleman."

Siringo chuckled around the stem of his pipe. "That's one accusation nobody never made before. I don't own a stick and I'd rather cut my throat than put on a stiff collar."

"Prettiest man I ever saw in a dinner jacket cut up his wife and shipped her to Boston in a trunk. It isn't a question of dress."

Siringo had on the new Stetson he'd bought with Earp's money to replace his disreputable old one, his canvas shooting coat with cartridge loops on the breast over his ribbed trousers, stovepipe boots without spurs; he'd left them at home under the impression his riding days were behind him. Hammett wore a slouch hat, old work boots, and the bottom half of a retired pinstripe suit, worn shiny in spots. He carried a .38 Smith & Wesson revolver with a four-inch barrel in one deep coat pocket and a set of brass knuckles in the other, the material sagging under their weight. They had five guns between them and Siringo's mare, which was having trouble making peace with the scabbarded Winchester slung from the saddle. It kept trying to reach back and bite through the strap, but couldn't get inside range, like a man with an itch in the middle of his back.

"Why be coy about Earp? He didn't hold back on your account."

"I done my damage. No use raking it up again."

"I thought all you old-timers were braggarts."

"I strangled the truth around my share of campfires, but I growed out of it. Earp never did, and that's one of the differences between us."

"Well, then, tell me about Billy the Kid."

"He's dead. Anything you hear to the contrary's horseshit. He ain't selling dry goods in Chicago and he wasn't seen last year in South America wearing a plug hat and smoking a cigar. He never left that hole they dumped him in down in Fort Sumner."

"You met him, though."

"I was the first to call him Kid."

Siringo was riding fence for the LX Ranch in the Llano Estacado. He spotted a cut in the wire, the ends still shiny, and followed fresh hoofprints to where he found the Kid rounding up LX strays inside Palo Duro Canyon. He wouldn't have thought anything of it except for the cut fence and the fact that he'd never seen the slender youth around the bunkhouse.

The Kid was seventeen then, and the pistol on his hip was largely there for ballast. Alone and concentrating on the uncooperative longhorns, he wasn't aware of the twenty-two-year-old ranch hand's presence until he rode right up on him, threw his lasso over his bony shoulders, and jerked him out of the saddle. Siringo dragged him twenty or thirty yards to take the fight out of him, then disarmed him, bound his hands to the horn of the Kid's own saddle, tied a lead, and towed him into town and passed him over to the marshal.

He'd never known a pleasanter journey. The Kid was affable, remembered every joke he'd ever heard, told it with just the right pauses, sometimes in dialect—he had an ear, Billy had—and sang in flawless Spanish in a bell-clear tenor, interrupting himself in mid-lyric to insert a piece of conversation:

"You snared me good, cowboy. When I was in the air I thought I was struck by lightning. You must've been born with a lariat in your hand."

"I was for a fact. It made all the medical journals."

"My name's Henry. What do they call you?"

"Charlie."

"Charlie, you reckon you can teach me how to throw a loop like you?"

"I'd admire to, kid, if they don't put the rope on you first."

"Every ranch started with somebody else's beeves. They can't hang you for that."

"Can and have. Also that horse you're riding wears the LX brand."

"I got a bill of sale somewheres."

"I believe you, kid, I really do; but that saddle's got my boss's initials carved in the fender."

———

"Why'd he give you a false name?" Hammett asked. "I never heard where he skulked."

"He didn't. He was Henry McCarty. I reckon he lived to regret changing it. What politician worth the graft would bother to put a price on somebody called Henry the Kid?"

"Hard to believe he was good company. I thought he was blood simple."

"I can't answer for what come of him later, though I rode down two good horses going after him for the reward. I'd of brung him in, too, instead of shooting him in the back in the dark. I do know the first time he was arrested it was for stealing clothes from a Chinese laundry."

"Gooseberry lay, no kidding? I didn't read that in your book. It was all shoot-outs and midnight rides."

"It'd be a shame to write a whole book and not make one sale."

"Did you know Pat Garrett?"

"His letter got me into the Agency, though I never liked him. He was tall as Abe Lincoln but not half so honorable. He became a tax collector after he assassinated the Kid. He got himself shot by nobody knows who while he was pissing on the side of the road."

"Were you there?"

"Not guilty. But folks will talk, and I'm a good listener."

"I'm starting to think everything I ever read about the West got it all backwards."

"Not everything. But when they say it's both true and authentic, you can bet it's neither."

"I thought writing was honest work. It's why I left the Agency."

"No wonder you can't find a publisher with a flashlight and a map of New York City."

"It's worse than dishonest. It's a waste of experience."

"Experience is like rhubarb. You got to add sugar to make a pie."

"Huh." Hammett threw his cigarette overboard and started rolling a fresh one. "How'd the Kid get away from that town marshal?"

Siringo grinned.

"Shinnied up the jail chimney and lit out black as Old Joe for New Mexico. He was skinnier'n your boy Feeney. They never made a pair of cuffs that fit him."

"Was he as ugly as his picture?"

"That wasn't him. He wasn't any longer on brains than most outlaws, but he was smart enough not to get his picture struck with paper out on him all over New Mexico Territory, like them dumb sons of bitches in the Wild Bunch. Some slick photographer paid a tramp to pose with a prop pistol and carbine, made plenty of copies, and sold 'em like French postcards. The Kid had nice teeth and he was generous with them. That's what made all the señoritas wet their drawers the minute they laid eyes on him."

"I'm beginning to see what you mean about rhubarb. The truth may not be ugly, but it can always use a boost."

"I'll make a writer out of you yet, Mr. Hammett."

9

The Sonoma Valley was as alien to an old plainsman like Siringo as a lunar landscape—which may have served as Jack London's inspiration to call the location of his ranch *The Valley of the Moon*—with strange bare rounded hills standing shoulder-to-shoulder. Riding up one side, down the other, and up the side of the next grew monotonous in a bluetick hurry. Even the horses were bored.

"When do you calculate this country'll get tired of jumping up and down and stretch out?" he asked.

But Hammett was unresponsive. A sidelong glance showed a pallid and sweating rider hanging on to his saddle horn as if it were a life preserver. His slouch hat was soaked through, and although he'd shrugged out of his coat and secured it behind his cantle, his shirt lay plastered to his chest. Siringo could practically count his ribs.

"You ain't fixing to die on me, are you? 'Cause I ain't packing your carcass back over these goldarn hills."

"Don't worry about me, old-timer. I'm sandier than I look."

"You'd have to be, or I'd have you half-buried by now. What possessed a man with your affliction to set down in a wet place like Frisco?"

"I tried that desert air in Los Angeles, but Hollywood just made me sicker. What they're doing to Fatty Arbuckle shouldn't happen to a dog."

"Think he's innocent?"

"He's guilty of throwing a party that got out of hand. If you're asking me did he rape that girl with a Coca-Cola bottle, the answer's no. It's just an excuse to throw him in jail so the studios won't have to pay him his high salary."

"I'd expect a Marxist would say he got what he deserved for being a capitalist."

"Well, I don't make a religion of it." Hammett fortified himself from his flask. His color improved.

It was well past noon when they mounted a hill between rows of staked-out grapevines. The smell of the ripening fruit was overpowering. It made a man woozy.

"Reckon they're for grape juice?" Siringo asked.

"Oh, that and the Catholic Church. You can't feed a worshipper three-two beer and tell him it's the Blood of Christ." They topped the rise. Hammett drew rein. "There it is, Beauty Ranch."

"You don't say. I never would of figured it out on my lonesome."

Beyond the base of the hill, the furrowed road passed under an arch fashioned from among the redwoods that lined it, the wood carved in a twisting configuration spelling the single word BEAUTY.

"We'll put on our best behavior from here. It's a female household since Jack's death. Not that you might think so when you meet the widow."

"Which I take it you have."

"Oh, she's a force of nature. You can't miss her when she's in town."

"Then what in thunder was that Walter Noble Burns business? She'll know you by sight and have us both thrown off the spread for imposters."

"I'd read in the *Examiner* she was in New York, dealing with Jack's publishers. That's what I get for believing everything I read."

"What makes you think she ain't?"

Hammett was rolling a cigarette. "Because that's her coming this way."

Siringo saw a lone rider approaching the gate from the other side at full gallop. The figure wore riding breeches, a white shirt and broad-brimmed hat, and knee-length boots. He drew his spyglass from the bedroll, snapped it open, and focused on the horse and rider. "Holy jumping Jesus, it *is* a woman."

"What'd you expect when I said 'her,' a sow bear?"

"I never seen a woman ride straddle."

"The better you know Charmian, the more things you'll see you never did."

"I don't figure we'll get on, then. I don't burn tobacco in a woman's presence and I expect the same sort of decency from her."

"If you did, she'd probably bum some off you and burn it in yours."

"You do all the talking. I'm likely to say something rash and waste the trip." He folded the glass with a bang.

She was an uncommonly good rider, he'd say that for her. The horse was a fine one, a sleek sorrel with a blaze, and together they raced down as bad a stretch of road as he'd seen without a single misplaced hoof. He himself wouldn't have dared it in his prime: One loose rock, one small hole, and half a ton of mammal rolled over on top of you like a rockslide.

"God spare me from a reckless woman," he muttered, not low enough to avoid one of Hammett's nasal snickers.

Twenty yards from the top of the rise where the two men

waited, the woman leaned back on the reins, slowing the animal. It was a stallion, Siringo knew then; that snort when it caught the scent of his mare couldn't be mistaken. The mare in its turn tossed its head and shook its mane. *Two* reckless females, he thought; just what the situation was missing. He choked up on the bit and his mount settled itself.

The Widow London switched from a canter to a walk and drew alongside the visitors. "Welcome to Beauty Ranch, gentlemen. You're Mr. Hammett, if I remember correctly. Dear Eliza's a conscientious manager, but she gulls easily. Would you introduce me to your friend?"

"Charmian London, Charles A. Siringo."

She brightened considerably. A striking woman rather than a pretty one, she had a boyish figure and a turned-up nose in a long horse face and buck teeth that altered her appearance greatly when she smiled. He judged her to be nearer fifty than forty—senior to her late husband—but fit, with no gray in the dark hair that hung in a bob to the corners of her jaw. The hat, he saw, was a Montana Pinch, with dimpled crown and a broad silk band, considerably weathered, and too big for her; it must have taken at least a section of newspaper stuffed under the sweatband to keep it from sliding down over her eyes. He seemed to remember having seen a similar rig on Jack London's head in a rotogravure. Quite probably this was it. It made her look younger somehow, like a little girl playing dress-up.

"Not *Charlie* Siringo, the cowboy detective?"

"I was. Now I'm just plain Charlie Siringo."

A slender hand took his in a man's grip. "How Wolf would have loved this moment! He enjoyed *A Texas Cowboy.*"

"Wolf?"

"My dear Jack. If you like, I'll show you his copy, all scribbled in the margins with his praise."

He was flattered despite himself, and sad suddenly. He'd have enjoyed discussing his work with the most famous writer in the world, even if the man was a Socialist. Before he could respond, she turned to Hammett.

"Now. What is this Burns business? We met, I believe, at a demonstration calling for the release of Eugene Debs. You told me then you were a writer of fiction, not history."

"Habit. I was a detective myself, but no cowboy, and I learned early on to lie first and apologize later. I didn't think you were home."

"I was delayed. The lawyer for Jack's literary estate is in Los Angeles, threatening to shut down a moving picture company if. it proceeds with its plans to film *The Sea Wolf* without the courtesy of paying for the privilege. I thought it best to stay close."

"I dealt with their like," Siringo said. "I should of brung a rope."

She slid her hat to the back of her head to study the gathering clouds. "Rain's coming. You can tell me in the cottage why you're here."

They rode three abreast through the open gate and between more redwoods. To the right, after they'd been riding a while, rose the charred timbers of Wolf House, Jack London's dream home, gone up in flames years ago. Siringo had read of the disaster and felt bad for the owner. He himself had been flush then, and had considered building a place of his own on a more modest scale; the incident had made him put off the project, the only thing predictable about the future being its uncertainty. In retrospect, he wouldn't have been any worse off than he was had he gone through with it. There wasn't a dime's worth of difference, worry-wise, between a man who was flat broke and one who was so deep in debt he'd never climb out.

Farther on, they came alongside an enormous boulder that

looked out of place in a clearing in the woods. Charmian removed her hat as they passed it. Hammett followed suit, and signaled to Siringo to do the same, which he did, hoisting his eyebrows in a silent question.

"London's grave," Hammett whispered. "They rolled a rock on top of it to keep the coyotes from digging it up."

There was something about the ranch, beautiful as it was in its sylvan setting, that depressed Siringo. It was a holy shrine. Nothing had been overlooked, from the widow's dreamy tones when she spoke of the late writer to the still-standing remnants of the great ruined house, which ought to have been torn down the minute the ashes cooled, and now this rock. He wondered, impiously, if London had come out from under it after three days.

Hatted again, they passed a Fordson tractor idling by a silo built of concrete blocks and then an extensive series of pens where Siringo's nose told him, well before he saw the animals rooting around inside, hogs were raised. Beyond that was a stable. He became alert as Charmian stepped down to hand her reins to a boy who came out from inside.

"Rub down these gentlemen's mounts first, please, Abner. They've ridden all the way from San Francisco."

The men dismounted. Hammett put his coat back on with the weapons in the pockets. The boy who took their reins was a sullen-faced youth of about nineteen, with a mop of brown hair that needed soap and shears, in filthy bib overalls and rubber boots crusted with manure: Abner Butterfield, who had presided over Wyatt Earp's stables the day his prize racehorse had disappeared. Siringo noticed the young detective appraising him as he led the animals into the stable.

The first drops of rain were plunking their hats when Charmian London led them up a flagged path to the porch of a whitewashed cottage. She was shorter than Siringo, a surprise; she had a long torso and the kind of bone structure that usually belonged to a woman of stature, all loose-limbed, with long narrow hands and feet to match. She pulled open a screen door against the pressure of a noisy spring, hung her hat on a peg, and ran her fingers through her boyishly short hair. Her guests took up two more pegs, Siringo adding his sourdough coat, and scrubbed their feet on a sisal mat after her lead.

They entered a room that took up most of the ground floor, which served as both dining room and parlor, with a plain table under a ship's helm hung with chains from the ceiling, oil lamps mounted on the varnished handles, and rockers for relaxing.

"Eliza's gone to the village for supplies," said their hostess. "That's good luck for you. She's guileless, as I said, but she can be a fierce old dragon when she realizes she's been taken in. She'd have had a hand throw you both out, and no mistake."

"And you, Mrs. London?" The cozy domesticity of the arrangement, with the rain hissing now on the roof—a roof without holes—brought out Siringo's soft-talking side; but he was rusty and groped his way.

Her face became homely when it wasn't wearing a smile. "I'm not sure yet. If it turns out you've come to pick my brain for stories you can sell, I'll do the ejecting myself. I was Jack's favorite sparring partner in the ring he built, and he taught me to shoot and fence." She inclined her head toward a pair of foils with basket hilts crossed on one wall. "I could run you through before you raised either of your weapons."

10

He had to smile at that. The woman had sharp eyes. The Colt was plain in its worn chamois holster, but even Hammett had missed the Forehand & Wadsworth under Siringo's shirt. "We're not here for ideas."

"We'll see. Are you hungry? We have sandwiches and beer. Becky can't abide turning away even a plagiarist on an empty stomach."

"Becky?"

"Jack's youngest, by his first wife. She's here on a visit." She raised her voice. "Becky?" No answer. "She's probably upstairs, reading."

"One of her father's books?" asked Hammett.

"One of Dickens'. *David Copperfield*, I believe. She's on the second volume. She started the first in January. She makes it a point to read Dickens every winter. A determined child, Mr. Hammett. And no longer a child, as I must keep reminding myself. Sandwiches, gentlemen? Beer? Something stronger? Jack left us well-stocked."

"Thank you," Siringo said. "I could eat a horse, and as you can see, Hammett plumb disappears when he turns sideways. And a beer would go good right about now."

She looked at Hammett, who nodded.

"I'll get them. Make yourselves at home meanwhile." She left them, her English riding boots clip-clopping on the redwood floor.

Hammett sat, coughing quietly into his fist, while Siringo toured the room. China settings in every design filled a row of glass cabinets. Jack London had been nearly as well-known for his hospitality as for his writings, but they looked neglected now; although not a speck of dust showed, they bore the air of objects that hadn't left their places for weeks, months, maybe years, like books in a library owned by a semiliterate man who wanted to appear educated. The trophies on display—swords, boxing gloves, long guns and pistols, a pick worn to nubs, probably during prospecting days in Alaska—all contributed to the sensation that they were visiting a museum, or more particularly a mausoleum.

Hammett, apparently, had been thinking along the same lines. "Scatter a few heads around and the place might have belonged to Teddy Roosevelt."

"I met him once." Siringo lowered himself into a rocker and squirmed around on his saddle sores. "He didn't have anything good to say about London. We shared the same opinion of radicals."

"He'd've thrown me down the White House steps." The young man looked around. Reassured, evidently, by a framed photo of London writing with a cigarette drooping from his mouth, he took out his makings. "Hell, I'm out of tobacco."

Siringo tossed him his pouch.

He examined it. "What is it, horsehide?"

"Buffalo."

"I thought buffalo'd be coarser."

"It is, till you get to the balls."

Hammett smiled. "What happens if I rub it?"

"Turns into a pair of saddle bags."

He laughed his snarky laugh, opened the pouch, and sprinkled some tobacco onto a paper. He was lighting the cigarette when a young woman entered. She stopped when she saw the two men, who rose, Hammett just behind Siringo.

"I'm sorry," she said. "When I smelled someone smoking, I thought it was one of Father's old friends. I've missed that smell."

She looked just under twenty, a pretty, grave-faced girl with blond hair that curled inward at her shoulders, in a sheath dress with an unnaturally low waist, the way women her age were wearing them now. There seemed to be a good figure underneath. Her feet were small in patent-leather pumps that buttoned to the ankles.

"I'm Mr. Siringo, and this is Mr. Hammett. We're guests of your stepmother's. I'm sorry to say we never knew your father."

"You missed something, I assure you." A wisp of a smile lightened her features, and Siringo saw the resemblance then. She had her father's deep-set eyes and strong brow, but the shy upward twist at the corners of her mouth had appeared in hundreds of photographs of the oyster-pirate-turned-sailor-turned-prospector-turned-vagabond-turned-world-traveler-turned-bestselling-writer. They were very modern faces, Siringo thought; not at all the grim visages of his contemporaries, men and women resigned to hardship, who only smiled when something amused them. Very little had.

The smile vanished then, like breath from a mirror. "You call yourself guests, but that's no comfort. As long as I can remember, guests in this house have taken advantage of my father's good nature. They borrowed money and didn't pay it back, stole his ideas and sold them to other writers—one of them even left with a dozen of his silk pajamas in his suitcase. Pajamas! Death hasn't stopped them. You're not movies, are you?"

"Movies?"

"Moving-picture people. They're the worst of all. They make away with Father's experiences and imagination and hard work like thieves in the night."

"Mr. Hammett and I are here only to ask the favor of a few minutes' conversation. We're detectives."

"You mean like Nick Carter?"

Hammett laughed, this time without sarcasm. "Not as heroic as that; but if it's all right with you, we'd prefer to discuss the details with the lady of the house."

She beamed—genuinely beamed—and clapped her hands. "A lady! Oh, she'd be amused by that. She says that's Mother's area of expertise." She leaned forward, lowering her voice. "She voted for Debs."

"So did I," said Hammett. "We met at a rally."

"Riot, you mean." Siringo frowned.

"There you are, you willful girl. I could have used help with this tray." Charmian entered, carrying a silver tray containing a pile of sandwiches, a pitcher of beer, and two schooners gray with frost. It was a feast fit for a troop of cavalry.

"I'd have offered encouragement," Becky said.

"Sauce! Since you've obviously all met, you may as well join us." The widow placed the tray on a low table carved from pale wood and filled the glasses from the pitcher. A thick head grew on each. "Brewed on the premises, gentlemen, from hops planted by Jack; for private consumption, hence legal. Thank the Lord Congressman Volstead doesn't prohibit us from drinking, only selling. The sandwiches are liverwurst and ham. Old Pete, dear," she told Becky. "He died in his sleep last week."

"Not Pete! Father caught me riding him once and said it was time I learned horsemanship. He was the gentlest thing." She perched herself on the edge of a rocker, helped herself, and bit into two slices of coarse bread with a thick slice of Old Pete in between.

Siringo fidgeted, disapproving of the girl's presence; what if she took it in her head to warn Abner Butterfield they'd come for him? Readers of Nick Carter got all manner of things into their heads about injustice and such. But Hammett caught his eye and gave his head an almost imperceptible shake. *We're outnumbered*, it seemed to say.

"Abner?" Charmian, who'd taken neither food nor drink, stopped rocking her chair. "But Mr. Earp gave him a sterling character."

Siringo responded before Hammett could; settling women wasn't for a man who considered them the enemy. "That was at our suggestion, ma'am. We had to be sure he'd light someplace he could be found."

Becky stopped chewing Old Pete. "You let us invite a thief into our home?"

"Calm yourself, dear. We don't live in the stable. However, it is a point. I had to sell most of the stock to settle Jack's debts, but I kept his favorites, Washoe Ban and Neuadd Hillside. They're past their prime, but I've turned down offers for them recently. If they were to vanish—"

"That's why we didn't waste our time getting here," said Hammett. "The sooner we can talk to him, the sooner he'll be off your hands."

"What makes you so certain he's guilty?" she asked.

Siringo said, "We ain't, but he was the last to see Spirit Dancer before she went missing. Every case starts there."

"He came here afoot, Eliza said. He told her he'd hitchhiked from San Francisco."

"He wouldn't be likely to ride a stole horse, ma'am. Chances are somebody bribed him to sit on his hands while it was took. We're here to ask him who it was."

"Will you arrest him?" Becky seemed to have forgotten all about the sandwich she was holding.

"We don't have that authority," Hammett said. "All we want is a few minutes' conversation."

Charmian's lips pressed tight.

"You were wise to give Eliza a story, and had I known your mission, my reaction would have been the same. But let's get this over with and send Abner on his way. This ranch has sheltered more than its share of brigands as it is." She rose. Siringo and Hammett scrambled to their feet.

"No need for your presence," Siringo said. "It may be unpleasant."

She laughed shortly. She had a smooth rich contralto, and even mirthless laughter was musical in her case. "I nearly died of malaria, lost two babies in the hospital, sailed through fierce tropical storms, and nursed the finest man I've ever known through his last agonies. I'm no stranger to unpleasant adventures. No, Becky, stay here and put away these things. Your mother thinks little enough of me now. She'll never forgive me if you come to harm."

Becky, who had risen, colored and set her jaw, looking more than ever like her father; but after a moment she acquiesced. "I shall expect you back in a quarter-hour. If you haven't returned, I'll come for you, with as many hands as I can muster."

"And a fine lot of pirates they are. Gentlemen, you are forewarned." Her stepmother removed one of the revolvers from its glass case, rummaged in a drawer until she found a box of cartridges, and loaded the cylinder, wasting not a moment in the operation. She thrust the weapon under her belt in the small of her back and concealed the handle beneath her shirt-waist.

The rain had let up, and the clouds to the west had parted to release a shaft of copper-colored sunlight. A mist continued to fall. It was a combination of conditions Siringo disliked intensely. *"Devil's whipping his wife, Charlie,"* Shanghai Pierce had said in that situation; although what Mrs. Satan could possibly have done to rile up her husband, Siringo couldn't guess. He'd invented disloyalty along with all the other vices.

Charmian insisted on leading the way along the flagged path to the stables. The two detectives stayed as close as they could without stepping on her heels. The old cowboy admired her trim waist, on top of all her other attributes; he could have used her reloading for him in that Gem shithole. She wasn't that much younger than him, he decided.

Step down, Charlie. You don't hunt vermin with your bump of romance up.

———

They found Butterfield in the tack room, sitting on a milking stool and eating sardines from the can with his fingers. A single window with four discolored panes let in all the light there was. The detectives' gear was there, including Siringo's Winchester in its scabbard. He hoped the stable boy hadn't monkeyed with the rounds.

"Abner, these men would like to ask you some questions. I'd consider it a favor if you'd answer them truthfully."

His sullen face pulled into a scowl and he leant his weight forward, ready to spring upright. He hadn't risen on her entrance, which to Siringo's mind settled the point about his character. But he folded that thought out of sight and put on his most amiable expression.

"Abner, is it? I had a horse by that name. Damn fine mount; beg pardon, Mrs. London. I'm Charlie. This here is"—he hesitated; *Dashiell* seemed to him to strike the wrong note.

"Sam." Hammett had adopted a curt attitude. Pinkerton hadn't invented the ploy, but it had been around so long Siringo reckoned it went back to Pharaoh.

"Sam's from around here. I live in Los Angeles. You come from there, didn't you?"

"What if I did?" The boy went on chewing with his mouth open, strings of fish caught between stained teeth, one of them gold, but he set aside the can and wiped his hands on his overalls.

"I wouldn't hold it agin you. There are worse crimes. Abner, it's Spirit Dancer we want to talk to you about."

Butterfield started up from the chair, his expression bent on flight. Hammett placed the flat of his hand against the boy's chest and shoved him back down. The stool balanced precariously on one leg, then righted itself with a bang.

Siringo hooked his thumbs in his belt, spreading his coat casually so that the butt of the Colt showed. "We ain't here to accuse you. All we want to know is who paid you to go pick daisies while the horse went and vanished."

"You calling me a hoss thief?"

"What if we did?" Hammett spread his feet, hands balled into fists at his sides.

"Easy, Sam. Nobody said that, son. I know Wyatt Earp from way back. He can pinch a penny till the buffalo bawls. There ain't a soul living wouldn't give a better offer the courtesy of a listen."

Charmian, standing near the open door that led toward the stalls, smiled kindly, without showing her teeth. "It's all right, Abner. I give you my word these men won't take you away. You're under the protection of Beauty Ranch. As my husband used to say, there's no sanctuary more reliable."

"I don't know what that is, but there's no call—"

"Balls to sanctuary," spat Hammett. "You can talk, or ride double back with us to the Frisco jail, or come tied belly-down over the saddle. It don't make no difference to me which you choose. This offer expires in—ten, nine, eight . . ."

"Listen to reason, son. You don't want to see what happens when he finishes the count."

"Six." Hammett reached up and took a coiled bullwhip off a nail. "Five." He uncoiled it.

The boy's dirty face paled. He looked up at Charmian. "You gonna let him flay the hide off of me? Who is it I work for, you or them?"

"All you have to do is what I asked." Her smile was still in place.

"Three. Hell, I forget what comes next." With a move so swift it impressed even Siringo, who'd seen Bill Cody clear leather in the arena and thought only a locomotive was faster, the young detective flicked the whip in a side-hand maneuver. A sharp crack, and the right side of Butterfield's overalls tore open. He howled, clapped a hand to the rip. Blood slid between his fingers from a gash on his rib cage. *"Jesus!"*

"Never met the man." Hammett drew back the whip, this time higher, on a level with the boy's face.

"Nobody paid me! It was my idea! That skinflint Earp; wouldn't advance me a penny on that puny bit he paid me, for cigarettes and other incidentals. I figured—"

"Get down!"

Dropping the whip, Hammett moved in two directions at once, kicking out a leg of the stool and twisting to grab Charmian London around the waist and bear her to the floor, falling down on top of her. Butterfield crashed down at the same instant, his legs indistinguishable from those of the stool. Siringo, whose reflexes were rusty, moved an instant slower, but got himself clear of the window just as one of the panes exploded. The report followed, warped by wind and distance.

11

"Rifle!" barked Hammett. "I saw the sun flash on the scope." He was still lying on top of Charmian, who had the sense not to struggle.

"Figured that. Where?"

"One o'clock."

"I asked where, not when."

"Top of that rise." He pointed.

Butterfield was stirring, trying to disentangle himself from the stool. Siringo laid the barrel of the Colt alongside his temple, stilling him. The old detective holstered the weapon and reached out to catch his rifle scabbard by its strap and drag it over. He slid out the carbine, levered a shell into the chamber, and crawled over the unconscious stable boy, creeping up to the sill of the shattered window.

As he watched, exposing only one eye inside the frame, something moved among the redwoods standing at the top of the hill.

He ducked just as another bullet passed through the missing pane, burying itself in the wall opposite with a sound like an axe chopping wood. He sprang up on his knees then, obliterated the rest of the window with the Winchester's barrel, and fired three times fast, working the lever in between.

"You can't hit anything shooting like that," Hammett said, as the echo of the third shot growled away over the hills.

"I don't expect to, just announce there's somebody in here with an iron. Everybody all right?"

Charmian said, "I'm fine. Is Abner dead?"

"Maybe. I didn't hit him gentle."

"You *hit*—?"

"He was a distraction."

"I'm swell," Hammett said. "Thanks for asking."

Siringo shushed him.

The sound of a motor sputtering to life reached them. He'd ducked again after firing the salvo, but now he rose into a cautious crouch, in time to see a battered Model T truck come bucking out of the woods, its flat windshield flashing in the sun as it turned in the direction opposite the stable.

His face was wet on one side. He swept the back of his hand across his cheek and looked at the smear of blood. A shard of glass had brushed past just close enough to break the skin.

Then something heavy struck the backs of his bent knees and his legs folded in on themselves. He had sense enough to twist his body and avoid plunging through the window with its border of razor-sharp glass. As he did so, he opened a path for Abner Butterfield, who'd knocked him off his feet, to scramble over him and dive through the opening with his arms crossed in front of his face.

"Stand clear!" Hammett got to his knees and leveled his .38 at the stable boy, who was running toward the tree-topped slope, his arms pumping.

Siringo bumped up the pistol with his elbow. A round crashed into the rafters overhead.

"He ain't told us what he done with the horse!"

"Sorry."

"You yonkers got too much lead in your pencil and no brains in your head." He threw the Winchester at Hammett, who dropped his gun to catch it in both hands.

"What—?"

"Cover me in case that flivver comes back." He looked at Charmian. "What's the best horse you got? I don't mean the prettiest."

The widow had pushed herself up into a seated position. "Washoe Ban," she said. "He was Jack's favorite. He's old, but he's in excellent shape. First stall."

It was a suspiciously beautiful black gelding with sleek haunches and a deep chest, which at least was something. He grasped its mane in both hands and heaved himself astraddle. He hadn't ridden bareback this century, but some things you never forgot, especially when you were in a hurry. The animal grunted in surprise and pique, but bolted out of the stall when he put his heels to it. A lariat hung in a stiff coil outside the stall; he snatched it off its nail as he passed.

Charmian—no slouch herself when push came to shove—was already at the double doors leading outside. She unlatched them and flung one open just as the horse got to it. Siringo had to duck to avoid cracking his skull on the top of the opening.

Once outside, the old gelding caught the fresh air in its nostrils and went into full gallop without any urging; all he had to do was point it toward the running figure growing smaller in the distance and they were off, gobbling up the yards.

The ground was wet, he'd been too long out of the saddle, and he hadn't thrown a rope since the LX Ranch; as who would? It wasn't a skill that translated into other occupations. Not that it signified: He'd get thrown and bust his neck long before he came within lasso range.

Washoe Ban laid back his ears and thrust his head forward,

making a silhouette like a speeding arrow. His hot wet breath flew back into Siringo's face. The rider hunkered low, but the wind found his untrained hat anyway and snatched it off his head.

———

"I got a cartwheel dollar says Curry fades you in the stretch."

Cassidy was grinning, chewing a cedar toothpick. With his big jaw and his bowler cocked to one side he always looked like an Irish prizefighter. The brogue he affected to go with his alias contributed to the illusion.

"Just a buck? Why not one of them double eagles you got up in Montana, you're so sure?"

"I hear you talking, but your words don't mean horseshit. I like you, Charlie, but you ain't rode with us yet. You could be a Pinkerton for all I know, burrowing your way into our little fambly."

"That's a laugh, that is." Siringo frowned. *"Why are you boys always racing your horses? What if the law shows up and they're bottomed out?"*

"That's why this place is called Hole in the Wall. They got to ride in single-file, where Sundance can Winchester 'em off one by one. Meanwhile we keep lean. You ought to trade that bitty mustang. They might win races, but a big stud carries more."

"You mean like a Wells Fargo box?"

Cassidy laughed and almost choked on his toothpick. "You keep after a man, Charlie, that you do. I'm starting to think you are a Pink."

He won, too, by three lengths; Kid Curry, the cross-eyed son of a bitch, hated him for that even more than the other thing.

———

The blamed fool boy was running square toward his would-be killer. Siringo was sure Butterfield was the target, or the slug would have passed through an upper pane, aimed at the three people who were standing, and not one on the bottom, which had been in line with the seated stable boy's head. The old cowboy dug his heels deep into the gelding's flanks, and the horse found more bottom with a lunge. The wind stung Siringo's eyes. He felt a tug on his cheek; nothing stopped up a cut like a good hard run.

But, hell's bells! The fleeing boy stayed the same distance away, like a tree in the desert, its promise of water forever beyond reach no matter how straight you rode nor how long. One of those dreams where time was getting dearer by the minute and you were running in place.

And then he began to make progress.

The horse was galloping flat-out, leveling the slope, and Butterfield was losing steam. He looked back over his shoulder once, which slowed him even more. The burst of speed he put on in his fresh panic wasn't enough to maintain the gap. Siringo swatted his mount's right haunch with the coiled lariat. The animal snorted—contemptuously, Siringo thought—and their pace quickened. Where did the old ball-less wonder keep it all? It didn't seem fair somehow.

The youth slipped in the mud, but caught his balance in midstumble and made for the trees, his torn overalls flapping. But that little loss was a big gain for the man on horseback. Keeping his eye on Butterfield, he straightened, raised the rope, took a couple of swoops, paying out hemp between his thumb and palm, steered soft right with his knees as the boy zigged that direction, took a swoop, calculated the wind by the movement in the redwoods' branches, took a swoop, grinned in concentration, took a swoop, and let fly.

The stiff loop flew high and straight, the rope whizzing through his hand; but it drifted left. It was going to miss. The horse was slowing now, just a little, but clearly it had touched bottom at last. Age was their common enemy. If Butterfield made it into the trees and over the top of the hill, Siringo wouldn't get another chance.

But God abhors a horse thief.

The wind caught the rope, the boy zigged left, and the loop dropped over his head like a horseshoe scoring a ringer.

As soon as it cleared his shoulders, Siringo leaned back hard with a fistful of mane. With a painful whinny the horse ground to a stop, plowing furrows in the ground with its hooves as the rider gave the lariat a mighty backward jerk.

"That's the boy, Charlie!" Shanghai Pierce called out from outside the corral. "Set the hook deep! I got to take you with me fishing one of these days."

The world flew out from under Butterfield's feet. He executed an inverted U two feet into the air, lit on his tailbone, sprawled onto his back, and before he could recover from the stun of it all the man on the other end of the rope heeled Washoe Ban around and headed back toward the stable at a brisk lope, dragging the fight plumb out of the stable boy. Holy Christ, but life was a beautiful thing.

Then, as he slowed to a walk, he spotted the group of strangers standing between him and the stable, ugly bastards in dungarees, steel poking through the toes of their workboots. They were armed with scythes and sledgehammers and pitchforks. Siringo's hat was skewered on one set of tines.

12

He took a dally around the saddle horn to free his hands and drew the Colt, cocking it and pointing it at the man in the center of the line. The man had black whiskers that appeared to grow straight up from his neck all the way to his eyes, whose whites shone through the thicket. He held a sledgehammer near the end of the handle in throwing position.

"Six rounds, seven men," Siringo said. "Which one of you thinks it's his lucky day?"

No one moved.

"Stand down, gentlemen. This man is my guest."

Charmian had emerged from the stable behind the men, to stand beside Becky London; the plucky little squirt had made good on her promise to bring on the cavalry. She'd added a hat to her ensemble, with a velvet brim tilted toward one temple. Her stepmother held her late husband's revolver against one hip with the hammer eared back.

"That how you're fetching a man to supper now?" Black Beard pointed his hammer at the stable boy on the ground. He held the heavy tool straight out; three feet of hickory ending in four pounds of steel. Siringo would not want to take him on at wrestling.

The old detective let the others do the talking. He kept the pistol aimed at the man's breastbone.

"He's wanted in L.A. for horse-stealing," said Hammett. He was inside the building, leaning on his forearms on the sill of the broken window. "You can come with us if you want, and share the charge. Me, I never made friends that fast."

Black Beard turned his head far enough to see the .38 in the young detective's hand. He let the hammer slide through his hand until he was holding it more casually near the head.

The tension went out of the group then. Weapons lowered. Obviously the man with the sledgehammer was the leader.

"You can step down, Mr. Siringo," Charmian said. "Yuri, help him with the prisoner."

One of the other men, slope-shouldered, with a fine set of imperial whiskers, leaned his scythe against the stable wall and came forward.

Siringo uncocked and holstered his Colt and dismounted. Together he and Yuri got the dazed Butterfield to his feet and free of the lasso. The bib of his overalls hung down where a strap had broken, but he appeared unharmed except for scrapes and bruises. Black Beard dropped his hammer and took Washoe Ban's reins while the two men escorted the stable boy toward the building, a hand on each arm.

The man with Siringo's Stetson raised his pitchfork for the detective to jerk it loose of the tines. Siringo paused, scowled at the punctures, slapped the hat against his hip to knock loose the dirt, and put it on. As he stepped past the man with the pitchfork, he curled his free hand into a fist and swung. The man's nose collapsed and he sat on the ground.

"Respect a man's hat."

Hammett laughed his snarky laugh.

Charmian hung up the gallows telephone in the combination dining room and parlor and went back to her seat. "That was a Sergeant Conifer with the San Francisco Police, returning my call. A horse answering Spirit Dancer's description was found half an hour ago in the livery stable of a man named Soo Lok."

"That sounds like the place where we rented our mounts," Hammett said. "We could've saved ourselves a trip."

"I ain't complaining." Siringo sipped beer, spat a hop back into the glass, and sat back in his rocker, admiring Charmian London. It was dark out, and lamplight was uncommonly kind to her cheekbones. "I was pretty sure Butterfield told the truth this time. No one wants to be drug by a horse twice."

"That was barbaric." Becky London didn't look up from *David Copperfield* open in her lap; on the other hand, she hadn't turned the page in twenty minutes.

Her stepmother ignored the interruption. "The resemblance wasn't so close at first, but the sergeant was thorough enough to apply a piece of wet burlap to the horse's forehead. He found Spirit Dancer's star-shaped blaze under the paint. Personally I doubt Abner had the intelligence to think of that; but I doubt the police will be able to prove it was Soo Lok, unless Abner implicates him. It was probably a crime of opportunity. He saw his client was nervous, guessed theft was involved, and took steps to protect himself and whatever profit he might draw from the situation. In any case, the fact someone went to all that trouble certainly redounds to the theory's credit."

"Who goes to jail over it don't signify, though Earp'll likely want somebody to pay; he's vindictive. But he's more interested in getting the horse back. Now all we got to figure's who benefited from putting Butterfield in the ground before he could tell his story."

"We know *who*," Hammett said. "*Why's* the question."

Charmian looked from one to the other. "What is it you think I'm too delicate to know? If having an assassin on my property doesn't entitle me, I don't know what would."

"Mr. Hammett's just speculating. I'd like to run it past your sheriff before we go around casting stones. Can you trust your hands to make Butterfield stay put till he comes?"

"They're used to harder work. As I said, they're a fine bunch of pirates." She looked at the clock on the big stone mantel. "He should have been here by now. What's keeping him?"

"Shaking every hand on the way," muttered Becky. "He started running for reelection the minute he was sworn in."

"Patience, child. You've a lifetime to learn about the world of men." Charmian returned her attention to Siringo. "You know, you didn't have to break Ivan's nose. He and his brother Yuri have been working here since Jack brought them from a Russian settlement up north. They're sawyers by training, and between them they do the work of ten men."

"It's a self-defense issue. In Texas, a fellow's hat can be the only thing between him and a set of fried brains."

"Need I remind you this isn't Texas?" This time Becky met his gaze. She still had her own hat on, as if she'd forgotten about it. He thought she looked comical sitting around her own house wearing a hat.

Hammett turned from a shelf of books whose titles he'd been examining and smiled over his beer.

"Don't be too hard on him, miss. He's got an allergy to lynch mobs. And he could've shot Butterfield and saved himself effort."

"He's a brute. This is Beauty Ranch, not some filthy mining camp."

"All the more reason to see you came to no harm for harboring a thief without knowing it."

Siringo could see his partner was sweet on the girl. He changed the subject before things got any more complicated.

"You pull a good brute yourself, Hammett. For a minute there in the stable I thought you was going to skin Butterfield like a jackrabbit."

"It's the moustache." He touched his upper lip. "All the picture villains wear them."

"You're all impossible! I'm going home to Mother in the morning." Becky snapped shut her book, got up, and left the room.

"She inherited Jack's temper," Charmian said. "The rows he had with her mother were known to all the neighbors, but he never laid a hand on her. He was all blow, and so is Becky."

Hammett said, "I think she's just about perfect."

Pistons clattered outside. Charmian put aside her cup of tea.

"That will be the sheriff in his Dodge."

The sheriff's name was Vernon Dillard; and five minutes' acquaintance was sufficient to make Siringo suspect he'd changed the spelling, substituting *i* for *u*.

He wore a town suit and a homburg like the president's, but that was as close as he got to looking like a man in a responsible job. His coat barely buttoned across his paunch and his big ham face was red and streaming by the time they got to the top of the ridge. He squatted over the tread marks the truck had left, and made as much noise getting back up as a cow giving birth to a calf with a full set of horns.

"Good luck finding the man that belongs to that rig," he said. "Half the property owners in the county own a Ford truck."

Hammett shook his head. "The eel doesn't live in this county. He sleeps in the Frisco sewer and eats raw fish."

"You big-city detectives read too many cheap magazines. If it's this eel character you keep jawing about, he's probably working for one of London's creditors. He left a lot of bills unpaid when he croaked."

The young man opened his mouth again, but Siringo stared him into silence.

"Thanks for coming out, Sheriff," he said. "You'll put a man or two on watch, in case he comes back?"

"Just for a day or two, and I don't mind telling you it's a waste of time. He was just trying to put a scare in the widow, and now he's done that, he won't be back. I'm short-handed enough sending men all over these hills hunting down alky cookers. I can't spare one to wet-nurse a couple of skittish women all spring."

"Spoken like a true servant of the people," Hammett said. "You can't step ten feet out your office door without stumbling into a speakeasy. What's the going rate to eliminate the competition from the sticks?"

Dillard's face reddened another shade. "How's about I run you in for lugging around that flask in your pocket?"

"Go ahead, sweetheart. The law says I can drink all I want, as long as it doesn't catch me selling any. It's been a long time since I lost sleep worrying what a tin badge thinks of me."

The sheriff dug a sap out of his hip pocket and slapped his other palm with it. "Maybe I offered to take you in for questioning and you put up a fight."

"Don't lie on my account." Hammett reached into the pocket containing his brass knuckles. Siringo's hand shot out and clamped down on his wrist.

A tense moment followed. Then Dillard grinned, straining the bulge of tobacco in his left cheek, and returned the sap to its pocket.

"It's a lucky man's got a friend he can count on in a pinch," he said. "But the sun don't shine on the same dog's ass all day. He might not be around next time."

"You like to pick your teeth with dynamite, that it?" said Siringo, when the sheriff was halfway back down the slope.

Hammett had his makings out, but his hand shook so badly the paper fluttered out from between thumb and forefinger. He looked down at the hand, laughing. "Whew!"

When Dillard left, with Abner Butterfield manacled in the Dodge's backseat, Charmian invited her guests to stay the night. Siringo shook his head. They were back in the parlor. Becky London had gone upstairs.

"Mr. Hammett can, if he wants. I'll be hanging around Frisco a couple of days."

"Yeah?" Hammett's brows raised.

"If it's Becky and me you're worried about, shouldn't you stay here?"

"Your sheriff's dead wrong about his intentions, but I think the shooter got what he come for, even if it didn't go the way he had figured. I doubt he had anything to do with stealing horses. He, or the man he's working for, had something on, and a couple of private detectives sniffing around was bad for business, whatever it is. Like a lot of folks he thought if he put our only witness out of the way we'd lose interest. You got to snuff out that kind of thinking right at the source.

"Also I don't like being trailed. I want to get to the bottom of this eel business before I head home."

"Who—or what—is the eel?" Charmian asked. "Gentlemen, I think by now you know I'm no shrinking violet. I demand to know why my house was put under assault."

Hammett looked at his partner. Siringo rocked back and forth, pulled on his pipe, nodded. "Local character," Hammett told Charmian. "He's affiliated with a man named Clanahan."

"That scoundrel." Her face was grim.

PART TWO

OPERATING UNDER THE INFLUENCE

In the early 1920s . . . Hammett was not a writer learning about private detectives, but a private detective learning about writing.

—Joe Gores

13

Samuel Dashiell Hammett was tall and gaunt, with a barbered moustache that made his expression unreadable as a cat's. His hair was pale rather than blond, and when he took off his hat it sprang up into a tall mane as if it had never been held down. His nose was straight and his chin cleft. He looked like a fair-haired Lucifer.

When his landlady called up to say he was wanted on the telephone downstairs, he bounded down the steps and picked up the receiver she'd left dangling from the black box. "Yes, angel?"

"Sam, darling. How did you know it was me?" Jose's mezzo tones crackled, broken up by a thousand miles of interconnecting cables.

"It's always you. No one else knows this number—or wants it. When are you coming out?"

"Just as soon as the doctor says it's safe for me to travel. You know, the first three months are the most crucial."

"I thought it was the first three minutes."

"Don't be coarse. Do you miss me?"

"Sure, but we better not go against doctor's orders."

"You could try to sound disappointed."

"You know I miss you."

"You could come back to Montana."

"I'm stuck here just now. Do you need money?"

"Did you sell something? Why didn't you tell me?"

"No such luck. I took a job."

"What sort of job? A detective job? Sam!"

"It's almost wrapped up. I'll wire you a couple of hundred later today."

"You told me you were done with all that."

"I said if I never worked another case it'd be too soon. It got to be too soon."

"Were you going to tell me?"

"I just did."

"After I pried it out of you. Sam, are you taking care of yourself?"

"Sure." He tucked the earpiece under the corner of his jaw and rolled a cigarette.

"Not smoking?"

"Promise." He held the match without striking it.

"Drinking?"

"Not a drop." He left the flask in his pocket.

"Are you writing?"

"I was, when the phone rang."

"Don't be cross. How's it going?"

"I'm having a little trouble with the plot. I can't figure out what the villain's got in mind."

"Well, you will. I know something the publishers don't."

"What's that, how to answer your mail?"

"No, silly. I know you never quit."

"I quit the Agency. I quit my tomcat ways when I met you. A guy can get used to this quitting business with an angel to help him out."

"Banana oil. Are you sure you can spare two hundred? What will you live on?"

"Love, sweetheart. Like the song says."

"I'm serious. You're not eating, I can tell. You even sound skinny."

"I'm fat as a slug. The client's loaded, don't worry."

"Who is it?"

"You know I never talk about that."

"Is it a woman?"

"Sure. Swell dame. She looks like Theda Bara and dances like Nazimova."

"I'm serious. If you won't tell me, I'll burn up every penny of that money on this call."

"Okay. It's Wyatt Earp."

"So you really won't tell me."

"Someone else wants to use the phone. I'll call you in a couple of days."

"Who's waiting, Jesse James?"

"Crazy about you, Jose."

"Promise me you'll take care of yourself."

He promised, and hung up the receiver just in time for a coughing jag.

He walked to the States Hof Brau and ordered pickled pig's feet and a bottle of near beer. Charlie Siringo entered just as he dug in.

The old detective stood just inside the door, glancing around while his eyes adjusted to the dim light, then spotted Hammett and came over. He was slight, with a few black hairs in his silver moustache trimmed at right angles like a carpenter's square. He wore parts of different suits, gray trousers with a striped vest and black coat, but they were carefully brushed and a green cravat added a touch of color. His face was dinged all over from pox and he limped slightly from some old injury.

He took off his hat when he reached Hammett's table. His hair was thin at the temples, bald at the crown, and parted in the middle. "Eat the rest of that hog while you was waiting?"

"Take a load off. Try the Wiener schnitzel. It's the best in town."

"Can I get a steak?" He drew out a chair and sat down, frowned at the holes in his hat, and set it at his elbow.

"Big John!"

A great rolling zeppelin of a man came their way, draped in acres of gray worsted. A yard of gold watch-chain hammocked his belly. "*Ja*, Sam." The counterweight of his muttonchop whiskers added resonance to his Prussian accent.

Hammett asked Siringo how he took his steak.

"Any way it comes, so long as it's quick."

"Make it bloody, John. And squeeze out two more bottles from the moose in back." He pointed at his beer.

John squinted at Siringo. "Prohibition agent?"

"Pinkerton," Hammett said. "Retired, like yours truly. What's in back?"

The big man leaned over the table and lowered his voice. "I just took delivery on a case of Canadian."

"Who's on the seal, Pancho Villa?"

"It's good schnapps, Sam. Come on into the back room and sniff the sawdust. Lodgepole pine from Alberta."

"I'll have a beer," Siringo said. "And throw in a mess of grits. I missed breakfast."

"*Was ist* 'grits'?"

"If he doesn't know it, he doesn't have it," Hammett said. "Give him fried potatoes and onions. Beer for me, too. But hang onto a bottle of that Alberta, will you?"

"Sure thing, Sam."

"That's the biggest man I ever saw," said Siringo, when they were alone.

"Wait till you meet Paddy Clanahan." Hammett ate. "What kept you from breakfast?"

"You hit on it when you said Clanahan."

———

They'd left the ranch late. Charmian had told them her experience of Sean Patrick Clanahan, boss of San Francisco.

"Jack was short on cash, a chronic condition," she'd said. "His books and stories weren't selling as well as they used to, and to be frank, he was—"

"A spendthrift," Hammett had offered.

"Extravagant. *Profligate* would not be too strong a word; yet there are extenuating circumstances. He came from nothing, gentlemen: born out of wedlock, forced to scrounge a living on the wharves of San Francisco at fourteen, working all day in a cannery and robbing oyster beds at night to support his mother and older sister. He stoked coal aboard tramp steamers, sweated in laundries, nearly perished of scurvy in the Yukon, where he hoped to find gold and an end to his labors. That failed, and when he came home hoping to sell his experiences to the popular press, he was rejected a hundred and sixty times in the first year. Surely you can sympathize with that, Mr. Hammett."

"Sure. I know the feeling."

"And surely, Mr. Siringo, you must understand his reaction when suddenly his books and stories began to sell, in numbers no one could have predicted. He married, had children, showered his family with gifts. After the union ended in divorce, Bess couldn't understand when his fortunes turned and he couldn't provide for her and his daughters as he had in the past, and drenched him in guilt and scorn. His work brought him less money, so he slaved to replace what he'd lost—a thousand words a day, gentlemen, no matter where he was, here in the cottage or sailing to Japan or touring the country on the lecture circuit. When the *Snark* sank, when Wolf House burned to the ground, he went deep into debt just trying to hold on to what he had, what he'd built.

"Since his death, Clanahan has been buying up all his notes for pennies on the dollar, scheming to gain ownership of the ranch. Some of Jack's creditors have remained sympathetic, and have promised to hold off on selling until I can gather the capital to redeem the notes, but they can't wait forever. They have bills to pay and mouths to feed too. I'm negotiating with Jack's publishers, hoping to persuade them to bring out new editions of all his works, and advance money against royalties; but with pirated copies floating all over and now the moving-picture people hijacking the property of his imagination and labor, it's a slow process, and Clanahan works swiftly."

"What's his object in getting hold of the ranch?" Siringo had asked. "Beg pardon, ma'am, but it don't look prosperous."

"Only because Jack was foursquare against pressing his grapes into wine for commercial uses. He supported Prohibition since before it had a name. I can see you're skeptical, gentlemen; Jack was a bibulous man, and made no secret of it. But if you've read *John Barleycorn*, you know how much that habit cost him and how hard he tried to cure himself. He kept drinking until nearly the end, when his kidneys failed. But he was determined to do what he could to prevent others from following his example, before they started, while they could still be saved. Just before he died, he made me promise I would never permit the fruits of Beauty Ranch to appear on the market in the form of wine. The same holds true for the beer we brew. Our small store of spirits is for personal consumption only."

She leaned forward. "Needless to say, Clanahan doesn't feel

bound by that vow. He intends to flood the bootleg market with Jack's private label and make millions corrupting the future of a generation."

She got up and left the room, to return carrying a bottle of red wine. "From our private stock." She showed them the device on the label, a pen-and-ink rendering of a wolf's head staring balefully face out.

"He'll drag that symbol, Jack's personal totem, through every dive, gin mill, and blind pig in the country, and with it the good name of Jack London. Gentlemen, can you stop him? I promise you, you will not find the estate ungrateful."

"I been to the library, improving my mind," Siringo told Hammett. "Went through every newspaper in San Francisco going back six months. Couldn't find hide nor hair of this Clanahan. Even checked the funny pages."

"I could've saved you the trouble. He doesn't hold any political office, and what he does is only news if you still haven't got the dope on Santa Claus."

"There's got to be one reporter with a backbone in this town."

"Not if he wants to keep it in one piece. The last one who tried to get an interview wound up in traction."

"Who put him there?"

"The man himself. He does his own strong-arm work. He saves the eel for serious errands."

"I thought all that Barbary Coast business was finished."

"It did. Back then everything was out in the open, like the gimcrackery on all the buildings. The ones built since the Big Shake are smooth as a steel rail and so's the grafting."

A waiter came with Siringo's meal and their beers. Siringo tucked his napkin under his collar and cut into his steak. Blood ran out. "I could save this cow with a tourniquet."

"You said you wanted it quick."

"I wasn't complaining." He forked a piece into his mouth and chewed. "Buying up London's debts is an underhanded way of taking over his spread, but it ain't illegal. I can't figure why he bothered with us."

"Clanahan's got all the money one man can ever use. When he sets out to make more, it's for seed. Whatever it is he wants to finance—*that's* why he wanted us to stop turning over rocks in Sonoma County."

"Tell me more about this Teapot Dome business."

"Wyoming's just part of it. The Elk Hills oil fields here in California are just as productive. The word is Albert Fall, that old cowboy I told you about, is behind the move to turn government control into private profit. He's the president's secretary of the Interior."

"I don't know what that is, but it sounds like some varmint's been burrowing where he oughtn't."

"He pushed Harding into signing an executive order transferring responsibility for the reserves from the navy to the Interior. He didn't pop much sweat pushing; that dope's the worst thing to happen to the Union since Bull Run. Everybody in Washington knows he's got a piece on the side, including Mrs. Harding."

"How do you know so much about Washington?"

"The superintendent of the Pinkerton branch there is an old partner. We keep in touch. Where the president dips his wick won't affect the price of beans, but too many people know what Fall's about. When it breaks—"

"Does this story have Clanahan in it?"

"Sorry. I told you politics is a hobby. But if there's a dirty dollar floating around this state, you can lay odds Paddy's not far behind it. A thing like this can sweep the Republicans clean out of office. I think our native son's got a bad case of claustrophobia."

"He wouldn't be the first cow got too big for its pasture," Siringo said. "I still got a flea on my tail?"

"Can't you tell?"

"I got a sting in the middle of my back, but you're the one with the eye."

"Not this time, which means either Clanahan lost interest after the horse turned up or it's the eel. He's as good a shadow as I know, and I was the best in the Agency. One time, I circled all the way around the bird I was following just because I got bored. He never tipped to it."

"I used to play dumb jokes like that. It got me a bullet in the knee."

"You didn't give Charmian London an answer. You staying or going?"

"I like to size up the other side before I commit. What's this muckety-muck look like?"

"John!"

The proprietor came rolling over and stood over the table swaying against his moorings.

"You still carry around that clipping?"

"*Jawohl*. A man must remind himself he is not invincible." He took a wallet the size of a branding book out of his suit coat, licked a thumb, and started paging through the notes and other papers inside.

"Clanahan didn't used to be bashful around the press," Hammett told Siringo. "You just didn't go back far enough. John was the Bay Area arm-wrestling champion nine years' running before he tangled with the mick." He accepted a square fold of yellowed newsprint from the German and held it out. Siringo pushed aside his plate to take it.

He handled it carefully; it was tattered at the folds and flakes fell to the table as he opened it. It was dated 13/10/18 in faded pencil on a margin. In the grainy picture, two men sat facing each other across a table, elbows braced on the top and hands clasped, surrounded by a crowd of spectators. John's whiskers were darker and he had a little less belly. Siringo looked at his opponent.

"That ain't a man. It's a whale with feet."

"He hasn't gotten any smaller. His breakfast is a side of pork and two loaves of toast slathered with lard."

"Why ain't he dead?"

"They don't make coffins his size."

"Who's the shy jasper?"

One of the onlookers, a medium-built man in a dark suit, stood holding a straw hat in front of his face.

"That'd be the eel. He's superstitious around cameras. Wears a Sunday boater every day of the year, they say, just so you know who's responsible for your sudden loss of life."

Siringo returned the clipping to John, who looked at it briefly, then refolded it with a sigh. "Friday the thirteenth. A man should know."

"It was Friday the thirteenth for him, too," Hammett said.

When they were alone, Siringo ate potatoes and fries and washed them down with beer. "Worse comes to worse, he's a hard target to miss."

"Does that mean you're taking the job?"

"If you come with it. You're faster on the draw."

"It would've been awkward if you'd said no." Hammett picked his hat off the table, removed a telegraph flimsy from the sweatband, and gave it to him. It was from Charmian London, instructing the Bank of San Francisco to pay the bearer a thousand dollars from her account.

"You went behind my back?"

"She did. I think she didn't want to give us time to decide to turn her down."

"Thought she was strapped."

"So she sold some hogs and fired a hand."

"Hope it was the son of a bitch ruined my hat." He gave him back the telegram and picked up his Stetson. "Let's get on to the bank before it closes."

14

The building appeared to have been carved out of a single chunk of marble, with twice as many fluted pillars necessary to hold up its porch roof and a two-mile hike to a paneled yellow-oak counter holding up more marble yet. It put one in mind of what a Catholic cathedral would look like if the Church of Rome had as much money as the Bank of San Francisco. Once inside, Siringo's voice fell to an involuntary whisper.

"If you told me about the place, I'd of rented a set of tails."

"Frisco's all show," Hammett said. "That's new money for you. Rockefeller was already in long pants when the first sourdough saw color."

"Can you lay off that Red talk just for today?"

The teller, morning-coated with a pair of egg-shaped lenses clipped to his nose, looked dubiously at first at the tall pale tubercular and the short man with holes in his hat, but brightened a bit when he saw the Western Union draft. "Will you be opening an account?"

"Two," Hammett said.

"The vice president will make the arrangements." The teller handed back the flimsy and pointed out a pebbled-glass door to their right.

Behind it sat a well-upholstered man in his fifties, also in a morning coat and striped pants, working the black handle of an adding machine the size of an anvil on his desk. He got up to shake their hands, peered through a pair of half-glasses at the draft. "One moment, please." He got up and went out carrying the sheet, leaving his door open. They watched him cross to the opposite wall and enter another pebbled-glass door marked PRESIDENT.

"Next they'll yell for the guard," Siringo muttered.

"Maybe if you left the artillery behind. Your coat sticks out on that side like a bad liver."

"I didn't know I was going to the bank when I strapped it on."

"This place has come up in the world. First time I was here, you only had to go through two people to do business."

When the vice president returned, all smiles, they each opened an account and made arrangements to deposit four hundred in each, asking for the remaining two hundred in cash. The man went out again, to return carrying a bank envelope with an engraving of the building in a corner. He counted the money into two neat stacks and pushed them across the desk, then rose to grasp their hands again. "Welcome, Mr. Hammett; Mr. Siringo. I hope this is the beginning of a lengthy and prosperous relationship."

On the way out of the building, they passed three portraits hung in gilt frames: George Washington, Abraham Lincoln, and Warren Gamaliel Harding.

"Wonder which denomination they'll stick his picture on," Siringo said.

"Probably a three-dollar bill."

———

They held their first war council in a speakeasy on Mission Street, where the owner of a face that was too big for the narrow window behind the iron-grille gate recognized Hammett and let them in. At that early hour the place was only half-full and the little bandstand was deserted. They hung their heels on the brass rail at the base of a mahogany bar. The back bar, carved intricately from the same wood, glittered with bottles, siphons, and glasses of every description.

"I know this place," Siringo said, looking around. "The bat-wing doors throwed me for a minute."

"There aren't any bat-wing doors."

"There used to be. That's what throwed me."

"It was a saloon during the Alaska Gold Rush. It's just about the only one left from the old days. It was called the Golden Slipper then."

"It was a shithole. I saw Crooked Mouth Hank shoot Jed Corcoran over there by the cigar corner in ought-one. It was over a woman named—let's see—Buffalo Mattie."

"It's usually over a woman, though they're not always named Buffalo. Big girl, was she?"

"No bigger'n your thumb; but she once swapped her favors for a buffalo coat because the fellow was tapped out. Poor Jed Corcoran was only nineteen. He didn't last long enough to acquire a colorful name."

"Why'd they call a place like that the Golden Slipper?"

"The Bucket of Blood ain't as good for business."

The bartender asked what they'd have. His hair was slicked back from a center part and he wore waxed handlebars and garters on his sleeves. The place prided itself on its Gay Nineties origins.

"Scotch," said Hammett.

"Rye," said Siringo. "Mind you don't pour 'em from the same bottle."

"We do all our business from Canada, mister."

Hammett smiled. "You know Big John over at the States Hof Brau?"

"Can't say I do."

"You should make his acquaintance. You're both honorary citizens of the Dominion."

Their drinks came. Hammett paid for both and the bartender slid his rag down the bar toward a party near the end.

"What brought you to town in ought-one?" Hammett asked. "Catch the gold bug?"

"I got my fill of all that digging in Gem. Someone said Ben Kilpatrick was here waiting to catch a boat to Central America and hook back up with the Wild Bunch; but either I missed him or it was a story. I never cared for the place. The Agency superintendent here had the notion he was a detective, went on every stakeout and jawed the whole time about his new baby boy. If Kilpatrick was in earshot it's no wonder I missed him."

"He was gone before I joined up. Mine kept goldfish."

"We here to palaver or drink a hole in another day?"

"Where better, if we're still being watched? If we shut ourselves up in my apartment or your hotel room, they'll know we're plotting. Here we're just two birds dipping their beaks."

"Where's Clanahan hang out?"

"You want to brace him?"

"I want to know him. All I got now is he had his pitcher took once and he can eat and Indian wrestle."

"You expect him to tell you his life story?"

Siringo smiled grimly. "His woman might."

"How do you know there's a woman?"

"There's always a woman."

"Not *always*."

They shared a look.

"Any reason to think it's like that?"

Hammett shook his head. "A man of politics? It would've come out."

"You said he don't care about money, just power, but they're just the same. When you got the one you got the other. You need to spend the money on somebody besides yourself, and power's not worth a thing without somebody to brag on it to. I got into one robbery outfit through a woman, and if it wasn't for my luck in that line I'd still be in Colorado, growing mushrooms at the bottom of some shaft."

"I don't mean to insult you, but that was a long time ago."

"Meaning I lost my good looks?" He stepped back from the bar and stood in front of him. "I ain't put on more'n six pounds since I joined the Agency. I didn't have as much snow on top, but I still got most of my hair, and I weren't Doug Fairbanks even back then. I've had these death-dimples since New Mexico in '90, where I near died; it didn't slow me down none with the ladies. All's you need is sound teeth and a smooth line of talk."

"Well, you've still got the teeth."

"You think I talk to a gal the way I talk to you? Do *you*?"

"Hell, no. I learned how to lie before I got my first paper route. Unfortunately, the likeliest place to find Clanahan without him tossing us both down his front steps is the Shamrock Club on Pacific."

"Irish joint?"

"If it were any greener you could shoot golf there. That's where he beat Big John back in 1918."

"His own patch? That was bright of John."

"He knows how to run a restaurant and cook sauerbraten. I never said he was Tom Edison. Clanahan cheated, by the way, but you couldn't expect that crowd to notice he braced one heel against the wainscoting."

"Who told you?"

"I saw it."

"You was there?"

"Tailing an Irish gunrunner. I won twenty bucks on the match. I didn't see the eel, if that was him in the picture."

"You bet against Big John?"

"We were at war with Germany. I should get myself lynched over a double sawbuck?"

"I reckon not. I reckon also John don't know."

Hammett smirked.

"You know what the Agency pays. Who do you think put up half?"

"He throwed the fight?"

"I wouldn't go that far. I think he gave it his best shot; but dough has always been as important to him as his reputation. Let's say he hedged his bet." Hammett put away the rest of his Scotch. "Welcome to Frisco, Charlie."

"Siringo. I ain't on a first-name basis with radicals and card cheats."

"It wasn't cards."

"That makes all the difference, don't it?" He rolled a slug of rye around his mouth, frowned. "This ain't half bad. They put a little brown sugar in the formaldehyde."

"They start with the best: Braun and Sons Mortuary is where all the local gangsters go to see off their friends, and Dolf Braun has an understanding with the joint." Hammett got the bartender's attention and twirled a finger. The man nodded and turned to the shelves in back. "The Shamrock's strictly men. Not likely you'll meet Clanahan's dame there, if there's one."

"I had a standing membership in all the best clubs in Denver and Santa Fe. They're where men go to talk about their women."

Hammett watched Siringo, waiting until the bartender served their drinks and moved off.

"I didn't know you old-timers spent so much time thinking about—"

"The gentle sex?"

"Sure. Let's call it that."

"The problem with your generation is you don't understand the power of an empty compliment. You can't get no place nowhere calling 'em dames and tomatoes and twists and what you was just now thinking. You think it's plain speaking, but the only thing plain about it is dumb. There ain't one of them thinks she's Lillian Russell or Dorothy Gish, including Lillian Russell and Dorothy Gish. They got mirrors, and they see what's in 'em, not like us. It's our job to convince 'em otherwise, or at least make them think we're convinced ourselves.

"What was we thinking about? Son, the winters was seven months long and there was one woman for every ten men. You think those ole boys was working out sums all the time they buggered the calves?"

Hammett colored. That hadn't happened since he'd stolen his first cigarette.

"Not that I ever done that, understand," Siringo said, pouring the dregs of his first drink into the second. "I was saving myself for marriage."

15

"I used to know my way around this neighborhood blindfolded," Siringo said. "Now it looks like Mars."

"The quake moved like a crumb-scraper, sliding everything this side of Telegraph Hill clear into the ocean. So I'm told," Hammett added. "I was twelve at the time, failing geography in Baltimore."

"I was living it while you was studying it. What's the point? One shake and it's gone."

They were standing on the corner of Front Street and Pacific Avenue. Siringo pointed across Pacific. "The Old Ladies' Club was there, in a shack built from ships run aground. I don't recollect its real name. They called it that on account of all the girls were older than thirteen."

It was a brick hotel now, five stories high.

"You've got a good memory."

"You never forget where you caught your first dose of clap."

"Backseat of a Pierce-Arrow for me. Her father's Pierce-Arrow. Here's the joint."

It was an Edwardian house, gabled all over, with four chimneys and eight different shades of paint. Its only identification was a sign suspended by chains from the semicircular porch roof, shaped like a four-leaf clover.

"Looks like an undertaker's parlor."

"What's more respectable than that?" Hammett opened the wide front door and they stepped inside.

The foyer had been partitioned off with tongue-and-groove boards into a broad corridor ending in a gracefully curving staircase, at the base of which and to the right stood a podium supporting an open book the size of a ledger. Behind it on a high stool sat Mr. Pickwick: bald as an egg, with side whiskers combed straight out from their roots, a starched flaring collar, and a swallowtail coat and checked trousers. He looked up from his feather quill to blink at the visitors. "Names?"

"Mr. Hammett and Mr. Siringo," said Hammett.

"Visiting whom?"

"Mr. Sean Patrick Clanahan."

"Reason for visit?"

"Social call."

"Expected?"

"No, we're just dropping in."

"Members don't entertain unexpected visitors." He returned to his writing.

Siringo said, "How come it's easier to bust out of jail than into a gentlemen's club?"

"I believe 'gentlemen' is the word in operation." He didn't look up.

Hammett took the roll of cash he'd gotten from the bank, peeled off a dollar bill, and smoothed it across the pages spread out on the big book. The book snapped shut on it so quickly it nearly caught his hand. "Card room. Top of the stairs, first door on the left."

"So that's what it takes to be a gent," Siringo said on the way up.

"Always did. You were just out in the wilderness too long to see it."

The door stood open to a room occupying fully a quarter of the second floor, paneled in cherrywood, with massive portraits of cardinals, bishops, and bearded men wearing judicial robes in elaborately carved frames leaning out from the walls. Below them hung sporting prints in smaller frames: boxers, baseball players, jockeys, and track-and-field men striking competitive poses. Another frame held a brown and chipped poster advertising the Fitzsimmons-Maher fight in 1896. No date or place was mentioned.

"I recollect that one," Siringo said, pointing. "Judge Roy Bean put it on down in Langtry after the U.S. and Mexico outlawed boxing. I was assigned to accompany the Texas Rangers sent to stop the fight. The train carrying the lumber for the ring and bleachers stopped there for water, then went on without unloading. I smelled a trick, but the ranger captain told me to stick with the train. It was scrap wood; the real order had already been delivered and nailed up. By the time I got back to Langtry, the fight was finished. The judge just winked at me and paid me my winnings."

Hammett laughed, startled. "You put down a bet?"

"Well, sure. Anybody with half an eye could see it was Fitzsimmons all the way."

"Is there a soul you *didn't* meet on the frontier?"

"I just missed Belle Starr. She was dead a week when I got to the Injun Territory."

The room was furnished with a bar and round tables with green baize tops, around which several parties of men were playing poker. There wasn't a bare head in the place and a pall of cigar smoke hung just below the high ceiling like overcast. It stung the eyes and blurred all the well-fed bodies in the room into one.

"I ain't seen so much beef in one spot since I quit running buffalo," Siringo said.

Hammett went straight to the bar and ordered Scotch. The man in charge, built along Siringo's slight lines but with a hard face creased sharply like crumpled brown paper, asked if he was a guest of the club.

"Nope. Just visiting."

"Sorry, mister. Only members and guests get served."

Siringo said, "We're here for Clanahan."

"Who is?"

Hammett spoke before Siringo could. "Ed Doheny."

"Mr. Doheny's a member. You ain't him."

"Tell him we're here on Doheny's business."

"Tell him yourself."

"Which one's Clanahan?" Siringo asked.

"The one with all the chips."

At first, the man the bartender had pointed out seemed to squat on his haunches. His bulk entirely obscured the shake-bottom chair he was sitting on. He wore black broadcloth, enough for a half-dozen suits of ordinary size, and a bowler the size of a wash-basin, but a snug fit for that. The hand of cards he held looked like stiff postage stamps in his hands, the fingers swollen-looking and the color of lard, with the nails rounded and glistening with polish. His broad face grew straight up from his shoulders, with rings of flesh overlapping one another to conceal whatever collar and tie he might have been wearing.

A rumbling, somewhat flabby bass issued from deep in his well-upholstered chest.

"Well sir, the time has come to lay aside subterfuge and disclose all assets."

"Talk English, Paddy."

"That's precisely what I'm speaking, my dear fellow. Lay your cards on the table."

The other man, fat as well but not in Clanahan's class, spread out his hand flat on the baize. "Read 'em and weep, you fancy-talking bag of wind." His brogue was far more pronounced than his opponent's.

One of the other players, shorter than the man who'd just spoken but fully as wide, threw down his cards with a disgusted snort. "Aces full, damn your eyes."

The fourth man shook his head with a grim smile. He was younger than the others by at least a decade, in a tailored suit and glasses with tortoiseshell rims. "I folded just in time. O'Neill doesn't bluff."

"Nor does he play well, or he'd have been aware the essence of the game is not the cards, but rather the man who holds them. Four queens of Erin, Seamus: As you'd have known had you paid attention and knew how to count." Clanahan laid his pasteboards faceup with a circular gesture that shaped them into a perfect fan. As O'Neill stared, the huge man scooped the pile of chips in the middle of the table to join those he had stacked neatly in front of him.

"You son—" O'Neill reached a hand inside his coat.

Hammett wasn't watching the players, but the crowd gathered around the table. An arm moved, but then whom it belonged to was lost in the shuffle of bodies straining for a closer look at the cards. In any case, when O'Neill's hand came out holding only a wadded handkerchief to mop his face, the movement came to nothing. All he saw was that the arm wore a black sleeve with a charcoal stripe, among half a dozen men dressed identically.

He looked at Siringo, also watching the crowd. "Anything?" he murmured.

"Not to act on. Life was simpler back when all the hardcases didn't dress like bankers. I reckon he checked his straw bonnet today."

"No cameras this time. Eels like to blend in with their surroundings."

The enormous man sat back, mining a heavy watch on a platinum chain from his folds of fat. The chair beneath him creaked like a galleon under full sail. "My friends, I have time for one more hand. Who among you wishes to deprive me of the burden of carrying away all this plunder?"

"Not me. I can't beat black magic." Seamus O'Neill shoved back his chair and pushed himself to his feet. "You're a slippery one, Paddy, but I'll flour my hands and have you yet."

"I welcome the challenge, sir. Good day." He turned his attention to the other fat man. "Mr. Clancy? Has your angel awakened?"

One of the young men in the crowd helped Clancy to his feet; the effort turned both their faces bright red. "I'd need a Ouija board for that. Good-bye, and to hell with you."

"Mr. Kennedy?"

The bespectacled man nodded shortly. "Sure. I'm in."

"Me, too," Siringo said. "If you don't mind playing a stranger."

Clanahan looked up at him, taking in Hammett at the same time.

"And the name of my challenger, sir?"

"Charlie Siringo."

"A melodious name. Irish?"

"Half. But not the Siringo side. Does it signify?"

"Have you the wherewithal?"

He took out his wallet, removed the sheaf of bills, and riffled them with a thumb.

"Then it does not signify. And your friend? Is his angel awake as well?"

Hammett showed his roll.

Clanahan smiled, his fat cheeks riding the creases, and inclined a blubbery hand toward the remaining player. "Allow me to present Joseph P. Kennedy, a visitor from Boston, and a fellow with a rare sense of humor. Please indulge me, sir, and tell our new friends what you told me earlier."

But Kennedy wasn't smiling. "I never joke about politics. I intend to make my son the first Roman Catholic president of the United States."

16

A steward in a green jacket with gold buttons brought a tray of chips, which he traded to Siringo and Hammett for cash. Shortly afterward, a waiter arrived with setups for the players and a bottle of Kilmartin's Crest with the wax seal in place. Clanahan did the honors, and when they all had drinks, he shuffled the deck and dealt. Siringo waited until he had a complete hand before saying anything.

"If you don't resent a fellow speaking his mind, Mr. Kennedy, that's a tall order. Most folks think a Catholic president would take his orders straight from the pope."

"You've nailed the main hurdle on the head, Mr. Siringo. It will take years to set people's minds at ease on the point; many years, and I may not live to see the thing out. In any case, my oldest boy is far from the age of eligibility. But Joseph, Jr., has a sound head on his shoulders for a boy, and if it isn't to be him, he'll have the patience to carry on until we succeed."

Kennedy spoke with a broad New England accent, with no trace of a brogue.

"It'll take more than patience," Hammett said, arranging his cards. "What do you do for a living, if I may ask?"

"Mr. Kennedy is a man of many parts," said Clanahan. "He's

come here to produce picture plays with his own money. Ante up, gentlemen."

The man from Boston threw his chips into the center of the table with the others. "I'm an investment counselor, and I've taken my own counsel so many times I'm in absolute danger of having to give half of it to Mr. Harding's government. It seems I must lose some in order to keep more, and the motion-picture business promises quick action in that department."

"Tom Ince said the same thing. Two cards." Siringo discarded a deuce and a trey, leaving himself with two queens and a jack. "Since he was already setting himself up with an excuse not to pay me, I sent him on his way."

Clanahan, evidently a serious poker player, said nothing until he'd dealt the two cards. "Are you in pictures, Mr. Siringo?"

"I just said I ain't. But they was pestering me for a while to sell 'em my memoirs. I was a cowboy and a detective, and they can't make up their minds which one they want more; though they don't want neither bad enough to make a decent offer."

"Indeed! I hadn't thought the two professions had much in common."

"Just me. Far as I know I'm the one and only."

"And you, sir?"

"I'll stay with these." Hammett tapped his cards.

"As you wish, but that was not the question I had in mind. It's your vocation I'm curious about."

"I'm a writer."

"Splendid! A writer, a cowboy-detective, the father of a future president, and your humble servant all seated around one table. Our little club has come up in the world from its shanty origins. Have I read your work, sir?"

"That depends, Mr. Clanahan. Have you ever been an editor back East?"

"I've been many things, including a hod carrier and a street sweep, but never that."

"Then, no."

"Unpublished? If I'm not being too curious, how do you cope?"

"I take the odd job now and then. I used to be a detective, like Siringo. We both worked for Pinkerton."

A look passed between Kennedy and Clanahan. Hammett saw that Siringo saw it as well.

The political boss dealt Kennedy a card at his request, concentrated hard on his own hand, and discarded three for a new trio from the deck. "Such a variety of talents. Mr. Kennedy was being modest earlier. He didn't mention we're drinking his stock."

Siringo took a sample from his glass. "This is good sipping whisky. I'd of got around to asking who your bootlegger was eventually."

"Importer," Kennedy corrected. "Just one of the interests in my portfolio. The shipments are purchased lawfully from the distiller in Edenderry, Ireland, carried with other legal cargo to Nova Scotia, where it's approved by Canadian Customs and brought legitimately by rail across the country and then by truck to San Francisco."

"It's that last two hundred miles the law cares about," Siringo said.

"I'm in for a buck." Hammett threw a chip after the others. "This is the third time today Canada's come up in a drinking conversation. They ought to crank down the bear flag in Sacramento and run up the maple leaf."

"It doesn't spend enough time in Canada to pick up any French," Kennedy said. "I'll see that and raise you five."

All three of his opponents met the raise.

Kennedy met Siringo's gaze over his cards. "My father came

here during the Famine. He learned the Constitution and the Declaration of Independence by heart, and could recite whole sections of American history; every family meal was a lesson at school. Prohibition isn't the first ludicrous and unjust law the people of this country have been moved to protest. In the past, they did so by sending delegations to England and, when peaceful means failed to change the situation, through civil disobedience. You can't live in Boston any length of time without being reminded constantly of how the early patriots disposed of overtaxed tea. I see no difference between my activities and theirs."

"Good speech," Hammett said. "Your son—or grandson— should work it into his inaugural. He might leave out his ancestor was the first to turn his patriotism into profit."

Kennedy colored slightly. Siringo chuckled.

"I'll ask you to excuse Mr. Hammett's poor manners. He's opposed to capitalism."

"A lesson, young man, in economics." The investment advisor's complexion had cleared. "Money is only scraps of paper and bits of metal. People who pursue it to its own end are miserable creatures, which is why they spend it on country houses and private railway cars and women who would otherwise be unobtainable to them, to fill a hole that has no bottom. When you have money, you have power, and those things will come to you in the course of events without your having to spend a penny. The mere reputation of wealth is sufficient. Meanwhile it grows and grows, along with the perception that goes with it. That's a lesson you won't find in Mr. Wells's history, and there are many who would pay any amount to learn what I've provided you free of charge."

"Thanks. Where do I pick up my diploma?"

"You've led your horse to water, Mr. Kennedy," Clanahan said. "A man can do no more."

Siringo grinned at his cards. "Sure he can. All you need do to make it drink is stick its head in the water and suck on its ass."

Even Kennedy laughed.

They played for an hour, and the stakes climbed. At one point Siringo was up a thousand, Hammett three hundred, but Kennedy performed more consistently, doubling his bets when he'd lost a hand and halving them when he won, attracting a fresh crowd of spectators from the other tables and making Clanahan forget what he'd said about having time for only one more hand. At length, the man from Boston pushed all his chips into the center of the table.

"Trying to buy the pot?" Siringo asked.

"Then call it."

Clanahan shrugged, smiling, and threw down his hand.

Siringo counted his chips. He was short a hundred dollars.

Hammett folded and shoved his own chips forward. "I'll back your play."

"You haven't seen his cards," said Kennedy.

"I don't play cards. I play the man playing."

"How about you, Mr. Siringo?"

"This here's for Texas." He tossed the rest of his chips into the pot and laid down his hand faceup. "Four ladies."

Kennedy placed each of his cards side by side, one at a time. "Ace high flush. I bet only when I have the cards."

"Your lessons get more expensive all the time," said Siringo.

Clanahan consulted his watch. "Let's be off, Edgar."

A man in a black suit with a gray stripe came forward as the rest of the crowd was retreating. His glossy black hair lay flat and his small ears were flush to his skull. Apart from a permanent blue beneath the skin of his cheeks and chin, there was nothing about his description that would ring a bell with anyone it might have been given to. He was holding a brown Chesterfield coat with black velvet patches on the lapels and a glistening white-silk lining, which he held while Clanahan pressed his palms on the table, reddening a shade, and levered himself to his feet.

"My personal assistant, gentlemen," he said, pushing his fists into the sleeves of the coat. "Edgar Edison Lanyard. Edgar, Mr. Charles Siringo and Mr.—I apologize, Mr. Hammett; I don't know your Christian name."

"Dashiell."

"Colorful and heraldic. And Mr. Dashiell Hammett: Pinkertons emeriti."

"I don't know what that is." Lanyard's speech smacked of the flat Midwest. He finished helping the fat man into his coat, but he didn't offer his hand.

Clanahan adjusted his bowler. "A most entertaining afternoon. In future, gentlemen, you must wait for an invitation rather than bribing Mr. Perkins downstairs. The club bylaws are adamant on the point. Mr. Kennedy." He touched his brim and turned away, followed closely by Lanyard.

"What was the point of all that?" Hammett asked as he and Siringo descended the staircase. "I mean, apart from cutting our grubstake almost in half."

"We got to meet Joe Kennedy," said the old cowboy. "You like coincidences too much if you think he ain't in this thing."

"You don't really believe he meant that about making his boy president."

"Well, he ain't much for bluffing. What it has to do with oil in California and Wyoming and shooting at a stable boy at Jack London's ranch, or if it's got nothing to do with 'em at all, is what we need to find out. You can't work a riddle without all the parts."

"Trouble is we don't know how many parts there are."

"I reckon there's as many as Kennedy's got dollars. He needs more or he'd be on about his business instead of juggling paste-boards with the kind of mick his old man left Ireland to get away from."

"That's why he went from being an investment advisor to running liquor. We know from the way he gambles he doesn't take risks."

"Sure he does. That's why it's called gambling."

A block from the Shamrock Club, Hammett took off his hat and swept his handkerchief around the sweatband.

"Where?" Siringo asked.

"Hundred feet back. I wouldn't have spotted him if I didn't get to meet Edward Edison Lanyard. The eel's something more we got out of that poker game."

17

Wyatt Earp was in a better mood than Siringo had ever seen him; he said as much to Hammett later.

"Come to study on it, it's the first time I saw him in a good one."

They dined in the backyard of Earp's modest ranch house overlooking a stable and corral, the whitewashed wood standing out against green grass. His wife Josephine was visiting family in San Francisco, leaving him in the care of a Mexican cook. Abner Butterfield's replacement, a thick-bodied youth in a flannel shirt and dungarees, was walking Spirit Dancer around the test track, cooling her down after a hard run. It was the first glimpse either guest had gotten of the beast that had caused so much fuss.

"She's my ticket out of debt," Earp said, slicing a coarse loaf of bread. "I've had the longest string of bad luck since Odysseus."

"Never heard of the fellow." Siringo blew on his soup. "I know I been stretching the same dollar since I came to California."

Hammett steered the subject away from argument. "I'm no judge of horseflesh, but it looks like a fine animal."

Siringo said, "Looks chesty to me. My experience is a horse

built for the long stretch takes a while to get going. The Derby's only a mile and a quarter. Hope she likes dust with her oats."

"Care to lay a wager?"

"Nope. I got a roof needs patching."

Hammett asked Siringo how sure he was about the horse.

"Sure enough to bet your money, but not my own. I ain't much for gambling."

"Charlie and I have that in common, at least," Earp said. "We left all our luck in the streets of every cow town worth talking about."

"No, I tend to win at cards and such. The way I see it, a man's born with only so many lucky breaks. There'll come the time I need one to save my hide. I won't waste it on games of chance."

Hammett said, "I didn't see any of that luck in the Shamrock Club."

"You think I lost by accident?"

"What were you two doing in a place like the Shamrock?" Earp asked. "You need to be Irish on both sides going back to St. Patrick just to get in the door."

Siringo wiped his moustaches with his napkin. "The money we slipped the doorman was green enough. We got us a lesson in poker from a fellow named Kennedy."

"Don't know him." Earp's tone was oddly strained.

"He was a guest of Paddy Clanahan." Hammett watched the old lawman's face congest.

"Was he with a man named Lanyard?"

"You know the eel?" Siringo asked.

"I saw him just once, crossing Market behind his boss. I knew Clanahan, and I saw Lanyard for what he was the second I laid eyes on him: Man walks a pace behind and a step to the right, looking all around while the one he's with looks straight ahead—

because he can, in that company—you know what the connection is.

"Bat Masterson was with me, visiting from New York. He knew them both from sporting circles, writing for the *Telegraph*. He hasn't been a journalist so long he forgot what he learned in Dodge City and Adobe Walls. 'Wyatt,' he said, 'in the old days we'd've come up on someone like that from two sides. I'd strike up a conversation while you buffaloed him and threw him aboard the outbound train.'"

"'I saw him for a killer,' I said.

"Bat said, 'No ordinary kind. You recollect some are close-up murderers, like Luke Short, while others work from a distance, like Jim Miller. The eel—that's what he's called, on account of his initials—doesn't have a preference. And he'll use a blade or his bare hands as like as an iron.'"

They were seated at a plane table covered with a red-and-black-checked oilcloth. Hammett played checkers on it, using biscuits for men. "That's him, all right. We got a sample of his long-range work the other day."

"You mean at London's ranch? You never gave me any details beyond where to find Spirit Dancer."

"That was another deal," Siringo said. "It's still going on, which is why we invited ourselves here."

"I wondered about that. I never knew you to step out of leather unasked."

"I don't trust the telephone. There's too many people shouting down the line. We just wanted you to know what we're about, in case they fish us out of the harbor."

"I'm doubtful aid. I haven't carried a pistol in public since the Sharkey-Fitzsimmons fight. I got into a mess of trouble for forgetting I had it on when I took off my coat to referee."

"I hadn't straddled a horse in years until just recently. My ass is one big blister, but I didn't fall off. It makes me less jumpy knowing somebody who knows how to crack a cap knows my business. Mr. Hammett was against it."

"I don't like working with civilians." Hammett crowned one of his biscuits. "They're where stray bullets come from."

"Earp hits where he aims."

"You said that. You also said he doesn't always aim at the right party."

"You're still telling that lie?"

"I ain't here to dig up old bones." Siringo glared at Hammett. "I wouldn't of come clear back here, even to recruit your gun, except it seemed a good idea to let Clanahan think I come back home to stay. I left a trail a blind man could see, to draw the eel off Mr. Hammett. Him showing up here would of tipped our hand."

"No need. I was the best shadow man the Agency had, and I'm just as good at throwing off someone else's."

"It seems to me you told me that when I hired you." Earp looked at Siringo. "How much of what this sprout says he can do can he do?"

"Hammett's young, and substitutes talk for reputation. He did a fair job of doubling back on Clanahan's man Feeney in Frisco, and he spotted the sun flashing off the eel's long gun at Beauty Ranch. I reckon I can stand his jawing so long as he continues to back it up."

"You're saying the eel followed you here," Earp said.

"Me for certain. We took separate trains, and like I said, I put on a good imitation of a mama bird faking a busted wing."

"But did you see him? Bat said when you spot him behind you he means to be spotted."

"Bat says a lot of things, most of 'em hogwash. Anyway, he

never was a detective. You can change hats, put on or take off a coat, even hook on a false set of whiskers, but changing the way you move isn't something most people have practice in. I seen him walking away from me through the dining car and again when we stopped in Salinas, browsing a newsstand while I was buying fish wrapped in wax paper from a peddler. He thinks when he ditches the straw hat and puts on a pair of cheaters it makes him invisible. He's good, though. I didn't see him again."

"Maybe he stayed with the train when you got off in L.A.," Earp said. "Maybe he's on his way to Mexico to get laid."

"Maybe. Wouldn't be the first time I impressed myself with my own importance for nothing. On the other hand, a man Paddy Clanahan trusts to watch his back could probably bed a woman closer to home. Mexico heats up this time of year. If I'd been headed north towards Canada, I'd be more inclined to subscribe to your coincidence theory."

"I might be more inclined toward yours if you'd tell me what Clanahan's got planned."

"If we knew that, we wouldn't of had to come down here. It's got to do with oil in California and Wyoming, or it ain't. It's got to do with Kennedy wanting the White House, or it ain't. If Charmian London is right, it for sure has got to do with getting hold of her vineyards and soaking the country with wine, which is where Kennedy may figure, being a gentleman bootlegger. Whatever it is, it was important enough the eel tried to stop us from snooping around up there by killing Butterfield."

"This thing's nearly as complicated as Tombstone politics." Earp pushed away his plate and stood. "Charlie, let's take a walk. Hammett, I hope you don't take it an insult if I ask you not to join us."

"I didn't want to come here at all, but Siringo's only got eyes in the front of his head. I'll be swell." He took out his flask.

The others descended the slope toward the track, where the stable boy was letting the racehorse eat an apple out of his hand. "That man is ninety percent alcohol," Earp said.

"I don't know where he puts it, but I mean to order a case of his brand and give a bottle to everyone I ever work with again. If you tell him I said that I'll deny it; he's drunk enough on himself as it is. Also I wish his taste in politics was as good as his instincts."

"I had business with a Kennedy once. I didn't want to say it in front of Hammett. It reflected poorly on me."

"Tell me. If I can use it I will, if I can keep you out of it. If I can't use it, nobody need never know we had this conversation."

"I believe you." Earp leaned on the fence circling the track, stroking an unlit cigar. "It was in '71, and started in Fort Gibson, over there in the Nations. I was a yonker, but that's no excuse. Two fellows, Ed Kennedy and John Shown, and I got drunk and stole two horses from a man named Keys. Keys caught up with us in Arkansas. We were arrested: Kennedy stood trial and beat the charge, but I didn't have his same faith in twelve men good and true. I made bail and I haven't been back to Arkansas since, nor drunk more than a jigger of liquor in one sitting."

"Seems to me I heard something about that, though the details was muddy."

"There's more. My wife Urilla died the year before: Typhus, the doc said. She was carrying my child. They both went together. I lost my bearings for a spell."

He straightened, fished out matches, and puffed the cigar into life. "Well, it don't signify, and I won't hide behind it. But that one bad decision's chased me my whole life. Whatever mistakes I've made I made because I lost my good opinion of myself and I've been fifty years trying to get it back."

"We all put a foot wrong somewhere." Siringo shook his head. "It ain't the same Kennedy. This one's too young, and his name's Joseph. Anyway, Kennedy's Irish for Jones. But I respect you for telling me. I know how hard that is for a man like you."

"You're the first ever to hear it from my lips. I'd take it as more than a personal favor if no one ever hears it from yours."

"I promised that already."

"I know. I'm getting distrustful in my old age. You can trust everyone or no one and get in the same trouble either way." He raised his voice. "Bring her here, George. I want to introduce her."

The stable hand led the horse across the enclosure. The animal was a fair size for a filly, with a reddish-brown coat and a broad blaze on its forehead. Siringo reached up and stroked its muzzle. Spirit Dancer whickered and shook her mane.

"I take back what I said before. She's got winning in her eyes."

"Sure you're not just trying to duck out of a bet?"

"Yep. I put a lot of store in my bump of judgment."

"Rub her down, George. Mix in a little sour mash with her feed. She likes it."

Siringo chuckled.

Earp bridled. "Just because the country's dry doesn't mean she has to be. Nobody ever gave her a vote."

———

Hammett was rolling a cigarette when they returned. Earp excused himself, entered his house by the back door, and came out a few minutes later carrying a Smith & Wesson revolver. Hammett scrambled to his feet, groping inside his coat; but his host stepped past him, raised the weapon, thumbed back the hammer, and fired. The slug clanked against the weathervane atop the stable roof, a sheet of tin cut into the shape of a buffalo, and sent it spinning. The target was a good hundred yards away.

Earp lowered the revolver and smirked at Hammett. "Civilian, hell."

Hammett said, "Depends on whether you were aiming at the barn."

"Don't shoot him, Earp," Siringo said. "He's full of my moonshine and might explode."

———

"This isn't so bad," Hammett said. "I was holed up worse in Butte."

"That's 'cause it ain't raining." Siringo took the pot off his stove with a bandanna wrapped around the bail and spooned beans and sowbelly into the bowls on the table. He'd pushed the Smith-Premiere typewriter to one side.

"There's something strange about this machine."

"It's got twice as many keys as you're used to. The black ones are for the capitals. They hadn't got round to inventing the shift yet when it was made."

"Well, I'd trade you my Remington for it. It probably works twice as fast and gets double the rejections yours does in half the time."

"I don't need to counsel an Agency man about the virtues of patience." Siringo unscrewed the top from a Mason jar and poured an ounce into each of their cups of coffee. "Four, five years, you'll be rich as me."

"At least your view's better than mine."

"I wish somebody'd set fire to that sign. You shouldn't have to take up that much real estate to sell real estate."

Something thumped the front door. Hammett started, reached for his .38.

"Simmer down. It's the boy with the paper. I forgot to stop it, which is how I got the fire started in the stove. Get it, will you?" Siringo had just sat and picked up his spoon.

Hammett found the day's *Los Angeles Times* on the wooden front step and unfurled it as he shut the door behind him. "Good news for once. Harding commuted Eugene Debs's sentence."

"Do me a favor and don't spice up my stew with radicalism."

A one-column headline farther down the page caught the other man's eye:

BODY FOUND IN SAN FRANCISCO BAY
Police Identify Local Resident

He read the lead, looked up. "How do you feel about murder with your meal?"

"So long as it ain't mine."

"It's Mike Feeney."

18

Siringo snatched the paper from Hammett and read:

> SAN FRANCISCO, March 18—(AP) Michael A.
> Feeney, familiar to many local residents as a "job-
> ber" for the Democratic Party, has been identified
> as the man whose lifeless body was discovered float-
> ing beneath a pier in San Francisco Bay yesterday
> evening. It is believed he lost his way in the morning
> fog and fell in.
>
> Feeney was a familiar sight in establishments still
> associated with Barbary lore . . .

"We was still in town yesterday morning," Siringo said, tossing the paper on the table. "Time enough for the eel to run an
errand for Clanahan before he followed me to L.A."

Hammett nodded. "Dropping Doheny's name in the Shamrock Club was a bad idea. It tipped Clanahan off that we're sniffing around the oil scheme."

"I get a heap of ideas, half of 'em bad. How'd this one work its
way around to Feeney is what I'd like to know."

"That call I made to Beauty Ranch had an eavesdropper on

the line: Clanahan'd make it a point to know what goes on there. It isn't hard to trace a long-distance call, or to link the caller in this case to Pinkerton. That's when he put Feeney on us, to find out what we're up to. I'm local, you're not, so Feeney played a hunch and followed you when we split up. When Clanahan found out we knew the name Doheny, he knew we had to have gotten something out of his boy.

"You saw how easy it was to crack him open. After the eel got what he wanted, he threw Feeney into the bay like so much garbage."

"He'd of wound up there anyway. The Feeneys of this world always do."

"The question is, what's Clanahan got in mind for us?"

"He's a careful man, or I don't know nothing about playing cards. But there's a lot more ways to be cautious than there is to go off half-cocked. Is he going to watch how we play and figure out our hands before he bets, or is he going to play the percentages and serve us like he did Feeney before the odds change?"

"All I know is he won't waste time. Lanyard's too valuable an asset to throw away on a simple tail job. Clanahan's competition might get the bright idea he's left his flanks exposed. There's all kinds of new talent in town since Prohibition came in. They're not as discreet about disposing of an obstacle as the eel."

"I was in Chicago during the Haymarket riot. A bomb blew a company of police officers into so many pieces they still ain't sure how many was kilt. I don't see a nickel's worth of difference in slaughtering for politics and slaughtering for money."

"We agree on that at least. Mr. Siringo, I think there's a radical in you waiting to bust out."

The old detective gulped Irish coffee, looked sour; not necessarily in that order.

"That's the danger of living alone. You get a dumb idea,

nobody calls you on it, you get a dumber one later, nobody calls you on it, and before you know it you got a head full of dumb ideas and you run around like a blind horse till you smack up against the side of a barn. Where's that gal you're fixing to marry?"

"Montana, where she was raised. Why?"

"You ought to go pay her a visit. There's nothing like a woman or a slap with a two-by-four to right a man's thinking."

"Jose can swing a two-by-four. She's little, but she'll surprise you. She practically carried me on her back when I came down with TB in Tacoma. She was a nurse before I knocked her up."

"That was a right romantic story till the end."

"I didn't get to the end. The end part is I'm not hiding behind anybody's skirts while you deal with Clanahan and his gunny. They aren't as easy to buffalo as a common horse thief like Butterfield. That homemade hooch has got you thinking you're half your age and twice your size."

"I didn't say go to Montana. I said you ought to. If Clanahan knows you was with the Agency he knows your personal situation too. He won't think it odd you got a hard-on and decided to smuggle it east. The eel won't follow you any farther than the state line. He'll count that proof enough you're headed where it says on your ticket. Get off in Carson City, then take the next train back and meet me in Frisco."

"What good's splitting up?"

"While he's busy making sure you're a-courtin', I can pay a visit to this fellow Kennedy and ask him what kind of deal he made with Clanahan that's got Clanahan putting the boots to Charmian London for seed money."

"Why Kennedy?"

"Because Clanahan was head skunk till Kennedy spoke up. Paddy knows too much about us, and all's we know for sure about him is he's fat and plays a cautious game of poker. I aim to even the odds, but I can't do it with no eel wrapped around my ankle."

"Why don't *you* go east, see that little boy of yours, while *I* pump Kennedy?"

"Three reasons. One, I don't know where Lillie took him when she left. Two, how do I know while I'm gone you won't do something dumb to show off in front of Becky London? I seen you tripping on your pizzle every time she came into the room."

"I've got eyes too, old-timer. That wasn't Washoe Ban's ass you were admiring in the stable."

"Charmian turned out different from what I had pictured, that I'll warrant. I wouldn't object to making her the third Mrs. Siringo if she'd consider it. But the advantage of being an old-timer is you've learned to follow your brain instead of your pizzle."

"What makes you so sure she'd consider marrying a gimpy old saddle tramp with a roof full of holes?"

"I ain't, but there's no hobbles on either of us. You got a gal picking out kitchen curtains and a loaf in the oven."

"Are you telling me you never stepped out on your wife while you were on a case?"

"That was in the line of duty. Mamie never had a reason to think me disloyal; Lillie neither, if she'd only gave me half a chance to prove it. You're just a young goat with blue balls."

"I ought to knock you on your ass."

"I wouldn't."

"Yeah? How come?"

"'Cause it's still sore." Siringo brought his hand up from under the table and drew back the hammer on the Forehand & Wadsworth.

"You won't shoot me."

He raised the revolver an inch and fired.

The slug burrowed into a plank behind Hammett's head as the young man, moving already, launched himself across the table, tipping it over under his weight, while Siringo threw himself off his chair to the floor. They rolled around among the beans and dust bunnies, grappling for the gun. Hammett lanced his fist against the old man's jaw in a short right cross that put Siringo's eyes out of focus; but as he did so he loosened his grip on the wrist belonging to the weapon. Siringo bared his teeth and swung the revolver to the left, laying the barrel alongside Hammett's temple. A gong rang and the room broke up into black-and-white checks. The white checks kept shrinking until it was all black.

Something wet dashed his face. He sat up, his lungs turning themselves inside out, and tasted coffee and grain alcohol. He looked up at Siringo, standing with his feet spread, the revolver in one hand and his empty cup in the other. The old cowboy was panting with his hair in his face.

"Never back a man into a corner," he said. "He's got no direction to go but straight through you."

Hammett finished coughing, got out his handkerchief, wiped his mouth, and studied the square of linen. Then he applied it to his temple and looked at the pink smear. He stuck the handkerchief back in his pocket. "Any other wisdom?"

"Always make sure your left hand knows what your right's up to."

"Okay. Now I got one for you." Hammett placed his palms flat on the floor and butted him in the crotch.

The cup hit the floor first, followed a moment later by the man who'd been holding it. He landed on his knees and tipped over onto his side, hugging himself between his thighs, one hand still holding the gun.

"He-he-he," he said a minute later, in a voice that held no timbre.

"What are you laughing about, you old hyena?"

"I was thinking how bad this'd hurt if I still used it every day."

Hammett laughed then. It brought on another coughing fit, and for a while there was no telling whether he was enjoying himself or hemorrhaging.

"You all right?" Siringo asked, when he fell silent.

"No. You?"

"Tell you when one of 'em drops back down."

"Were you really going to shoot me?"

"I don't recollect. But it seemed to me you're pretty agile for a lunger."

"You're lucky I'd parked the thirty-eight."

"Not lucky. I seen you do it, though I wasn't sure about them persuaders you carry in your pocket."

He reached into it, felt the brass knuckles. "I forgot I had 'em."

"Then they're no good to you. See what I mean about dumb ideas?"

"You said yours was good for three reasons. What's the third?"

"I got it first."

"So what?"

"So you know what they call a writer who steals his ideas."

"Rich?"

PART THREE

THE BRASS KEY

Politics has got so expensive that it takes lots of money to even get beat with.

—Will Rogers

19

"See anything?" Siringo asked.

Hammett shook his head. "Just what I'm supposed to when it's the eel."

They went to the cigar counter in the station, where Siringo bought a pouch of pipe tobacco and Hammett his makings. The eastbound train pulled in just as they were paying for their purchases. Hammett picked up his satchel. Siringo scowled when he heard glass clinking. Hammett grinned.

"I helped myself to your cache. I'll bring you back a couple of jugs from Carson City. I know a bootlegger there whose Canadian doesn't speak with a Spanish accent."

"I can always get plenty. Just don't drink yourself overboard. Lanyard may take it into his head to split us up permanent."

"I hope you're right and he follows me instead of you."

"I know a trick or two if he don't. The Agency didn't start when you joined."

"It didn't stop when you quit." The whistle blew two short blasts. "There's Mother." He shook Siringo's hand and raised his voice. "I'll send you a postcard from Anaconda."

"Don't waste your penny." Siringo spoke just as loudly. "Them things always get home before you do."

He watched the young man board and took a step back on the platform to light his pipe, eyes working from side to side; but if Clanahan's man got on, it was in a scrum of last-minute passengers or under the cloak of steam as the train started rolling.

Six blocks from the station, he stepped onto a streetcar, walked all the way to the back, and got off on that end, without looking back to see if anyone followed. He entered an ice-cream parlor on the corner, a place of spotless chrome and enamel, ordered a strawberry sundae, and asked the counterman in the paper hat if he had a restroom.

"It's news to me if I do." He used his scoop.

"What about a phone?"

"Down that hall."

This was a narrow corridor with numbers penciled on the wainscoting next to the wall-mounted instrument. A tin sign read FIRE EXIT above a door at the end. He went through it, crossed an alley with trash cans bunched around the back doors of neighboring establishments, tried a door, found it locked, ignored the others as too time-consuming, and walked briskly around the end of the alley and into the first front door he came to. This belonged to a neighborhood movie theater. He bought a ticket to a William S. Hart western, took the aisle past the piano player, who was too busy trying to keep up with the action on-screen to notice, and let himself out a door reserved for employees. He changed cabs twice, kept the driver waiting outside his house five minutes while he packed some things, and watched out the rear window as they rattled away.

A Ford coupe fell in behind them after the first turn. It didn't have to mean anything, even if the eel had chosen the same model in a pickup truck when he drove onto Beauty Ranch; every third vehicle in California was a T. But some things never changed, not Butch Cassidy's proclivity toward dun horses (he claimed they were harder for posses to see in the scrub) nor Billy Bonney's liking for the small-framed Colt Lightning pistol that suited his lady hands nor Clay Allison's choice of Old Pepper when it came to a three-day drunk, like the one that finally broke his neck under the wheels of his own wagon. The Motoring Age just gave a detective a fresh handle on the preferences of outlaws.

He told his driver to make a right-hand turn, then another, and when the Ford stayed behind them, a third. At that point, the man behind the wheel of the cab squirted a stream of tobacco into the empty Quaker Oats box on the seat beside him and asked his passenger if he was lost.

"No, I'm arranging that for somebody else."

But after they'd made that turn, the Ford continued on its most recent path and disappeared beyond the corner. Siringo told his driver to pull over against the curb. They sat there, the motor idling and the driver chewing and spitting, for three minutes while Siringo watched the street beyond the back window. During that time, a Ford passed them, but it was a touring car going in the opposite direction.

Satisfied, he turned his head forward and directed the driver to an address on Cahuenga Avenue. It belonged to a saloon running wide-open despite the law of the land, with its door open in the southern California spring heat leading to a narrow passage with bat wings barely visible in the indoor gloom at the far end. A group of lanky locals dressed in ranch gear leaned in the doorway and against the front of the building, smoking and rolling cigarettes and watching a man in similar attire hopping in and out of the loop of the lasso he was twirling. The man wore a baggy grin and his Stetson pushed to the back of his head to expose a lock of dark hair spilling onto his forehead.

"That's a wicked-looking lot," said the driver. "You better slip the cash over the back of the seat. You don't want to flash no roll in front of that bunch."

Chuckling, Siringo paid him, adding a fifty-cent tip to make up for the inconvenience of an unusual fare. "You ain't far off the mark. That fellow abusing the rope's Will Rogers, and I owe him money."

Rogers looked up as Siringo approached; if anything his grin got broader and baggier, but he was spinning the lariat parallel to the sidewalk now and didn't falter. "How do, Charlie. You come to pay back that twenty?"

"You know goldarn well it's ten, you stump sucker." He held out a banknote. Rogers snatched it one-handed and stuck it in a jeans pocket without missing a turn of the loop. "I'd of been sooner, but I was down to my last chip till recent."

"I'm sorry to hear it: Your recent success, I mean. Lasky's getting set to shoot in Nevada and he needs a doughbelly."

"I'd wear out my welcome in a week. I can't cook nothing but beans and biscuits."

"I mean he's casting the part. He wants a stove-up old waddie with a bum leg. I don't know why I didn't think of you first off."

Siringo didn't dignify that with an answer.

"What you about here?" he asked. "I thought you was too busy putting together your own picture outfit to mix with these phildoodles looking for work."

"Hey!"

He squinted at the complainer, a gaunt man in flannels and denim with handlebars too black for the creases in his sunburned face. "Well, hello, there, Pete. I didn't recognize you in all that bootblack or I wouldn't of included you. Get too close to the lid when you was spitting in it?"

"I got to make out, Charlie. It ain't like the old LX, where they counted a man by his work. These directors don't hire you without cutting you in two first and counting the rings. I'm fighting these drugstore dandies for walk-ons."

"How you fixed?" Siringo reached for his wallet.

"Thank you kindly, but Will beat you to it. I'd just spend the extra inside. But I'll be thirsty again next week."

"I'll keep that in mind."

Rogers stopped twirling and walked Siringo out of earshot of the loiterers.

"It was produce pictures or starve," he said. "I'm a rope thrower, not an actor. But I try to get down here to the Watering Hole now and again. I don't want to come off all toney like Tom Mix. These boys show up here day after day, hoping a studio bus will come along, admire their hempsmanship, and scoop 'em up for a day's work on the set, just like ranch days. Only the bus don't come as often as it did. The western's shot its wad, they say: Harry Carey and Hoot Gibson has done beat that horse to death. Lasky's covered wagon picture is like to strand itself in the Nevada desert."

"I was wondering why Tom Ince stopped poking at me."

"He's shooting fox hunts on that spread of his." He circled the rope through his fingers. "Anyways, I like to come down and cheer the boys up with a little face-licking and maybe a turn or two they ain't learnt."

"And a stake."

Rogers scratched the back of his neck.

"I'd be obliged if that didn't get around. Even when old Pete gets a snootful, he just brags on hitting pay dirt. I'm grateful for that. Once you get that tramp sign on your front gate . . ."

"I know it. When my first book came out I got right popular with some old pards I never knew I had."

"I wisht somebody'd told me how expensive it is being rich."

"That's 'cause back then we never knew nobody wouldn't tip clean over sideways if he had a nickel in his pocket."

Rogers swung his lariat twice and missed the corner fire hydrant by two inches. "See it duck at the last second?"

"Horseshit. That was for the boys."

"Folks like it when you slip up. I tried telling that to Chaplin, but he couldn't hear me from way up there. What about you, Charlie?"

"Oh, I slip up just for practice."

"That ain't what I meant. You didn't take your dust to town just to square yourself with me."

"I didn't, nor to wet my whistle, neither. I need a place to change my duds." He indicated the valise he was carrying.

"You lose your billet?"

"Piece by piece, but that ain't the reason. I need to go in someplace Charlie Siringo and come out somebody else."

"Well, you're too old to run from a woman, and if you can give me back my sawbuck you can buy yourself time from the sharks. You ain't back with the Agency, by any chance?"

"They wouldn't take me if I tried, and I wouldn't like me if I did. I'm gathering information for a friend is all."

"A lady friend?"

"I ain't dead yet, Will."

"Working alone?"

"No, but I sent him wide while I drag a dead skunk crosst the trail. I don't suppose you'd know a man named Paddy Clanahan? He hangs his hat in Frisco."

"Not that I recollect, but I look forward to knowing him. I never met one I didn't like."

"I'm satisfied you ain't met. What about Edgar Edison Lanyard?"

"How many's that?"

"Just one. Some folks call him the eel, not necessarily on account of his initials."

"Nope."

"I wouldn't recommend making their acquaintance unless you want to test your theory."

"What are they, radicals?"

Siringo shook his head. When it came down to it, Rogers was just too amiable for this world.

"Don't ask too many questions, Will. It's the answers put you in the soup."

Will Rogers grinned.

"It's me you're talking to, Charlie. All I know is what I read in the papers."

20

The saloon Hollywood cowboys called the Watering Hole looked like it had been moved there by crane from a moving-picture location, complete with a half-naked woman reclining in a frame above the beer taps and brass spittoons along the foot rail. It was a piece here and a piece there of every cantina he remembered, all in one place for the first time. The only thing missing was the godawful stink of unwashed flesh and tracked-in horseshit.

The man behind the bar looked up as Siringo flapped through the bat wings, but not recognizing him as a studio representative went back to polishing glasses. Siringo put down his valise and ordered a shot of rye.

The bartender filled a jigger. He wore the uniform: striped sleeves, slick hair, waxed moustache.

Siringo paid for his whiskey. "Where's the rest of the barbershop quartet?"

The man glowered.

He drank, picked up the valise, and walked past Custer's Last Stand toward a pair of doors marked WRANGLERS and MARMS. WRANGLERS contained a pair of toilet stalls, a white porcelain sink, and a zinc trough where the men lined up like convicts to void their bladders. The room was unoccupied at present.

He hadn't been exactly square with Hammett. He had no intention of bracing Kennedy face-to-face.

He shut a stall door behind him, stripped to his long-handles, and put on the suit of clothes he saved for funerals, with a boiled collar and a necktie. Mothballs overpowered the stench of ammonia and disinfectant. He packed the clothes he'd been wearing in the valise.

When he came out of the stall, Pete, the sidewalk lounger with the dyed handlebars, was urinating noisily in the trough. Siringo opened his toilet kit and used the scissors to trim his moustache into a thin line, squinting at his wavy reflection in the mirror above the sink. This simple adjustment altered his features dramatically. He packed the kit in his valise, took out a bowler hat, polished the hard crown on his sleeve, and set it square on his head. As he was studying the result, Pete came over to wash his hands. He looked up at the man in the bowler.

"You from Paramount?"

————

The bartender did a vaudeville double take when a man he didn't recognize emerged from the restroom and put his valise and Stetson hat on the bar.

"You get another one of these when I come back for 'em." Siringo gave him a dollar and left.

————

"See anything?" Siringo joined the agent they'd partnered him with, a clean-faced youth who looked like the model in a shirt-collar advertisement.

"No. She must've missed the train." The young man was holding an Agency circular with a fair pen-and-ink representation of Laura Bullion, sometime companion of Wild Bunch desperado Ben Kilpatrick, in a fashionable dress with her hair pulled back into a bun.

They were standing on the train platform in Denver. The east-bound had stopped and passengers and greeters were mingling all around them.

"You can't expect her to look just like that. She knows we're af-ter Kilpatrick and that we figure she'll lead us to him."

"I know. I've been studying noses and earlobes like I was taught."

"You'd be surprised what you can do with rubber and wax."

"I know that too. I—"

"Hold your horses."

Siringo stepped past him and stumbled, knocking the slouch hat off a slightly built man in a Macintosh coat. A pile of auburn hair spilled to his shoulders.

"Beg pardon, sir; ma'am, that is."

Laura Bullion flushed, snatched up her hat, and hastened off, her flowered carpetbag swinging behind her.

The young detective came running up. "How did you . . . ?"

He pointed at her bag.

"She's carried that same one for months. It's a wonder how many slick characters think to change everything but their lug-gage. Let's get a move on before we lose her."

He bought a cheap cardboard suitcase in a secondhand shop on La Cienega, socks, shirts, and underwear in a haberdashery in the next block, packed them in the suitcase, and caught a cab. He felt naked and vulnerable leaving his dependable Colt at home with the Winchester, but the Forehand & Wadsworth hid better under the town clothes. He could send for them. He still had friends.

Just to satisfy his bump of caution, he changed cabs twice, drawing a ragged Z across that part of Los Angeles before finally giving the order to take him to the train station. He kept an eye out for imitators, but he was fairly certain the eel had taken the bait and was accompanying Hammett to the state line.

He overtipped the driver, getting a knowing leer in return. It was never too soon to get used to the role of a tenderfoot from back East.

He used the water closet twice during the trip north, and surprised himself both times when a city dude looked back at him from the mirror. He looked like a drummer selling ladies' unmentionables; not precisely the effect he'd been going for, but enough to pass for someone other than Charlie Siringo, at least to anyone who might have been furnished with just his description.

At the San Francisco station he spent a nickel. The telephone operator connected him with a reedy tenor voice belonging to the Pickwickian Perkins.

"Is that the Shamrock Club? I'm looking for Tammany." He used his best Irish brogue.

"This isn't it."

"I know that. I need the number."

"Who is speaking?"

"Charlie O'Casey from Chicago."

"Hold the line, please."

Siringo heard ambient noises a moment, then the little man came back on and gave him a number.

"Thanks. Say, is Paddy Clanahan there?"

"You just missed him."

"Can I catch him at Tammany?"

"I doubt that very much. He never goes there."

Which was better news than he'd hoped for.

———

Before he left the station he placed another call, collect, to a number he knew by heart.

"Hello, Bill," he said, when the charges were accepted. "I wasn't sure you'd take the call."

William Pinkerton, brother of Robert and son of the legendary Allan, exhaled audibly.

"I shouldn't, Charlie. You know how Bob feels."

"He favors your father. He's got the Pinkerton family tangled with the Pinkerton National Detective Agency. My beef never was with either of you, just with the way the business is run since you gave so much authority to little men."

"You could have prevented that. I offered you a superintendency."

"City work don't suit me. A telephone cord is just another kind of leash."

"Which makes this conversation ironic."

"Also a personal embarrassment, but I'm fresh out of choices. I need a favor, for old times' sake."

The West Coast branch of Tammany Hall met to elect candidates to office on the second floor of an enterprise on Kearney Street that Siringo knew for a fish market from across the street. A door propped open with a chunk of concrete probably shaken loose by the Quake belonged to a cramped staircase between beaverboard walls. He climbed it, breathing through his mouth the entire way. Just below the landing he paused to tilt his bowler to one side, like a comic in the burly-Q. That little act transformed his personality.

All the doors were open on the second floor, perhaps to vent the tobacco smoke that drifted in clouds like low-hanging fog. In the first room Siringo came to, a beefy, red-faced party in a straw boater, green suspenders to match his short necktie, and shirtsleeves rolled to his shoulders, sat on a wooden chair at a wooden table tallying figures from a long sheet like a publisher's galley on a scratch pad. The portraits on a wall of the otherwise bare room were of Grover Cleveland, Woodrow Wilson, and John L. Sullivan.

A typewriter clattered somewhere on the floor, and somewhere else a telegraph key was clacking. The place was a factory of sorts, cranking out city aldermen and delegates to Sacramento, without much contribution from the electorate.

At length the man behind the table sat back to consult the galley sheet, chewing on his pencil eraser. He didn't look up at the visitor.

"Pardon the interruption, friend," Siringo said in his Irish lilt. "The name's Charlie O'Casey. I'm just in from Chicago, looking for a billet."

"Try the Mariners Hotel at the bottom of Market. Two bits a cot, and the cockroaches stay for free."

"I don't mean a place to sleep. I'm here for the party."

"We ain't throwing any just now. Come back New Year's Eve."

"I'm talking about Tammany, of course." He jerked a thumb at his chest. "I got out the vote for Bathhouse John Coughlin in the First Ward."

The man was still looking at the sheet. "Chicago, you said? Jackie Coogan could deliver the ticket in the First Ward. The last Republican there starved to death twenty years ago."

"There was still plenty of 'em around in '93, which is when I done it the first time, and Bathhouse John's still in."

"What'd you do, tear down posters?" But this time the man favored him with an appraising look. He had a toothpick stuck in his mouth that if he took it out looked as if it would let all the air out of his fat face.

"I stumped. Loading dock, Rotary Club—hell, the middle of

the Loop; give me a box of Pear's to stand on and I can collect a crowd in the desert. I talked for five minutes in the Masonic Lodge before they threw me out on my ear."

"Why ain't you mayor?"

"That's the thing. They don't appreciate me back home, so I pulled up stakes and come out here, knowing you western types put store in a man's worth."

"Cut you out, did they?"

"I cut myself out." He leaned forward and lowered his voice. "Just between you, me, and John L. up there, Coughlin's through. He's got a string of squirts telling him he has to attract the youth vote, so he's replaced all his best men with green lads. He's opened himself wide to the guineas coming in from New York to take over the liquor business. Just last spring they shot one of their own, fellow named Diamond Jim, because he was standing in the way. Think what they'll do to the Irish. If I was Bathhouse John, I wouldn't waste my dough on green bananas."

"O'Casey, you said?" The man leaned sideways and pulled a gallows telephone attached to an extender out from the wall. "Who's your reference?"

"Pincus. Billy Pincus." Siringo gave him the number of William Pinkerton's private line in Chicago.

21

An Indian-head penny struck the floor on edge, caromed off it against the wall, and came to rest at the base of the wall, tails up. The next landed flat, but with enough momentum to bounce to the wall, ending up two inches away from the other with the Indian showing.

Hammett made a hissing noise between his teeth. He'd thrown the second penny.

"Odds are even, Slim. Call it." His opponent, a plumbing-fixture salesman from Dubuque—he carried a miniature toilet and sink in his sample case—juggled a third penny from palm to palm. He was short and thick-built, in a soft felt hat with the brim turned down over one eye and a gold toothpick glittering on his watch fob.

Hammett consulted his flask and swept a drop of Siringo's shine from his moustache with a finger. The baggage car swayed, and him with it.

"Heads."

The toilet salesman pitched.

The penny struck on its edge, spun once, leapt against the wall, and wobbled for a moment on the floor, a reddish blur.

"Tails," announced the salesman. "That's five you owe me."

"Just a second." Hammett seized the wrist belonging to a closed fist. The man struggled, but he applied pressure with his thumb and the hand sprang open as if a catch had been released. Hammett scooped up the coin and turned it over. It had Indian heads on both sides. Hammett brought his face close to the man's, whose wrist he was still holding, and grinned. "Double or nothing the one on the floor has more tails than a Broadway chorus line. You ought to give up tinhorning and put together a magic act."

The salesman cursed and tugged at his watch fob. Hammett spun him around by his wrist, jerked it up behind his back, and reached across him from behind. He pressed the pulse point on the man's other hand, and when it opened, he snapped the chain with a jerk, pushed the man away, releasing his wrist, and examined the nickel-plated derringer attached to the fob. He pocketed it.

"I'd look under your hat, but if there's no rabbit under it I'd be disappointed."

"You gonna call the conductor?"

"He'd throw us both off for gambling on his train." Hammett gripped the handle of the sliding door, heaved it open with a noise like coal tumbling down a chute, seized the salesman by the back of his collar and the seat of his pants, and hurled him through the opening. The man made a kiyoodling sound, arms windmilling.

The train was slowing for a curve, so he almost landed on his feet. His toes touched the grassy grade long enough for Hammett to root for him, but then the forward pitch of his body took him over onto his face and from there into three complete somersaults at least; he disappeared from sight while Hammett was counting.

He shut the door just as the conductor, an old campaigner

with white imperials and bad feet, let himself into the car from the passenger coach coupled in front of it. "What you doing here? Passengers ain't allowed in baggage."

Hammett made a sloppy grin and swayed too much for the movement of the car to be responsible.

"Sorry, friend. I got confused. All this motion makes me dizzy."

The conductor leaned close and sniffed. "If I was you, I'd put a cork in that motion the rest of the trip. You could confuse yourself clean over the side."

"Thanks for the advice." He started toward the door, but the man in uniform took a step in front of him, looking around. "You sure you're alone? I heard someone hollering."

"That was me. I was trying to remember the words to 'I Been Working on the Railroad.' No one ever mistook me for Caruso."

"Sounded more like Nora Bayes." But the conductor stepped aside.

Hammett had his hand on the doorknob when the conductor cleared his throat.

"Forgot your pennies."

He thanked him, bent over, scooped up the coins, and left.

He took his old seat in the smoking car where he'd met the salesman, propped his feet up on the sample case, and rolled a cigarette, stealing glances at his fellow passengers as he worked. None of them was Lanyard, disguised or otherwise.

He waited.

After five minutes, a farmer wearing a stiff hat and a rusty black suit coat over bib overalls came in from the next car, his Adam's apple preceding him, walked halfway down the length of the car, passing several empty seats, and took one across the aisle from Hammett. He stuffed a corncob pipe with tobacco from a Prince Albert can and sat smoking, looking out the window. He knocked the pipe out into the stand half-smoked, got up, and went back the way he'd come.

"Hope the eel gave him a flattering description," Hammett said aloud.

The conductor announced a ten-minute stop in Placerville. Hammett got off, entered the station, bought *The Racing Form* at the newsstand, waited for the man in the telephone booth to come out, and called Beauty Ranch. Becky London answered.

"Oh, it's you," she said.

"Don't get so excited. I thought you went home to Mama."

"Are you always this obnoxious, or am I special?"

"Is your stepmother there?"

"She's out riding. You can report to me. She filled me in on what you're about. I'm not in favor of it."

"You're good, you're really good. I think it's the way you talk way back in your nose when you disapprove." He gave her a short version of the case to date, including his current mission.

Her tone changed. "But what is Mr. Siringo doing?"

"Not over the wire, but I'm holding up my end. The man who probably shot at Butterfield's on this train."

"You saw him?"

"I saw the cat's-paw he paid to check on me after I dropped out of sight a few minutes. He was too cagy to do it himself. He's watching me now that I got off."

"So you can see him. I heard—"

"You heard right. But I can feel what I can't see. Whatever you think of Charmian, she doesn't hire a gardener when she needs a tooth pulled."

"I think she's wonderful, but I wouldn't admit it to my mother or my sister. They're professional martyrs since Daddy left."

"They won't hear it from me, angel."

"I wasn't asking you not to tell them! And don't call me angel!"

"Okay, sweetheart. You'll tell her what I told you? It's tough sitting around waiting."

"I'll tell her. And if you call me anything, call me Miss London."

The whistle blasted twice.

"That's my curtain line. I'll be in touch. Tell your stepmother if she receives word from a Peter Collins to get in touch with Siringo right away."

"Who's Peter Collins?"

"He's me." He paused. "He is I. I'm working on my grammar. It pays to keep your weapons cleaned and oiled. Clanahan's got a long reach. He probably knows people at Ma Bell and Western Union. No sense making it easy for him."

"Mr. Hammett, are you in danger?"

He suppressed a cough, grinned at the telephone box. "Don't worry, I'm used to it. But don't forget what I said. Oh, and angel—"

"Yes?"

He laughed his snarky laugh, said good-bye, hooked the receiver, and got back on board.

———

"Carson City, next stop!"

Hammett, who'd been dozing, tipped his hat back from his face. The conductor with the bad feet was just passing. "How soon?"

"Fifteen minutes." His gaze went to the sample case on the floor between facing seats. "I haven't seen your friend in a long time."

"He got off in Placerville. I didn't notice his case was still here till after we pulled out." He lifted it onto the opposing seat to be taken to the lost and found.

The conductor didn't take it. "He was paid through to Salt Lake City."

"Guess he changed his mind."

"Sixty bucks is a lot to pay for a last-minute fancy."

"Maybe he saw a girl he knew."

The conductor stroked his imperials, nodded. "Yep. Nobody ever broke his heart over money wasted." He picked up the case and moved on. "Next stop, Carson City!"

Hammett thought about his satchel in the overhead rack; but there was nothing in it of value except a couple of jars of moonshine, and he could always get it back from the railroad later.

He stepped out onto the car platform to build a butt. The smoking car was too crowded at that early evening hour. He leaned a shoulder against the front of the car and watched the slipstream shred the exhaust from his cigarette, the garbage alongside the tracks that always announced the approach of civilization. A coyote looked up from what it was munching, making eye contact for a tenth of a second, its yellow gaze lingering after the animal had passed from sight.

He flicked the cigarette into the stream of air and turned back toward the car. Something moved in the corner of his eye, he heard a swish, and black-and-purple light filled his skull.

———

Ties and jagged pieces of rock—the railroad cinder bed—whizzed past, inches in front of his face, black and white, like piano keys. His left arm was stretched to the breaking point, his hand clutching the bottom of the railing designed to prevent passengers from falling off the car platform, one foot braced against the coach chassis, the other bouncing off the ties. His reflexes had come around before his brain.

He drew up the loose leg, smelling the stench of scorched leather, then feeling the beginnings of a bad friction burn where the toe of the shoe had burned through. His head was filled with dirty cotton. Thinking was an act of physical exertion.

He realized he had another hand. He held it up in front of his eyes for a moment, making sure. Then he reached for the railing and with the assistance of his patient other hand, pulled against the wind of the speeding train, at the same time making a bicycling motion with his hot foot to find purchase on the platform. Pedaling empty air.

It was no good. A train cruised at forty miles per hour; a man was good for four at most, with both feet on solid ground and his brain working normally. The wind tore at his face, squeezing water from his eyes and pulling his flesh away from the skull. His hands had no feeling. If they held any grip at all it was news to him. A downward lurch told him it was slipping.

It wouldn't be like it had been for the toilet salesman. They weren't on a curve, and the engineer was making speed on the flataway, making up for two minutes lost somewhere along the way. A man could recover from a broken leg, shattered ribs, even a pelvis held together with wire and pins. A severed spinal cord was another thing, a fractured neck; the luck there was instant death. The alternative was someone turning him over from time to time to avoid bedsores, bathing him and wiping his ass, and waiting.

Jose would do all that, including the waiting. She would jump at it: no more empty bottles in the trash, no unfamiliar scents on his shirts, no more pacing the floor at night waiting for the phone to ring, the request to bail him out of yet another jerkwater can; just sheets to change, chamber pots that needed emptying. She was a nurse. His nurse, as it had been at the start, before it had turned into something else.

His nurse.

Not his wife, and certainly not his lover.

Until she wasn't any of those things.

How long?

He poised himself, using his last stores of strength to brace his hands and feet against the car. If he jumped high enough, far enough, landed hard enough, the rest was harps and trumpets, or more likely flames and accordion music. A man could live with those.

He flattened his palms against the resistance and took a deep breath.

A whistle blew. Westinghouse brakes hissed. The wind in his face grew less fierce. The train was slowing down for the station.

Hammett twisted his fingers around the railing, pressed a heel against the bottom of the platform, and hauled himself up hand over hand onto solid steel. Something slipped out of his pocket and rattled along the rail: the drummer's derringer.

"Carson City!" The conductor's voice, bawling above the slowing drive rods, the whoosh of excess steam. "Watch your step!"

He coughed—deep, hollow coughs, like mortars bursting behind a hill.

Then he wept.

22

The beefy man in the straw hat hung up the phone and stuck out a hand for Siringo to take. Having shaken hands with people in politics before, "Charlie O'Casey" shoved his deep into the big paw to spare his fingers, but it was still two minutes before circulation returned.

"I don't know Pincus, but he knows what a Tammany man should, and he says you're a hustler. We'll find out soon enough." He scribbled an address on his pad, tore off the sheet, and held it out. "Ask for Handy Muldoon. Tell him Ahearn sent you. He'll figure out something for you to do."

"I was hoping for a job with Clanahan."

"He's Paddy's all-around. You can't get closer than that. Why do you think they call him Handy?"

The address on the sheet belonged to a crazy-quilt house on Front Street, with porches and gables protruding in all directions, the oldest building in the block. SAILORS REST was the legend on a wooden sign shaped like a gull in flight pegged into the front yard: Frisco made allowances for the illiterate. The sailors resting in rockers on the front porch sat without rocking and only the occasional puff of smoke from their short-barreled pipes to show they were breathing. Siringo walked past them without interrupting their contemplation of the bay.

He went inside without using the bellpull, and nearly collided with a boy in knickerbockers running toward the door with an envelope in one hand. Siringo caught him by the shoulders and asked where he could find Handy Muldoon. The boy pointed toward the back of the house, ducked out of his grip, and ran outside.

Siringo passed the model of a schooner four feet long from stem to stern and three feet high from keel to topmast in a glass case on an oaken stand, and then more ships in pictures in copper frames, interspersed with fantastically bearded men in naval officers' caps, all photographed in three-quarter view so that they appeared one-eared. Certainly some of them were one-eyed; he'd seen fewer glass eyes in a taxidermist's studio. He wondered how they'd kept their vessels from always turning in the same direction.

The room he entered after passing the last cyclops was large, and might originally have held the house's library, although if there had been shelves they'd all been torn out and the evidence plastered over and painted institutional green. A huge blackboard decorated the far wall, so close to the ceiling that a tall stepladder stood at either end for the chalkers to reach. They were unused at present, and the boards were blank: but they'd been written on so many times, the names of more recent ward heelers scrawled over those of their predecessors and smeared by erasers nobody ever bothered to clean, that Siringo thought the city's governing history could be read there by some patient scholar, although it didn't signify why anyone would take the trouble. Folding wooden chairs were sprinkled about in no particular pattern, and ten feet of yellow-oak table bisected the room square in the middle, with a dozen or more telephones standing at attention its entire length. The room was like every betting parlor he'd ever visited, except the players in this one were betting on candidates instead of horses. The inevitable presidential portraits hung between blackboards, although Lincoln was the only Republican present.

"I told Paddy it was a mistake, but he said Honest Ape ran independent the second time, so he made him an honorary Democrat."

Siringo looked at the man who'd read his thoughts when his gaze had lingered on the sad ugly man in the painting.

Handy Muldoon—for it could be only him—stood behind the long table holding one of the candlestick phones with the earpiece tucked under his jaw. He was a tall man with an athletic, cylindrical build, in his vest and shirtsleeves with all buttons fastened and a red bow tie, the only color in his costume. He had a fine head of red hair and a chiseled face that would have been handsome enough to sell Palmolive soap except for the nose, which someone had objected to for some reason and pushed to one side. Tapes of scar tissue adhered to his eyebrows. Siringo grinned in sudden recognition, and nearly forgot his accent.

"I saw you fight Jack Johnson in '13," he said. "Keewatin, it was. Only it wasn't Muldoon then."

"I was Tiger Tim Conway. Anyway, that was the name on the robe someone left in a dressing room I used my first year on the circuit. It was a shame to waste it. Since I won the first six fights I wore it into the ring, I wasn't keen to change my luck." He spat his T's: a New York City borough rat from the ground up. "Jack was on the lam then, for taking a white woman across state lines for immoral purposes. He was having trouble digging up opponents in Canada: Half of 'em didn't want to fight coloreds, and the other half didn't want to fight Jack Johnson. I spent six months afterwards wishing I was one of 'em. This was the least of it." He touched a finger to his bent-over nose.

He stiffened then and cupped the receiver to his ear. "Al? Handy, in Frisco. No, I took one look at him and sent him back East on the next train. He never even got outside the station. Because I fired the lobsneak three years ago for stealing ballot boxes from the wrong ward. He was stealing 'em for them and us, too. Sure, he was Tom Coogan then, same as now; but you know goddamn well Tom Coogan is Irish for John Smith. Next time, send me a Rabinowitz. At least I'll know it ain't somebody I sacked already. No; hell, no, Al. How far back do we go? Fine. How's herself? Swell, keed. Good luck with the campaign."

"Al Smith," he told Siringo, hanging up. "He's running again for governor."

"Of San Francisco?"

"Hell, no, New York. You really do hail from Canada, don't you?"

"No, I was brokering a gun deal with some boys from Dublin." Which was partially true; he'd posed as a Home Rule sympathizer and the information he'd gotten had helped send the robbers of a U.S. armory to prison. "The name's Charlie O'Casey. I'm to tell you Ahearn sent me."

"And so you have. And who the hell is Charlie O'Casey, I'd like to know."

He told him about Chicago.

"First Ward, is it? Who's Bathhouse John's strong right arm?"

"Mike Kenna."

"Call him Mike, do you?"

"Nobody does. He was Hinky-Dink when I met him and always has been."

"Why do they call him that, do you suppose?"

"On account of he's too short to serve as a leprechaun. They named him after a shrimp in a comic strip."

"What about Bathhouse John? Cleanly fellow, is he?"

"He's a big fat slob, and you can smell him in Indiana; but he's a fine fellow for all that. He was a rubber in a bathhouse before he got bit by politics."

"How big's the First?"

"Big enough to raise a blister on a brogan. She runs from the river clear down to Twelfth Street."

The catechism continued for half an hour. Some of his answers had been supplied by William Pinkerton, consulting Agency records. Others he remembered from working out of the Chicago office. He'd hated the town; he hated towns in general as low spots where vice and corruption bred like leeches in stagnant water, but he knew it well. And he'd been through enough such interviews to know better than to answer every question correctly: He stumbled on some minor items, confessed his ignorance on some others. Nobody knew everything—unless he'd been coached.

They were interrupted frequently by one or the other of the telephones on the table. Muldoon purred into some of them, snarled into others, listened to the caller on still others, saying little. Siringo saw why he'd been installed in his present position. He conducted conversations the same way he'd fought.

Finally Muldoon ran out of questions. "I don't know why Ahearn sent you to me. I'm a persuader, not a politician. I make sure the polling places are safe for the party, keep the boys in line when they get a snootful the day after election: That kind of thing can hurt us come next round. When money's pledged and slow in coming, I remind the contributors of their promise. When they're still absentminded, I bring a couple of boys along."

"Don't the police interfere?"

"I go where they won't. Around here I'm known as the unofficial police chief of San Francisco."

"I ain't too old for a little dustup. I used to be pretty good at it and I can be again." Another ladleful of pure truth: It was the first good thing to come of doing that kind of work for Pinkerton.

"You're kind of little."

"I ain't got far to fall when I do get knocked down." He demonstrated his fitness by grasping the back of a folding chair with each hand and dead-lifting them above his head. He set them back down gently.

"We'll give you a try." Muldoon slid a hand inside his suit coat hanging on a chair behind the table and produced a folded sheet of paper, which he handed to Siringo. "Don't pay any attention to the names I crossed off. They're all true-blue. The rest need a gentle nudge. You heeled?"

He unbuttoned his coat to expose the butt of the Forehand & Wadsworth above his belt.

"Leave it with me. No rough stuff this far from November." Muldoon held out a hand.

Siringo hesitated, then took out the revolver and laid it in his palm. He felt naked immediately.

"Where you staying?"

"The Golden West." It was around the corner from the St. Francis, where he'd been registered under his real name, and just as handy to Hammett's apartment.

"I'll have it sent round." Muldoon laid the pistol on the table. "Don't come back here until I send for you. It helps when not all the birds who work for me know all the others."

"Jake with me."

He left, sticking the sheet inside his coat. The old sailors were still in their rockers, leaking smoke from their pipes and looking out toward Hawaii. Standing on the sidewalk, he unfolded the sheet and ran a finger down the names that were typewritten on it. A line ran through the one he most treasured:

```
Joseph P. Kennedy
Alexandria Hotel
```

23

A nurse was doing something to Hammett's foot.

"What's the name of this place?" he asked.

"Carson City Memorial Hospital." She was a tall woman with slightly Oriental eyes, a toneless professional sort of voice, and some citrus scent that clashed with the carbolic they'd used to disinfect the room. Nothing like Jose.

"How's the hoof?"

She finished dressing his foot and threw the old bandages into a metal rubbish bin with a pedal that swung the lid up and down.

"No peg leg for you," she said. "You're lucky. That's the worst friction burn I've ever seen. What did you do, try to brake the train the hard way?"

"You're close. Who told you I was on a train?"

"You did, when the cabbie brought you in. You were in shock. What happened to your head?"

He touched the bandage he wore like a pirate's bandanna. He couldn't remember when his head didn't ache. "I fell and landed on a blackjack. There a telephone in here?"

"No, and if there was I wouldn't let you use it. You need to rest."

"Get me a piece of paper, will you?"

Her smile was tight-lipped, more carbolic than citrus.

"Thinking about your will?"

"I need to send a telegram."

"I'll write it." She drew a pad and pencil from the pocket of her uniform. "Shoot."

"Can't. You took my gun."

"It's in the cupboard with your clothes. What's a nice-looking young man like you need with a gun?"

"You guessed it. I have to mow a path through the crowds of women or I'll never get anywhere. Send it to Charlie O'Casey at the Golden West Hotel in San Francisco."

She took it down:

DEAL FELL THROUGH STOP EXPLAIN IN PERSON
PETER COLLINS

"Who's Charlie O'Casey?"

"Shortstop for the New York Giants."

"No, he isn't. I'm from New York."

"Send it collect. I left my money in my pants."

He waited until she went out, then threw aside his covers and swung his legs over the side of the bed. He was naked under a thin cotton gown. Standing, he put his weight onto the wrong foot and almost fell back down onto the mattress. The morphine was wearing off. The foot looked swollen twice its size, but it was mostly bandage. He made his way to the iron footboard and used it as a railing to get to the narrow wooden cupboard on the side of the bed opposite the door.

There was only one shoe in the cupboard; he vaguely remembered someone cutting the other one off. He took off the gown, sat naked on the bed, and dressed himself slowly, molly-coddling the bad foot when he put on his pants. He borrowed a pillow slip, wrapped the foot in it for extra protection, and secured the slip with a sock garter.

He rose again, standing on his good foot, checked the chambers in the .38, and was working it in its holster onto his belt when a man came in wearing a white coat with a stethoscope draped around his neck. The man was young but balding and wore rimless glasses.

"What do you think you're doing?"

"Riding a bicycle. What's it look like?" He pulled his coat on and took his hat from the top shelf of the cupboard.

"You haven't been discharged. You're a sick man, Mr. Collins."

"Who are you, the ice cream man?"

"I'm Dr. Bartlett."

"Well, Dr. Bartlett, I've had this foot as long as I've had the other. I think I know how to take care of it. My head too."

"Obviously not, or you wouldn't need a hospital. But I'm talking about your other condition. You're aware of it, of course?"

"You mean the T.B.? Yeah. I caught it from a toilet seat."

"A man with your illness ought not to be jumping off trains."

"Did I say that's what happened? I was in shock. I *fell* off the train. All the jumping I did was to get back on."

"Someone hit you, you said."

"I'm a writer. I've got a big imagination. This whole business was for research." He put his hat on gingerly, at a tout's angle because of the bandage. He patted his pockets. "I had a flask when I came in."

"I had it taken away. This is a place of healing, not a speakeasy. It will be returned to you when you're discharged. You must get back into bed."

"Keep the flask. They grow on trees in this state. What do I owe you, Doc?" He found his wallet.

"You can pay your bill in the lobby. *When* you're discharged."

"Tell you what. I'll toss you for it." He took out the two-sided penny he'd gotten from the plumbing-fixture salesman.

"Do I need to have you put in restraints?"

He flipped the coin and put it away. "If I were you I wouldn't."

"Are you threatening me?"

"Nope. Just giving you sound medical advice. You know Pete Durango?"

"No."

"He used to run with Villa. Now he runs liquor up from Mexico and sells it here in Carson City. If the cops were to pay a visit downstairs and find a couple of dozen cases of Old Quezalcoatl marked Hydrogen Peroxide all packed up for shipping, this joint might run into a jam renewing its license. On the bright side, though, there's more dough in liquor."

"*Mister* Collins—"

"You don't even need to buy a truck. I used to drive an ambulance. You got any idea how much inventory you can carry in one?"

"How long are you prepared to go on in this vein?"

"That's up to you."

Bartlett's tongue bulged a cheek. Finally he palmed the doorknob.

"I'll bring you a cane," he said. "I can't have you stumping around on that foot and risk infecting it."

"Thanks, Doc. Send my bill to Apartment six, one-twenty Ellis Street, San Francisco, in care of Dashiell Hammett." He spelled the name. "He's my business manager."

———

He took a cab to the station, reclaimed his satchel from lost and found, and went into the bathroom to inspect the contents. The sympathetic driver he'd found in the taxi line had taken it from him and given it to a red cap; he couldn't support an injured man and carry his luggage both. Lanyard hadn't taken anything while Hammett was dangling off the train. Even his brass knuckles and the Mason jars filled with Siringo's moonshine were there. He unscrewed one and took a swig. It probably wasn't poisoned.

"Maybe he still thinks I'm dead."

But the man who looked back at him from the mirror above the sink wore a doubtful expression.

For the first time since before going to Beauty Ranch, he didn't look for signs he was being tailed. Lanyard would hightail it back to Frisco whatever Hammett's condition. He hadn't bought the Montana dodge and would want to know what Siringo had been up to in his absence.

Dashiell Hammett bought a ticket and sat on a bench, resting his bandaged foot on his satchel. His makings were in the pocket where he'd left them. He rolled a cigarette and waited for his train home.

24

The lobby of the Alexandria Hotel was all marble and mahogany with green fronds spilling up and over the sides of copper urns and the same snooty clerk who stood behind the front desk of every fancy hotel in town. Siringo approached him carrying a long white pasteboard box bound with red ribbon tied in a bow.

"Roses for Mr. Joseph P. Kennedy," he said, no brogue this time. He'd traded his bowler for a cloth cap he'd bought in a shop across the street from the florist's and wore blue-tinted spectacles that masked the color of his eyes. He'd left his necktie, collar, and suit coat at the Golden West Hotel.

The clerk took in his working-class attire. "Is he expecting them?"

"I doubt it. Ain't that the point?"

"Leave them here. I'll see he gets them."

"I'm supposed to deliver 'em in person."

The clerk sighed and went to the trouble of turning his head three inches to look at the key pegs. "He's out at present. He didn't say when he'd be back."

"Anybody in the room?"

"His son, I believe. I'll have to announce you." He lifted the earpiece off a house phone.

"Swell by me."

After a moment's conversation in inaudible tones, the man hung up. "Suite thirty-two. Third floor."

"Okie-doke."

The elevator car, located behind bronze doors and a folding cage, was automated, but operated nevertheless by a Negro in a pageboy uniform. They rode up on nearly silent pulleys and came to a gentle stop.

The door to Suite 32 was opened by a boy wearing a smaller version of the suit Kennedy had worn in the Shamrock Club. He had his father's firm jaw and spoke in an approximation of his broad Boston accent.

"Who sent them?"

"No card. Maybe he's got a secret admirer."

"None of my father's admirers keep their esteem secret."

He held out a receipt blank. "I need a signature."

"Come in. Put them down anywhere."

Siringo shut the door behind him, laid the box on a settee upholstered in green brocade, and followed the boy to a writing desk with a green leather top. The suite didn't lack for green. The boy opened the belly drawer and took out a fountain pen. His visitor scanned the inside of the drawer: It contained blank hotel stationery, a San Francisco telephone directory, and a brass key of a type different from those he'd seen hanging on the peg behind the front desk.

"You Joe Junior?" he asked as the boy was signing his name.

"Joseph."

"I hear your father sets a lot of store by you. You're about two feet shorter than I had pictured."

"I'm ten. What's your excuse?"

He stifled a grin. "He said you have a good head on your shoulders. I can see he didn't exaggerate."

"Do you know my father?"

"I seen him around, not that he'd remember me. He can't help but make an impression."

"Here you are."

Siringo took the receipt. As the boy returned the pen to the drawer and pushed it shut, the visitor grimaced and clutched at his chest, grunting.

"What's wrong?"

"Ticker." He fumbled a pill bottle out of his inside breast pocket. "Could I get a glass of water?"

Joseph P. Kennedy, Jr., hastened through a door that opened on gleaming tile. Water ran. Siringo reached across the desk, opened the drawer, snatched the key, and stuck it in his pocket. He closed the drawer just as the boy came out of the bathroom carrying a full glass.

Siringo indicated gratitude, put a pill in his mouth, and swallowed it with water. It was one of the aspirins he took to ease the pain in his bad leg.

"I thought heart medicine went under the tongue."

He squeezed his eyes shut, massaging his chest. At length he let out a gust of air and smiled weakly. "They're handing out medical licenses early back East," he said.

"You're all right now?"

"Sound as a dollar."

"I wish I knew who sent the flowers. My father doesn't like surprises."

"Who does?"

"May I have your name, in case he asks?"

"Peter Collins."

———

In the lobby he stepped behind a potted plant and looked at the key. It was a simple cutout with a round tab and slightly worn wards. On one side, the initials HAC were engraved above the number 12. The other side contained the legend DO NOT COPY.

A mahogany booth opposite the front desk contained a public telephone with a city directory on a shelf. He sat down on the leather-upholstered seat and thumbed through the *H*'s in the business section. Harriet's Advice Counseling seemed less than promising, as did Hassim's Arabian Caterers. Between them reposed, in medium type:

HARVARD ATHLETIC CLUB

Beside it was a telephone number and an address on Sacramento Street.

Three blocks from the hotel he entered a hardware store, waited for a man to pay for his purchase at the counter, and handed the clerk the key. The clerk, a young man in a canvas apron, turned it over and frowned. "It says 'do not copy.'"

"This says 'in God we trust.'" Siringo poked a folded five-dollar bill across the counter.

The bill vanished. The clerk found a corresponding blank on a pegboard, inserted the original in one slot of his machine and the blank in another, and switched on the motor. It ground and threw a shower of sparks. When it finished, the clerk held both keys close to his eyes, drew a rattail file from a bouquet of them in a tin cup next to the cash register, and spent a few minutes filing the wards on the new key to conform to the worn edges of the original. He inspected them twice before he was satisfied, then blew off the shavings. "That'll be two bits."

Siringo flipped a coin onto the counter. "Can I get an envelope to carry 'em in?"

The clerk handed him a No. 10 and Siringo left.

He returned to the Alexandria Hotel and Kennedy's floor. As

he stepped off the elevator, a maid in black-and-white livery emerged from another room to pluck a feather duster from a wheeled cart parked in the hall. He gave her the original key and a silver dollar to deliver towels to Suite 32, and while she was at it to drop the key in the top drawer of the desk when no one was looking. She looked doubtful, but bit the coin, nodded, and placed it and the key in an apron pocket.

Around the corner he stepped aboard a cable car and rode it nearly to the top of Nob Hill, home of more houses with clusters of porches and gables, but all in far superior condition to the Sailors Rest, painted in rainbow colors, with carriage houses behind. One, larger than most, had the year 1851 engraved in the stone lintel above the front door, and the address he was looking for on a gatepost. It bore no other identification.

A tall, white-haired porter whose Boston drawl made Joseph Senior and Junior sound like Midwesterners asked him in the entryway if he was a member. He shook his head and took out the envelope he'd gotten from the clerk in the hardware store. "I got a message for Mr. Kennedy. To be delivered in person."

The porter checked his registration book. "He's not in, sir."

"Know when he'll be back?"

"I'm afraid not, but if you leave the message, I can assure you he'll get it."

"Orders is orders. I'll check back later."

There'd been a risk Kennedy was in; but his leaving the key behind had been a hopeful sign.

Siringo took his time crossing the tessellated floor to the exit, and when he opened the door looked back. He saw only the top of the porter's white head bent over the registration book, possibly recording the visit. He closed the door and hustled on rubber soles to the other side of the winding staircase that separated the man's station from the rest of the room, found a door at the back, entered a narrow passage whose unpainted plaster told him it was used exclusively by staff, followed his nose past an open door belonging to a humid kitchen—moving fast to avoid attracting attention to a stranger—and came upon a plain staircase leading to the upper floors.

Instinct told him the gymnasium would be on the top floor, which contained the most windows and offered the broadest view of the city. There he detected the bleachy smell of disinfectant, heard water splashing, and stepped through a door into a room that took up most of the top floor, with a naked man doing the Australian crawl in a tile-lined pool and two others in trunks and undershirts sparring in a boxing ring. In the mouth of a corridor to the right he spotted the first of a line of tin lockers with louvered doors secured with padlocks.

He drew no interest from the swimmer or the boxers—both of whom, loose-bellied and shambling, were in no condition to fight professionally. It was always a wonder to him what lengths rich men would go to in order to make up for the exercise they didn't get by avoiding honest work.

Number 12 was indistinguishable from the locker on either side of it. He inserted the key he'd had made in the lock, cursed when it didn't work right away, wiggled it. The lock sprang loose. He tugged open the door and looked at some empty clothes hangers on a rod and a black satchel on the floor of the locker.

He lifted it out and set it on the long bench that ran down the center of the hallway for the out-of-shape athletes to sit on while they put on their socks and shoes. The satchel wasn't locked. He unlatched it and pursed his lips when he saw the contents, pantomiming a whistle.

25

"You look like a gigolo."

"I been called worse."

They were sitting in Siringo's room in the Golden West, the guest smoking a pipe, Hammett a cigarette. They were drinking Siringo's moonshine from hotel glasses.

"Tastes better from the jar somehow," Hammett said.

"Get used to it. Once you been to Nob Hill, you can't ever go back."

Hammett added the last slug of Scotch from his new flask, both secured in Sacramento.

"I don't trust a man who smokes a pipe," he said. "You ask a question, he fiddles with it for five minutes before he gives you an answer, and then it's usually wrong."

"I don't trust a man who blows up orphanages."

"I haven't blown one up all year. You think because you trimmed your moustache and put on different clothes it makes you invisible?"

"Not to a Pinkerton; but we ain't dealing with any, are we?" Siringo swallowed a slug of liquor. "You going to tell me what happened to your foot? You're too young and skinny for gout."

Hammett looked at the bundle of bandages covered by a pillow slip. "I should change the dressing." He told Siringo what had happened aboard the train.

"What about the toilet salesman?"

"I may have bought myself a day off Purgatory there, made an honest man out of a sow's ear."

"I doubt it."

"Me, too. Next time he'll just refine his methods."

"How's your head?"

"I'm working on it." Hammett took a long draught from his glass. "What about the other?"

"It appears we miscalculated. Lanyard didn't go for the bait."

"'We', nothing. It was your plan."

"I waited for you to come up with a better one, but then the train came and we ran out of time. Not that it was a total loss. We got him off our backs for a spell."

"He won't wander long. We need to get out of Frisco."

"For once we see eye to eye. I been hankering for that Sonoma country. Reminds me of the desert country along *La Jornada del Muerto*."

"And it's such a restful name. You going to tell me what you found out?"

"I hit pay dirt. There must have been right around a hundred thousand in that satchel, all tied up in neat bricks of C-notes."

"Let's divvy it up and retire."

"I left it there, the satchel, too. It came to me Kennedy might miss it."

"There goes South America and all its charms. What else might he miss?"

Siringo scooped something out of his inside pocket and flipped it into Hammett's lap.

It was a small notebook bound in green leather.

Hammett put out his cigarette and opened it, flipped through several pages.

"I can't make head nor tail of it," Siringo said. "Maybe he had a stroke."

"It's a number-to-letter cipher. If you gave me a year I might work it out."

"You got an hour."

"Why so specific?"

"That's when the next train leaves for the north country. I don't see no reason to dillydally, do you?"

"Go for a walk and take that stink-pole with you. I need to concentrate." Hammett got up from his armchair and sat down at the little writing desk.

———

When Siringo came back, the room was hazy with smoke. He opened a window. "You burn that camel shit and you beef about my pipe? What's the doc say about them coffin nails?"

"I got a second opinion in Carson City. He was against it." Hammett found a place to grind out his butt in the pile in the ashtray and tossed the hotel pad at Siringo. He caught it against his chest, opened it, and read:

> A. M. Fall: $10,000
> S. P. Clanahan: $5,000
> Harry F. Sinclair: $15,000
> Edward F. Doheny: $50,000

There were other names Siringo didn't recognize. "Who're the rest?"

"Search me. Punk players, by the amounts. Fall's got money problems, they say, so he'll take less than the oilmen. The bigger sums to Sinclair and Doheny are likely down payments. Those birds stand to make millions out of Buena Vista and Teapot Dome. Whatever Kennedy's got planned, he's in it for the long run, straight up to the cabinet."

Siringo lit his pipe, taking his time. He shook out the match and contemplated the charred end.

"I don't suppose it come to you we're in over our heads."

"Why should we be any different from the enemy? What do you think'll happen when Kennedy misses his account book?"

"He'll turn Frisco inside out looking for Peter Collins."

"Thanks for blowing my best alias. I was hoping to use it on a couple of stories I'm not too sure about."

"I couldn't use Charlie O'Casey. That would take him straight to Ahearn and Muldoon. No sense making things too easy."

"He'll trace it to my wire."

"Couldn't be helped. I've found it's easier to keep your lies straight if you hold them to a minimum."

"There's where we part company. You don't write fiction."

"You think not? When Pinkerton came down on A *Cowboy Detective*, threatening to break me in the courts, I spent weeks changing the name of the Agency and everyone I had anything to do with in its service. I paid back most of the advance to cover the extra typesetting. Whoever said a lie can't live never had to deal with lawyers."

"And you wonder why I'm an anarchist."

"I thought you said you was a Marxist."

Hammett shook his head. "I can't figure why you're not in public office."

Siringo pointed at the notebook. "That's why. It makes a man sentimental for the days of back-shooting in broad daylight."

"Another place where we see eye to eye."

"If you're waiting for a hug, I wouldn't advise it." The old detective puffed up a cloud of sour-smelling smoke. "Anyways, it's all the more reason to light a shuck north."

Hammett grasped his bamboo cane and levered himself upright.

"Arrange the tickets. I'm going home to pack."

"I wouldn't, unless you want to put the eel back on our trail. He'll default to your billet for want of nothing else. Pick up what you need on the way."

"Swell. Don't forget to pack the shine."

Siringo scratched at the stubble where he'd trimmed his moustaches. "What about that jug you was fixing to bring back from Carson City?"

"That bootlegger I told you about was Pete Durango. I blew him up at the hospital in Carson City. It was my getaway stake. I'll buy you a case of Jack London's best from Becky."

"Interesting how you went straight to her instead of Charmian."

"I won't seduce her till you give me the office. If you want to arrange it with her stepmother, you're a free man."

Siringo's pipe had gone out. He knocked it into a dusty basket of fruit courtesy of the Golden West. "In the old days, I'd horsewhip you."

"In the old days, you might try."

The old detective's face went black. Then it lightened by degrees. "I don't feature riding on the outside of a train's any picnic."

"If I'd seen it coming, I'd've packed a wicker basket." Hammett smiled then. "You weren't kidding when you said you've got luck in store. I guess you spent a deal of it when Clanahan and Kennedy weren't in residence when you ran those bluffs."

"I know it." Siringo looked sour. "From here on in I'm running on my wits and nothing else."

"In that case we're boned."

"Go to hell."

Hammett scooped up Kennedy's notebook and the notes he'd made.

"What you fixing to do with 'em?" Siringo asked.

"Keep the notes for show and rely on the good old U.S. Mail for the book."

"God help us all."

"He's had plenty enough on his hands just looking after us. I'm putting the rest in the hands of Uncle Sam."

"I just wisht the nephew wasn't Warren G. Harding."

Down in the lobby, Hammett got an envelope and a stamp from the clerk, put the notebook in the envelope, started to write *P. Collins* on the outside, made a wry face, crossed out what he'd written, wrote *S. D. Hammett* instead, added *General Delivery, San Francisco Post Office*, sealed the envelope, and dropped it in the chute. Then he went back up to find Siringo packed and dressed in his old outfit with the damaged Stetson on his head. His big Frontier Colt sagged in its holster on his hip. He was holding his Winchester by its scabbard strap.

"How'd you get your ordnance back?"

"Sent for it by way of a friend; the hat, too. You might know him. Will Rogers?"

"I never liked a man I didn't meet. I thought you'd've bought a new hat by now."

"It's got us this far. I've run clean out of my own luck. From now on I'm borrowing from my haberdashery."

"You're putting your faith in a hat?"

"I figure I got all I can expect from faith in Gem, Colorado. But if I'm going to die over somebody else's wine, I'd just as soon do it dressed like myself."

26

This time they took the train to Sonoma County. There was no one waiting for them at the station. It was late and there were no cabs at the stand.

"If you hadn't burned up Peter Collins, we'd have transportation," Hammett said.

Siringo shook his head. "It don't signify. Clanahan's bound to have somebody intercepting all the wires to Beauty Ranch. He'd of had a man here to meet whoever come off the train no matter what name we used. This way we slide in with the drunks from Frisco."

There was no shortage of them: men largely well-dressed but disheveled, many of them carrying bottles wrapped in paper sacks and walking with exaggerated dignity toward waiting personal vehicles. The detectives had blended in, with their coats buttoned wrong and hats pushed back to their crowns. Hammett had gotten rid of the bandage on his head, leaving the square of gauze stuck to the shaved patch with sticking-plaster.

Siringo watched him leaning on his cane. "You know, you'd get along better on crutches."

"You see to your bum leg and I'll see to mine. Where'd you get it, by the way?"

"Stepping into somebody else's business. We'll put in here and start out first thing in the morning." He pointed with his cheap suitcase at a four-story frame building across the street with a sign reading RAILWAY ARMS.

They entered the meager lobby, Hammett leaning heavily on his unsteady companion, both of them singing:

> *"Oh, see the train go 'round the bend,*
> *Good-bye, my lover, good-bye;*
> *She's loaded down with Pinkerton men,*
> *Good-bye, my lover, good-bye."*

The clerk, standing almost directly beneath an enormous moose head mounted high on the wall behind the desk, pasted a smile on his pale face. "You gents miss your ride?"

"We done that," Siringo said, slurring the words. "My young friend here's a newlywed. His wife ain't broke in just yet."

"She said if I got in after midnight, I could walk. On this leg!" Hammett indicated his bandaged foot.

"Women will be unreasonable." The clerk spun the registration book to face them, dipped a pen in the inkstand, and held it out. "What happened?"

"I bet him six bits he couldn't kick the top off a fire hydrant." Siringo took the pen and signed *Tom Horn, Cheyenne, Wyoming*.

Hammett said, "They make 'em stouter than where I came from." When his turn came he wrote *Booth Tarkington, Indianapolis, Indiana*.

"Will that be two rooms or one?"

"One," Siringo said. "My treat. I'm six bits to the good."

"Sam, I don't know what I can say to convince you I never throwed a wide loop in my life."

"That ain't what I heard, Charlie. Goodnight says a quarter of the LX stock is his and you put in more time on his spread than you ever did on Pierce's."

"He never. Bring him here and we'll see if he bears false witness. He's been taking the wrong advice from the wrong people."

"Well, he's sure enough paid me to fix your wagon, you stump-sucking bastard."

Which was as much warning as Siringo got before a bullet intended for his heart smashed his knee. Sam Grant was a sufficiently bad shot when he was sober, and after six hours sucking on a bar rag waiting for Siringo to show, the safest place to stand in Texas when he hauled out his Schofield—a brand new model nobody had any experience with yet—was in New Mexico.

Six weeks in splints, the better part of a year learning all over again how to walk, and a lifetime of reminding whenever he sat still long enough for the leg to stiffen up like a fencepost.

But the worst upshot of that affair was Siringo decided to give up the various life and limp into Kansas to open a mercantile.

"Charlie, wake up! You're chasing rabbits in your sleep."

He shot straight up in bed and had his hand on the Colt on the cracked nightstand before he realized he was in a hotel room in California and not the Lucky Seven Saloon in Tascosa, Texas. He left it where it was and sat back against the iron bedstead. Hammett, sitting in the room's only chair with his bad foot resting on Siringo's suitcase, was staring in the moonlight coming through the window.

"You okay? You were cussing fit to be tied."

"Forget it. And next time you call me Charlie I'll show you I'm a better shot than Grant."

"Who's Grant?"

He opened the drawer in the stand, took out his bottle of

aspirins, swallowed four, and washed them down from the Mason jar on the top. His leg was throbbing as if he'd just come out of the laudanum the first time. "Just a fellow they hung in Waco after his aim improved."

In the morning they breakfasted in a little restaurant patronized by farm laborers, whose conversation was predominately Spanish and Russian. The walls were redwood planks hung with Indian blankets and old farm implements. A tin sign with a pig painted on it advertised a brand of overalls that wore like a hog's snout.

Siringo found the Mexican food on a par with Los Angeles', and painfully inferior to Texas'. The cornbread tasted like cow patties soaked in axle grease.

Hammett, drinking coffee laced with Scotch from his flask, said, "How can a man eat beans and peppers in the morning? I can't face a fried egg before eleven."

"I never skipped a square meal on purpose in my life. You never know where the next one's coming from." He pointed with his tortilla. "I'd advise you to lay off that busthead before we go out to the ranch. Women can smell it on a man for a country mile."

"If you're such an expert on women, why aren't you back East letting your daughter take care of you?"

"Why ain't you in Montana, saying 'I do'?"

Hammett stopped up the flask. "On second thought, I think I'll try the liver and onions."

"Yes?"

As their cab rattled off, Siringo and Hammett took off their hats for the benefit of the woman standing in the open door of the cottage. She looked sixty, but was probably younger. Jack

London's large, melancholy eyes and well-developed forehead, prominent in photographs and well represented in his daughter's features, were even more pronounced. The woman wore her graying hair in a chignon and a black bombazine dress clasped at the throat with a cameo brooch. She appeared to be in bereavement.

"Good morning, ma'am. I'm Dashiell Hammett and this is Charles Siringo. Mrs. London may have mentioned us."

"Yes." The word sounded even more guarded when not presented as a question.

"She ain't expecting us, but it's important all the same," Siringo said.

"Yes?"

"We should be writing this dialogue down," Hammett told his partner.

"It's all right, Eliza."

Charmian, appearing behind her, wore a flannel shirt in a buffalo check and a suede skirt split for riding.

"Mrs. Shepard, gentlemen. Jack's sister."

"How do."

"Pleased to make your acquaintance."

"Yes." The woman withdrew.

"Talks your ear off, don't she?" Siringo grinned.

Charmian's eyes smiled.

"She practically raised Wolf. She's still looking after him even in death. We had an awful row after I told her about you. You lied to her at the start, and that's the story on you as far as she's concerned. You could push her out of the path of a runaway wagon and her impression would be the same."

"Can't say as I blame her. Telling her he's a historian was Mr. Hammett's notion, and I was darnfool enough to go along with it. I apologize for any unpleasantness."

"You have news?"

Hammett spoke up. "No. So far all we've been able to dig up is more questions."

"Can we talk inside? I'm worried about the hands. They worshipped Jack. They might do something rash if they overheard us."

"They got bark on 'em, that's certain," Siringo said.

"Your foot, Mr. Hammett. Did you have an accident?"

"No, ma'am, I didn't."

She hesitated, then stepped aside from the doorway. "We'll use Jack's den. These days it's the only place on earth where I feel safe."

When they entered the small room off the dining room/parlor, Siringo saw why.

It was a comfortable clutter of curling papers and lopsided books spilling off homemade shelves onto the surfaces of a small writing table and rolltop desk, and from there onto the bare plank floor; some of the stacks of sheets were tied with string—manuscripts, Siringo guessed—while others were loose, those not weighted down with native rocks, pine knots, sextants, and compasses stirring like cats awakening in the breeze through the curtained windows. Examples of the late owner's handwriting occupied the desk with a straight-back chair drawn up to it, and a portable typewriter with celluloid-inlaid keys in a battered wooden case with Jack London's name on the lid stood on the table facing a wooden swivel. It felt very much like a den belonging to a large and friendly bear, close and cozy and masculine. It smelled of cigarette smoke, sunk deep into every porous surface.

"Where's your luggage?" Charmian asked.

"Back at the hotel. We're traveling light." Siringo leaned the scabbarded Winchester in a corner. "This is a crackerjack room for a man."

"We've kept it as he left it, except for dusting and sweeping.

Eliza insisted. I thought it best to donate everything to a museum—a shrine can be a discomforting thing to live with—but I
came around to her way of thinking. Sometimes it seems as if
he's just stepped out for a walk, and will return in a few minutes
burning with ideas."

Hammett said, "I heard he was having trouble coming up
with them in the end."

"You mean because he bought them from struggling writers?
That was just his way of helping them out without insulting them
with charity. He had so many ideas of his own, he gave them away
to other writers. Sometimes I think it annoyed him when he had a
new one. They burned holes in his pockets like money, and he
was haunted by the premonition he wouldn't live long enough to
see them through."

"I know how he felt," said Hammett.

"I don't," said Siringo; "but I don't make stuff up. I write what
happened, and I'm running out."

Charmian shook her head. "I can't join your argument. I'm
not a writer myself, although I typed some of Jack's manuscripts,
on a horrible invisible typewriter I had to roll up the platen on to
see the mistakes I'd made. All I can say is, I feel nothing bad can
happen to me when I'm in this room."

"I'd keep the curtains closed," Siringo said.

27

"What does it mean?" Charmian looked at them over the tops of her reading glasses. She sat in the swivel chair with her back to the writing table, holding the notes Hammett had made from the green leather notebook.

Siringo, seated at the desk with an elbow resting on the blotter, said, "Hammett thinks they're payouts. I agree. Since I found them in Kennedy's locker, it stands to reason he's the one doing the paying. Question is what he's buying, and where's the money coming from."

"But you said he's rich."

Hammett stood by the window smoking. For some reason his foot hurt less than when he sat. "The amounts total almost five million. He might have that much, but investment advisors almost never put that much of their own money into a project. Not the successful ones, anyway. Since Clanahan's on the list, it isn't coming from him."

"I'm beginning to understand. He's being financed to buy up Jack's debts in order to control the liquor business: He answers to Kennedy. But who are these people who are getting such large payments?"

"Oilmen and politicians," Siringo said. "It don't say they got the money. Chances are he's counting his chickens early, waiting for Clanahan to come through with the stake."

"I know some of these other names."

"Mr. Hammett and I was hoping you would. That's one of the reasons we're here."

"They're local residents. Some of them were far from friends of Jack's. I suppose they may have some influence with the authorities, who could hardly be expected not to notice what Clanahan's about. You saw this name, of course." She turned the sheet their way and pointed to one near the bottom.

"Vernon Dillard," Siringo said. "Your sheriff. At about five bucks a pound I'd say he's overpaid. No wonder he weren't much help after the eel come to pay his respects."

Someone knocked on the door. Charmian took off her glasses. "Becky?"

It was her voice on the other side. "Aunt Eliza said those men are back. May I come in?"

Charmian looked at the detectives. Hammett grinned. "I won't be the one to try to keep her out."

Siringo got up and opened the door. Jack London's daughter wore a plain blouse and a skirt that left her calves exposed. The old Pinkerton would never get used to seeing women parading around half-naked.

"I've been out walking," she said. "I saw the taxi drive up. I don't suppose you've brought another murderer with you?"

"We're trying to break the habit."

She scowled at Hammett. "Why are you always grinning like a monkey?"

"You should see me when you're not around. I'm a regular sourpuss."

"Come in, Becky. Shut the door."

"Are you sure? It's always so stuffy in here."

"I'm very sure. These men have something to tell you and I'd rather it stayed in this room."

"But there's just Aunt Eliza."

"Who is a fine woman on whose face you can read her every thought. Please do as I ask."

She did, and noticed Hammett's bandages for the first time. "Have you been in a fight?"

"Yes, miss, with the Southern Pacific Railroad. The S.P. won." His face was pale despite the smile.

"Have you seen a doctor?"

"I've seen more than my share, thank you."

"When was the last time you changed the dressings?"

"I keep forgetting."

"Charmian, where is the first-aid kit?"

"In the kitchen, dear. Are you very much in pain, Mr. Hammett?"

"He'll live," Siringo said. "If you could die of a busted pin, I'd be six feet down in Texas."

"I wasn't asking you, Mr. Siringo."

Hammett said, "It can wait."

Siringo got up and held his chair for the girl. She sat with her back straight, her knees together, and her hands folded in her lap, her head cocked in a listening position. Her expression changed only once during the narrative, when Hammett described what had happened to him aboard the train. She clasped a hand to her mouth, but stayed silent until she'd been told everything her stepmother had.

"You left the money?"

Siringo nodded. "I won't say I weren't tempted. It's my opinion that cash was all Kennedy's, to prime the pump. Just because it came from his walking-around fund don't mean he wouldn't make me repay every cent with a piece of my hide."

"He's yellow, Mr. Siringo is," Hammett said. "And crooked as a roulette wheel."

"I think you're both marvelous," Charmian said. "Becky will see to Mr. Hammett's injuries and then we'll discuss what comes next."

Becky sprang to her feet and took Hammett's elbow. He offered no resistance; Siringo thought he leaned a little more heavily on her than warranted as they went out.

"You've trimmed your moustache, Mr. Siringo," Charmian said. "It becomes you."

"Much obliged. I always look better when I'm not supposed to be me."

"Charlie O'Casey. Peter Collins. I don't know how you both keep track of who you are at any given moment."

"Don't forget Horn and Tarkington. It's getting so when somebody calls me by my real name I look around to see who he's talking to."

"I can't blame you for taking precautions. These are dangerous men. There have been two attempts at murder, and may be more."

"I take heart that they keep missing."

She shook her head. For a homely woman she was uncommonly handsome. "I'm calling off this investigation. I'd rather let the ranch go than be responsible for your deaths."

"That's what they said in Colorado, when a puma that got too old to chase down wild game started going down into the local town and making supper out of the citizens. Instead of sending somebody after it and maybe getting him killed, they slaughtered a pig a day and left it at the town limits at sundown. The theory was the cat would fill up on pork and leave the folks alone."

"It's a reasonable assumption."

"See, that was the problem. Killers don't reason. Them pigs

was just appetizers. The town lost ten more from the population before all the men in good health rode up into the mountains with Winchesters. That puma's hide is still hanging in the lobby of the hotel there, and nobody's been ate since. You give a killer what he wants, he just goes on doing what he's been till you skin him and nail him to a wall."

"But this isn't your fight. Your lives are worth so much more than five hundred dollars apiece."

He smiled.

"I can't speak for Hammett, but I ain't doing it for just the money."

He watched her, expecting surprise or disappointment or loathing or maybe something encouraging. She smiled back.

"I guessed that, Mr. Siringo. I'm a grown woman and then some. I've gone through great loss, and learned from the experience. I fell in love once. It was wonderful and horrible and all things in between. I couldn't go through that again. But thank you for making a middle-aged woman feel once again like a desirable schoolgirl."

"We aim to please," he said after a moment.

She was still smiling. "I thought it was 'We never sleep.'"

"Oh, I catch plenty of winks off the job."

"Now you'll have your chance. I can't allow you to risk your life for something that can never be. That's why I'm ending this."

"I respect what you're saying. You got all the answers. You just need to ask yourself one question."

"Just one?"

"What would Jack do?"

Seated in a brightly lit kitchen with a pump-up gas stove, white-enamel sink, and an icebox big enough to chill a side of beef all at once, Hammett watched Becky London bathe his foot with warm water from a basin and pat it dry in her lap. The toes were blistered and peeling, but the new skin was radiantly pink. She inspected the damage from all angles with a frown of concentration.

"You're lucky," she said. "I don't know how you escaped infection."

"I medicate internally." He went on watching as she retrieved a roll of gauze, a bottle of hydrogen peroxide, and surgical scissors from a white tin box with a red cross painted on the lid. "Where'd you learn to be a nurse?"

"Charmian's the expert. She tended Daddy every time he took a spill and looked after him at the—at the end. She insisted on teaching me everything she knew. 'Men wrestle bears and fight wars, women patch them up afterward. That won't change just because we have the vote.' Her words." She snipped dead skin from his foot.

"You really do like her, don't you?"

"Daddy loved her. How could I not?"

"I guess she isn't one of those wicked stepmothers you read about."

"That would be my mother. I love her, but Daddy put up with a lot, before and after the divorce. I spend as little time with her and my sister as possible. They enjoy being miserable."

"Runs in the family. Sometimes I think a smile would starve to death on that pretty face of yours."

"I smile when I'm happy."

"I've got something to look forward to, then."

She used the applicator from the bottle of mild astringent to disinfect the wound, changing the subject along with the treatment. "You're a foolish man. Two stubborn women are nothing to lose your life over."

"I'm only doing it for one. I like Charmian, but I don't stick my neck out just for people I like."

"Are you saying you love me?"

"I don't know yet. You can want a new car bad enough to lose sleep thinking about it, but you don't know it's a good match till you drive it a hundred miles."

"Your opinion of my sex is why you've never seen me smile. A woman isn't an automobile."

"I only just said it."

"You didn't have to. In any case, you're promised to someone else."

"Siringo told you?"

"That wasn't necessary. I'm Jack London's daughter, Mr. Hammett. I don't have to see the hobbles to know when a horse is someone else's property."

"It's okay I'm a horse, but not you're a car?"

"You spoke of all women. I spoke of one man."

"Siringo'd say you didn't inherit Jack's bump of adventure."

"That wouldn't be an adventure."

"Sin, then. I read some of his books, and I read about him. I know which sins bothered him and which didn't. Ouch! Jesus!"

She'd begun winding gauze around his foot, and suddenly jerked it tight.

"Next I'm going to look at your head. There's a hole in it I'm sure. Get yourself killed if you want, but don't do it for my sake. Handsome men are bad for the heart."

"Your father was a handsome man."

"Exactly my point."

PART FOUR
MEN IN THE MOON

He solved the mystery a little sooner.
—Jack London,
on the death of a friend

28

They reconvened in the den. Hammett, his foot still smarting from the wrenched bandage, sat this time at the desk. The others stood. Charmian had sent the disapproving Eliza Shepard to town on an overnight errand.

"I still think we should abandon our course," Charmian said, "but Mr. Siringo has agreed to abide by your decision, Becky. The ranch is yours too. I was wrong to consider letting it go to Clanahan without asking you."

"Thank you. I—"

"Hang on," Siringo said. "This is about more than just real estate, or selling illegal goods. Kennedy means to control this country, and he ain't above hiring murderers to get what he wants. If we don't stop him here, history won't thank us."

"History's hooey."

"That's mighty enlightening, Mr. Hammett," Siringo said, "but maybe you'd care to go on for those of us who missed a class or two."

"What I'm saying is let's not pump the job up so big we can't see around it. Kennedy's just a politician, same as Clanahan, and when you get down to it Mike Feeney, may he rest in peace.

How many hands he's got doesn't count. You take out the head and the hands go with it."

"Are you suggesting assassination?" Becky's voice was almost inaudible.

Hammett shook his head.

"Mr. Siringo and I had our fill of that when we were with Pinkerton. It's why we left. I say we go to Kennedy and tell him the jig's up." He looked at Siringo. "You said yourself he isn't much for bluffing. He'll back off when he sees his plans are known. If he doesn't, we'll threaten to send his notebook to a Republican paper."

"We can't go to Frisco and leave this place wide open."

"We did before."

"Then we didn't have something Kennedy wants back. It won't take him long to match Charlie O'Casey to Charles A. Siringo."

"We'll manage," Charmian said. "We have the laborers."

"Oh, they can swing a sledge and snag a man's hat on a pitchfork, but they need to get in range first. Mr. Edgar Edison Lanyard'll pick 'em off with his long gun before they do."

"We'll send a wire," Hammett said.

"He'll never get it. Don't forget we agreed Clanahan probably owns the local Western Union office and the telephone switchboard too. He won't let anything go through to stop his payday. We'd just be telling him where he can send the eel."

"Kennedy will figure that out when he finds out his notebook's missing."

"Why save him time?"

Hammett had been sitting with his injured leg stretched out before him. Now he drew it back. "It doesn't matter one way or the other."

"Says who?"

"Says the man who knows the sound of a two-year-old Dodge when he hears it."

Siringo heard it then: the rataplan of pistons approaching the house. He turned and parted the window curtains.

"Could be worse," he said.

Charmian went to the window. "It's Vernon Dillard."

Siringo unstrapped the Winchester and levered a cartridge into the chamber. The noise made her spin around. "What are you doing? He's the sheriff!"

"Just a precaution, in case he forgot. You and Becky go out on the front porch and keep him busy. If he asks for us, you ain't seen us."

"Where will you be?"

"Attic. Better field of fire."

Hammett took out his .38 and inspected the cylinder. "I'll watch from the window."

Becky said, "You won't kill him in cold blood!"

"You've got me mixed up with someone else. I've never killed a man in my life."

"Me neither."

Everyone stared at Siringo.

"That I know of," he said. "A lot of us slung plenty of lead in the old days. We couldn't always keep track of where it all went. I ain't fixing to find out now, but that's up to Dullard."

"Dillard," Charmian said.

"Potato, po-tah-to," said Hammett.

A trapdoor led into the attic from the pantry next to the kitchen, with a ladder leaning on the wall nearby. He slung the carbine from his shoulder by its strap and climbed up.

"Brothers, you have allowed a spy to enter your ranks, and he now sits within reach of my hand. He'll never leave this hall alive. You know your duty."

He felt the Colt under his coat, the bowie stuck in his belt, a cold trickle of sweat marching down his spine.

Before he could get to either weapon, the men with the miners' union searched him as a new member, found a union account book, and noticed a leaf missing. He'd cut it out and sent it to Pinkerton headquarters.

They let go of him while they were studying the book. He got to his bowie first and cut a path through the crowd, making for the house he'd rented and fitted with locks and shutters.

After twenty minutes dodging wild rounds from the ports he'd cut in the shutters, they left men to watch the house and returned to the union hall to discuss strategy. All night long he heard their voices raised in violent argument, blows struck when words ran dry. Without being able to follow the conversation except by the fluctuating volume, he knew their decision by the harmony of the pitch near the end. As dawn broke over the raw earth of Gem, Colorado, the striking miners emerged from the building where they'd planned their revolt and surrounded the house, raw-boned men with the whites of their eyes glistening in their dirty faces, carrying picks, shovels, and dynamite . . .

That time he cut a hole in the floor and made his escape between the timbers of the foundation. This time he drew the ladder up behind him and lowered the trapdoor.

It was stuffy in the unfinished room under the rafters. Siringo opened the window, but not for air. He found an empty burlap sack, folded it, laid it on the floor, and knelt on it, resting the carbine's barrel on the sill and cocking the hammer.

He had a fine view of the sheriff's big touring car, and of the sheriff himself as he drew the brake and stepped to the ground, a big muscular man gone to suet, the star shining on the vest of his dusty black suit. He took off his homburg, mopped his red ham face with a handkerchief the size of a placemat, and started toward the house. He stopped when a screen door strained open at the end of its rusty spring and shut with a bang. The porch roof obstructed Siringo's view, but he recognized Charmian's voice.

"Good morning, Sheriff. Is this a social call?"

"'Morning, Miz London. How do, Becky. I'm afraid it's law business. I need to speak to your guests."

"Guests?"

"The hotel in town's part of my rounds. Fred, the clerk, told me two strangers checked in last night and out again this morning. The names they registered under didn't fit their description. I'd like a word with Siringo and Hammett."

Becky's voice answered. "What makes you think they'd be welcome here? The last time they brought a killer with them."

He scratched his burry head.

"*Killer's* harsh. The fellow was trying to throw a scare in someone, and he sure enough did. I got the location of that stolen horse out of young Butterfield before I got back to town. I figure the shooter's in line for a good citizenship medal."

"Even if he were, how would *you* find him?"

He showed his teeth in Charmian's direction: one grown-up to another.

"They left their bags behind. I searched 'em and found a couple of jars of contraband liquor, but I ain't here to make a federal case. It's enough to hold 'em till I get some answers."

"Be that as it may," Charmian said, "they're not here."

Dillard scowled down at his hat, appeared to notice for the

first time that it wasn't on his head, and put it on. It seemed to contain most of his authority, as his voice got louder and deeper.

"I see it's time to put my cards on the table. Somebody swore out a complaint against 'em for theft, which I reckon is why they faked their names this trip. Where are they if they ain't here, I'd like to know."

"You're the lawman," Becky said. "I'm sure you can figure it out. Perhaps not, on second thought. I forgot who I was talking to."

His face darkened a shade.

"There's no call to talk to me like that, little missy."

"You left two women here without official protection after someone fired a shot through our window. What is the call if not that, *I'd* like to know."

"You don't have any objection to me going in and looking around, I guess." He took a step toward the porch.

Charmian said, "You guess wrong, unless you've come with a warrant."

He stopped.

"I was sheriff when your husband was still digging up other folks' oyster beds. I never had to get a warrant to go in anyplace in this county."

"Never's a long time. You're not coming in and that's that."

"Who's to stop me?" He strode forward.

Siringo drew a bead and squeezed the Winchester's trigger. Dirt sprayed the sheriff's pants cuffs from the slug he'd placed at his feet. The echo of the report growled over the rolling hills of the *Valley of the Moon*.

29

He ejected the shell, chambering the next round, while Dillard was still reacting. The sheriff jumped back two feet, fumbling a big cedar-handled revolver from under his coat, looked around, heard the action of the lever, and stared up at the window.

"You're lucky you're slow," Siringo said. "You almost ran square into that first slug."

"Who the hell are you?" Dillard was shielding his eyes from the sun with his free hand.

"The deciding vote in the next election, if you take one more step toward the house."

"Siringo?"

"Yup."

"Where's Hammett?"

"The other end of this Roscoe," said a voice directly beneath Siringo's feet.

The sheriff lowered his gaze. "You men are in serious trouble, threatening an officer of the law."

"I see it as defending the Constitution. Get back in your car and don't come back here without a piece of paper signed by a judge. Your best bet's J.C. MacNamara. He's on Kennedy's list."

"You admit you stole it?"

"I did," Siringo said. "Hammett's just my accomplice."

A lazy grin spread across the red ham face.

"There's no call for all this gun stuff. Give me the notebook and we'll say it was all just a misunderstanding. Mr. Kennedy said he ain't interested in pressing charges so long as he gets back what's his."

"We'll take our chances in court, if it's all the same to you. The prosecutor can enter it as evidence."

"That'd be the Honorable Oliver Wentworth," said Hammett.

The sheriff's smile fled. "Be reasonable!"

"I thought that's what we was being," Siringo said. "You're the one standing out in the hot sun in a wool suit when you could be enjoying the breeze on the way back to town."

"How do I know you won't shoot me in the back?"

Charmian spoke up. "You have my word they won't. I know these men better than you do."

"A woman's word don't—"

A shot rang out below. Dillard's homburg flew off his head. He scrambled back into his automobile.

"This ain't the end of it!" he shouted over the roar of the motor. He swung the vehicle around and headed back the way he'd come.

"That was neat," Siringo called out to Hammett. "I didn't know you was a trick shot."

"I'm not. I was aiming at the car."

"How many of these guns work?" Siringo asked.

They were in the main room of the house, where most of London's collection of firearms was on display.

"All of them," Becky said. "I make it a point to keep them clean and oiled. Daddy showed me how."

"What about ammo?" said Hammett.

Charmian opened a drawer in one of the display cases. It was lined with cardboard boxes labeled with different calibers. "Do you think they'll be needed?"

Siringo said, "I hope not; but you can't hope your way out of a fix. I know Dillard. I met plenty of him in the old days. They do things the hard way. He'll come back with an army and that warrant—if he remembers to get the warrant."

"There won't be any trouble if you're not here when he does," Becky said.

Charmian scowled. "Don't be a child. They'll take us prisoner and use us to smoke Mr. Siringo and Mr. Hammett out into the open."

Someone knocked. Gripping his Colt, Siringo went to the window beside the front door. "It's just the hat-hater."

Charmian opened the door. The ranch hand had his own hat off and a slash of white bandage across his nose, sharply contrasted with his sunburned skin. He stiffened when he saw the man who'd broken his nose standing behind his employer.

"It's all right, Ivan. We're all on the same side."

"I heard shots."

"We're okay, but we're expecting trouble later. How many of the hands are conversant with firearms?"

"Convers—?"

"Can they shoot?" barked Siringo.

"I can work a gun if I have to, but I'm not an expert. Yuri is; he hunted tigers in Siberia. I can't say about the rest."

"Round 'em up."

Charmian said, "Tell them it's voluntary. I can't ask them to put themselves in danger just because I pay them to work the ranch."

"Miz London, there ain't a thing all them men wouldn't do for anybody named London. If it wasn't for your husband, I'd still be in San Quentin. Every one of 'em's got a story like it."

"Thank you. These men are in charge. I hope you can put any bad feelings behind you."

Ivan stared at Siringo for a long moment. Then he held out his hand. "Sorry about the hat."

"They don't last long here." Siringo accepted his powerful grip. "Sorry about the nose. I was saddle sore and took a bigger swing than intended."

The ranch hand grinned, displaying some gold plate.

"I guess where you're concerned a man has to look out for either end."

When he left, Hammett and Siringo began snatching weapons off the walls and from cases. When they were finished, the dining table was an arsenal of shotguns, rifles, revolvers, and semiautomatic pistols, representing many manufacturers from many countries. Siringo pulled the drawer filled with cartridges out of the display case and laid it across the arms of a rocking chair. "Start loading," he said.

All four got to work.

———

"What are you doing?" Becky demanded.

She found Hammett seated in her father's study, working his bandaged foot into a high-topped brogan he'd found in a cupboard.

"Working a jigsaw puzzle, can't you tell?" Wincing, he laced the shoe tight.

"You're going to make your injury worse."

He stood, testing his weight on the foot. "Time enough to recover after today. Meanwhile it gives me support." He grinned at the unmatching footwear. "I may not make the cover of a gents' magazine, but I'm no good to anyone wobbling around on a cane."

"What are you going to do?" She followed him into the main room.

"Mr. Siringo and I discussed it. I'm setting up shop in the stable. That way we can catch anybody who tries to charge the house in the crossfire." He selected a gas-loading Mauser rifle from the weapons on the table and hefted it. The boxes of ammunition had been sorted and placed beside the firearms they belonged to. He loaded the magazine, racked a cartridge into the chamber, and put the box in his pants pocket.

Siringo came in, accompanied by Charmian. "You was in the army," he told Hammett. "How are you at drill?"

"Better than I was at driving an ambulance. I never killed anyone on the parade ground."

All four picked up as many firearms and boxes of ammunition as they could carry and went out into the front yard, where the ranch hands waited in a ragged line. Hammett approached Yuri, the Russian with the imperial whiskers, and showed him a bolt-action rifle of Scandinavian manufacture. "Know how to load it?"

The slope-shouldered worker snatched it and the box from Hammett's other hand, slid open the breech, poked a long brass-shelled cartridge with a copper nose inside, and slammed the bolt home.

Hammett went down the line, handing out rifles, handguns, and ammunition until he ran out, then got more from Charmian and Becky. Standing there afterward, some holding long guns, others with revolvers and pistols stuck under their belts and in the bibs of overalls, they looked like peasant rebels.

Hammett had raided a dump in back of the house of empty coffee tins, lard buckets, and glass jars. He rammed kindling sticks from the fireplace into the ground, hung the vessels on top, ordered the men to stand thirty yards away, and had them fire one by one, indicating to each which target he was to shoot at. When everyone had fired six times, he told them to put up their weapons and inspected the results.

He signaled them to follow him to the yard where they'd stacked their farm implements in a pyramid. He disarmed Ivan and two men whose names he didn't know and told them to take their pick from the stack. "If you can get close enough to lop off someone's head with a scythe, do it," he said. "Otherwise I don't want any one of you birds within a hundred feet of a trigger."

Siringo took command, sending Ivan to the house to watch the back and sing out if anyone tried to dry-gulch Yuri while he guarded the front, Ivan to the stable for the same reason regarding Hammett, and distributing the others among the pigpens and other outbuildings.

"And you, Mr. Siringo?" asked Charmian. "Where will you be?"

He pointed at the concrete-block silo. "I saved the best view for myself."

She glanced down involuntarily at his bad leg. He grinned.

"I trust my old complaint over Hammett's new one. Anyway, last time I was under siege, I had to go down to get out. This time I'm going up."

"And I?"

"You and Becky load for Yuri and lay low."

She raised her chin. "I'm as good a shot as Jack was. We hunted pheasants together from the time they were imported from China until he was too ill to go."

"Pheasants ain't men."

"I agree. They're twice as fast and they can fly."

"Okay, I know when I'm licked. Becky, you're loading for your stepmother. Ivan can load for Yuri. That way we got guns on both sides of the house, which I like better."

"I can shoot, too," Becky said.

"Somebody has to load."

"But why me? Why not Roberto?"

"Who's Roberto?"

"I am Roberto." This was a stocky Hispanic who had proven as inept with percussion arms as Ivan. He was armed with a hay hook.

Siringo shook his head.

"Roberto scares the pants off me with that corkscrew. That's worth something. Anyway, you're the youngest here, and out-ranked."

"Very well." But her eyes blazed defiance.

Hammett cradled his Mauser and took out his flask. Siringo scowled.

"If that don't improve your aim, put it up."

"What's the difference? It's a suicide play any way you look at it."

Siringo took the flask from him and raised it. "Pinkerton men." He drank.

"Good-bye, my lover, good-bye." Hammett took it back and swigged.

Charmian held out a hand. He lifted his brows.

"Jack taught me to drink, too." When she had it, she smiled. "Gentlemen; Becky. To the call of the wild." She emptied the flask.

30

Siringo slung his Winchester over his shoulder, made sure his Colt was secure in its holster and the Forehand & Wadsworth belly gun under his belt, and climbed an iron ladder up the side of the cement-block silo. When he clambered onto the roof, he was grateful to find that it was concave rather than convex, giving him a sounder purchase and a circular rim that concealed him from anyone on the ground when he lay on his stomach behind it.

It was more than twenty feet high and gave him a spectacular view of the ranch with its rolling hills, towering redwoods, and miles of vineyards. The thick vines curled about the pickets that supported them, resembling battlefields he'd seen in photographs taken during the Great War, decorated with coils of barbed wire. He hoped they'd slow down the assault the same way they had in France.

He saw the ranch's old wooden silo a hundred yards off, the great boulder beneath which Jack London slept off his roistering life, the jagged ruins of Wolf House sticking up like the petrified bones of some great animal dead since before Man, and wished again that Charmian would have the gaunt rafters bulldozed and buried instead of shackling herself to a corpse.

Everything he'd read by and about London celebrated life in its full ferment and decried death and destruction, while here in the heart of his chosen country, disappointment and loss was on exhibit as if it belonged to an extinct civilization. Dwelling on the past did no one good. When Siringo himself wrote about it, it was gone—except when it came bounding back from cover like a rebel bushwhacker.

———

Tom Horn made a tight six-foot-five squeeze through the trap into the cattle car on the A.T. & S.F. The Agency had advanced him a hundred in cash to ride the rails on a robbery investigation, and he'd lost it all on one turn of cards.

Siringo was "Charlie Cully" then, sent by the Agency to spell Horn, who was needed to testify in Albuquerque. He lent Horn money to get there, but he managed to lose that, too, and the last Siringo saw of the big jug-eared galoot was when Horn gave the brakeman his last dollar to put him in the stock car and then his shorn head lowering itself through the hole. He would spend the rest of the long trip from Coolidge hanging onto the hay rack to keep from being slashed to pieces by the longhorn steers below: a Horn among horns.

Then again, when Tom was braiding a lariat in a cell in Wyoming, killing time while waiting to mount the scaffold, Siringo supposed he looked back on that journey with a wistful expression.

———

No sign of intruders yet. He sat with his back to the rim, the carbine across his lap and his legs stretched out, waiting for the blood to stop pumping pain to his knee. When he turned his head to survey the grounds near the cottage, he saw the barrel of Hammett's Mauser sticking out the stable window that the eel's bullet had shattered—was it only a week ago?—Charmian's Greener, a handsome English shotgun that could finance rebuilding Wolf

House, if only she could bear to part with it, and the pigpens bristling with more artillery. From his position he saw far more than anyone else on the spread, legitimate residents and otherwise.

He took out his pipe, but he didn't charge it. There was no good purpose in calling anyone's attention to his smoke. The stem felt good between his teeth and took his mind off his knee.

Charlie Siringo reckoned that he'd had a good ride any way you studied it. He'd looked into Kid Curry's cross eyes, the eyes of a killer, and lived to write about them, sung range songs with Billy Bonney, cheated a lynch mob in Gem, survived smallpox, and stood close enough to see men blown to pieces with dynamite, coming away with only a ringing in his ears that came back on quiet nights. If it all ended here, he came out ahead on points.

"Leastwise it beats sitting around the house watching the roof leak," he said aloud.

———

Hammett, sitting on Abner Butterfield's milking stool, leaned his Mauser against the windowsill and reached down to loosen the lace on the brogan. He rolled a cigarette, didn't light it, hung it on his lower lip, and looked out the window, scanning the buildings and terrain. Siringo was out of sight atop the silo, but the man who looked for them could spot the weapons belonging to Charmian and the men on the ground. As he was watching the house, Becky bent to say something to her stepmother, caught his eye, and straightened when he raised a hand in greeting, removing herself from his line of sight.

He grinned wolfishly and listened to the horses snorting and shuffling in the stalls on the other side of the partition.

A high harsh whistle pierced the air, coming from atop the silo.

Siringo took his fingers out of his mouth, removed his Stetson, and rolled over onto his stomach, peering over the metal rim at the line of motor vehicles coming up the ranch road, Sheriff Vernon Dillard's big Dodge in the lead. He rested his Winchester on the rim and drew a bead on its tombstone-shaped radiator, but he held his fire. The procession wasn't inside range of the firearms at ground level, and the cars were passing between thick stands of redwoods; if the sheriff and his posse comitatus decided to bail out and take to the trees, there would be no smoking them out. He hoped the others wouldn't be tempted to start the ball early.

With that thought in mind he watched anxiously as the motorcade continued at walking pace. Besides the touring car there were a couple of Ford roadsters, a Hupmobile, and a T truck. He wondered if it was the same one in which Lanyard had made his escape after shooting at Butterfield, and if it was the eel driving.

He counted five in the Dodge, two in each of the roadsters, and six more in the truck, including four in the bed, clinging to the stakes. The light caught shiny bits of metal he took for badges, but they wouldn't all be deputies: The county wasn't rich enough to afford that many on the payroll. Dillard must have deputized half the village.

Amateurs, then, most of them; or at least not full-time lawmen.

Which didn't encourage him, not even a little bit. He remembered the trigger-happy p.c. shooting bloody hell out of that line shack that was supposed to contain Billy the Kid and getting nothing for all that expenditure of lead but one dead armadillo. And since there were no armadillos handy, that left two ex-Pinkertons, a parcel of ranch hands, and two women.

At length the last car cleared the woods. He leveled the

carbine again, aiming low at the Dodge. The sheriff was a dumb lug and belonged to Joseph P. Kennedy instead of the voters who put him in office, but Siringo had no interest in finishing out his career as a murderer of policemen. He centered his sights on the left front tire and tightened his finger on the trigger.

Something struck the iron rim not six inches to his right, striking a spark and peppering his cheek with bits of rust. He heard the shot then, belatedly, bent by distance and wind, and dropped flat.

The report had not come from any of the automobiles, which were still moving, the noise of their motors probably having drowned it out to the ears of the occupants. Nor did it belong to the defenders: Looking up at the rim where it had been struck, he saw a scallop-shaped nick on its top, shiny where the bullet had scraped off the rust. It had to have come level.

He took a deep breath, mustering sand, and went up on his knees, shouldering the Winchester and snapping a shot at the top of the other silo. He hadn't dared take time to aim, presenting as he did so clear a target, and although he couldn't tell from that distance whether he'd hit anything, it didn't matter, because it got the result he wanted. He saw a tiny billow of smoke atop the wooden tower and went flat again, just in time to hear the slug crack the air inches above his head.

The damn dime novelists had gotten it right for once. The criminal had returned to the scene of his earlier crime.

31

When the first shot rang out, Hammett looked first at Charmian, then at the other guns inside his range of vision, including the one on top of the concrete silo. Siringo's hatless head appeared suddenly, then the spurt of flame from his Winchester. He didn't see where the third shot came from, but when Siringo ducked, he didn't have to.

"Mr. Hammett!" It was Charmian. "Who's shooting?"

"Mr. Siringo and the eel," he called back. "They both took the high ground."

"But, when—?"

"Get away from the window!"

Her head vanished below the windowsill just as something struck the frame, followed closely by the sound of the shot.

Hammett got up, moved the stool farther from his window, and laid the Mauser's barrel on the sill. "He's been here since Dillard's last visit!" he shouted. "The sheriff must've dropped him off before he drove in sight and worked his way around to the other silo. He didn't get into position till just now or he'd've picked at least one of us off when we came outside."

"Is Mr. Siringo all right?" came Becky's voice from inside the cottage.

"Hang on." He put his thumb and finger inside his mouth and whistled sharply through his teeth.

Another whistle answered from atop the near silo.

"He's fine!"

"What can we do?" Charmian asked.

Hammett reached down and tightened the lace on the brogan. "Start shooting!"

"At what?"

"The silo."

"It's too far! This shotgun—"

"Stop wasting time!"

The Greener bellowed, spraying pellets that fell many yards short of the wooden silo.

Hammett shouted again, cracking his lungs. "Everybody shoot!"

The salvo from the weapons in the hands of the laborers sounded like an army of axes chopping wood. Hammett clambered out the paneless window and charged the wooden silo, firing the Mauser from the hip. The powerful semiautomatic rifle pulsed in his hands. Something struck the ground at his feet, throwing a clump of dirt and grass at his pants cuff, but he didn't slow down. The next shot made a snapping noise in the air past his left ear. He ran and fired; and now Siringo was returning Lanyard's fire from the top of the concrete silo, as fast as he could lever in fresh rounds.

Hammett's hat flew off his head, either from his own slipstream or carried away by a bullet. The Mauser's magazine emptied with a click. He threw it aside, drawing the .38 from his belt, and fired it at the top of the wooden silo, which stood well beyond pistol range.

And now more guns spoke. Dillard and his posse had taken up positions and were throwing lead at the running figure.

He was wheezing, and his pace grew uneven; his injured foot had entered the fight on the other side. He was close enough to the silo to be aiming almost straight up. The ladder attached to the side was nearly within reach. He was lunging at it, groping with his free hand, when something struck him from behind with the force of a catapult. His fingers grazed a rung of the ladder as he fell.

———

Siringo saw him fall, but only on the periphery of his vision. He was concentrating on the silo opposite, firing until the Winchester clicked, then ducking below the rim to reload. He cursed as he fumbled more cartridges out of the box he'd brought, forcing himself to fill the magazine before resuming.

The wooden structure was just within range; he could hear the slugs chunking into the boards, see splinters flying, but the man atop it was careful not to present much of a target against the sky; when Hammett had gotten too close for Lanyard to shoot at him without standing up and aiming almost straight down, he concentrated again on Siringo, and his shots were placed closer to his target. He must have had a telescopic sight and a gas loader with an enormous capacity, because the reports were so close together they sounded like one extended roar and he never stopped to reload. Siringo changed positions between shots, confounding the man's aim through the glass aperture, but his bump of good luck, and the eel's bump of bad luck, couldn't continue.

The sheriff and his men had found cover in scattered trees. They couldn't shoot up at Siringo's silo with any hope of hitting him, so they'd started snapping at the man running on the ground. There wasn't an expert shot among them, but then one of them got lucky. The old Pinkerton couldn't tell where his partner had been hit, but either it was a heavy round to knock him down at that range or it had found something vital.

Hammett's bump of courage must have been the size of a pumpkin. Siringo had never known a man—not Wyatt Earp or Pat Garrett or Billy Bonney or the whole goldarn Wild Bunch put together—who would run straight into crossfire when he could have stayed put and gone on breathing a little longer. He'd never see anything to compare with it, even if he survived that day.

And then—hell's bells!—he did see it.

Hammett breathed dirt.

He lay on his face with something hot and wet streaming at a leftward angle from his right shoulder and his pulse centered where it started. All the shooting now was coming from the cottage and pigpens and both silos; the sheriff and his men had stopped when their only real target had fallen.

Without obvious stirring, he groped for the .38 where it had fallen and thrust it under his belt, covering the movement with his body.

The ladder was useless. It stood squarely in the sight of the posse: If their aim hadn't improved except by luck, neither had his odds, and a man climbing a twenty-foot tower was hard to miss. He filled his lungs, emptied them, filled them again, coughed, pushed himself onto his hands and knees, and scuttled around the base of the silo, putting it between him and the sheriff's party just as a slug from their direction banged against the wood near the ground.

He rolled over into a sitting position, resting his back against the silo, and groped behind his right shoulder with his left hand. The skin of his back jumped when he found the wound. He dragged his handkerchief out of his inside breast pocket and stuffed it into the hole, gritting his teeth. Then he looked up at the silo, rising and narrowing for miles toward empty blue sky.

London's mania for innovation and modernization had not stopped with his writing. The storage building was rigged for automatic filling, with an electric motor on a concrete base, connected to an open bin and a copper pipe as big around as a man's arm running from the bin to the top of the silo: The silage was shoveled into the bin and propelled by suction up the pipe into the silo. What the pipe lacked as a ladder it made up for by its placement.

But a man had to be fast. He had to climb twenty feet of slippery copper before the posse grew bold enough to come after him and before the pain of the bullet in his shoulder paralyzed him.

He reloaded the .38 from his pocket, pulled himself to his feet, and began shinnying.

————————

"You dead, Hammett?" Siringo called out.

He didn't expect an answer. Thinking aloud kept a man alert. There was a lull in the shooting; either the eel had run out of ammunition finally or he was playing the waiting game, counting on Siringo to forget himself and present a better target.

Hammett had vanished behind the wooden silo, whether to die or work some angle couldn't be known.

The posse was getting curious. Siringo saw the sheriff lean out from behind a redwood, sweeping an arm in the direction of Lanyard's silo. The man he was looking at, a badge-wearer crouched at the base of a neighboring tree, shook his head violently.

Siringo grinned. In every party of manhunters there was always one who placed his life before his job.

It was the volunteers you had to watch for: ordinary men who got a boot out of playing cowboys and Indians.

This time it was a skinny runt in a tweed suit and an argyle sweater, a bank clerk or sub-assistant postmaster. He waved to Dillard from behind his tree and started off at a slow walk, bracing his rifle against his hip like a great white hunter stalking a wounded lion.

Siringo decided not to wait for the man to trip and shoot himself in the head. When he was halfway to the silo, the old Pinkerton chucked a round past his head that sent him swiveling and running for cover, throwing away his weapon in favor of speed.

It was such an amusing sight Siringo forgot the eel.

A blow to his mouth rattled his bones and he ducked below the rim, the stem of his pipe still clamped between his teeth. He'd forgotten it was there until the bullet shattered the bowl. He spat out the stem and checked for more damage. A molar wobbled when he tested it. It was one of only two he had left. His luck; it was the good one.

He told himself to concentrate on the work. Eating soup at every meal got old fast.

———

People who talked about climbing a greased pole had never tried it.

Hammett had to stop every few feet, wrapping an arm around the copper pipe while he wiped his other palm on his coat, then reversing arms and wiping the first. The hands shook, not from fear but from increasing weakness. His wound was bleeding again despite the handkerchief he'd stuffed into it. How long a man had before he bled out was something Pinkerton didn't teach.

The first shot in a while barked on the other side of the silo. The shot that came behind it was much closer; the vibration of the recoil made his hands buzz on the pipe.

It had nothing to do with him. He resumed climbing.

———

The sun was closing in on the western tree line. He figured the men on the ground were waiting for darkness before storming both silos. Lanyard would be waiting for the same thing. Siringo would have to show himself to stop the assault, and the sky offered no promise of a night without stars and moon.

He hoped Hammett wasn't dead, and not just because he'd miss the man's company.

———

His hand slipped. He caught himself with the other, but the movement brought the heavy brogan on his bad foot banging against the copper pipe. He was close enough to the top now to hear planks shifting when the sniper walked his way to peer over the rim.

There was no cover. Freeing one hand to grasp at his .38, Hammett slipped six inches and gripped the pipe again with both hands. He clung to the pipe and looked square into Edgar Edison Lanyard's eyes and then the muzzle of his rifle, a Browning semiautomatic with a magazine as big as a toaster. The man's straw boater was a flat disk pushed to the back of his head.

32

Hammett wasn't dead.

Siringo knew it when the silhouette of the other silo changed and he made out the outline of a man rising above the rim on the side opposite Siringo. The eel had detected someone approaching from that side. The darn yonker must've been part housefly.

This wasn't like plugging branches and scraps of waxed paper by the HOLLYWOODLAND sign. When you missed, they waited motionless for the next shot. He was only guessing that Lanyard's back was to him; he was just a shadow against the reddening sky. Siringo had to expose himself to draw a clear bead, and if he'd guessed wrong . . .

"God hates a coward, Charlie."

Jimmy McParland, the greatest Pinkerton who ever lived: hero of the Molly Maguire case, superintendent of the Denver office, and Siringo's personal idol, was walking square down the middle of Boise's main street, heading for an interview in the penitentiary, with dozens of eyes tracking his progress, and probably nearly as many firearms from behind cover.

The I.W.W. had blown up Idaho's ex-governor in his own home and the Wobblies had made it clear the Haywood-Pettibone-Moyer trials would nol-pros or others would join him.

And here was the old man bold as Biddy's garters, wearing the trademark bowler that had become part of the Agency uniform based on his preference, swooping handlebars, and gold-rimmed glasses, swinging the gold-headed stick that had been presented to him personally by Allan Pinkerton at the close of that affair. All that was missing was a bull's-eye painted on his chest.

"He may hate a coward, but that don't mean you have to be in a hurry to make His acquaintance."

"They're the yellow ones. They know if they try anything in a crowd they'll be kicking air long before those men in the dock. Look at Orchard: the worst murderer since John Wilkes Booth, and he didn't have the sand to plant his charge any closer than the front gate."

Harvey Orchard had killed twenty-six men for the miners' federation, including thirteen scabs in one dynamiting in Colorado. He was testifying against his accomplices in the Governor Steunenberg killing in return for a commutation of his death sentence, and it was him McParland was going to see. Siringo had been assigned to bodyguard the superintendent throughout the court proceedings. Every creak of a wagon, each slam of a door had him clutching the handle of his Colt fit to bust it.

"I guess cowards was smarter in your day. I knew plenty dumb enough to think he can outrun a mob."

"Maybe so, but if we show the white feather, who's to avenge our murders?"

Well, McParland survived, Orchard got life as a reward for turning state's evidence, and Haywood, Pettibone, and Moyer were acquitted anyway. It was after that McParland gave Siringo the gussied-up Colt he'd left behind in Los Angeles.

"It's a parade piece, but I expect it will brighten up that little room of yours."

"What for? The trial was a bust."

"You weren't. I'm alive."

"I didn't do nothing."

"Sure, you did. You walked a foolish old man down Capitol Street not six yards away from four sticks of dynamite."

"How can you be so specific?"

"We got a tip the next day."

"Why didn't he touch 'em off?"

"I sent men to ask him, but he blew himself up in his house when he saw them coming up the walk. Told you they're yellow."

───────

He wished now he'd brought that fancy rig along. Three guns didn't seem near enough under the circumstances.

He rose to his full height, such as it was, spread his feet, shouldered the repeater, aimed at the center of the silhouette on top of the other silo, and fired.

───────

Hammett shifted his gaze from the Browning's muzzle to the telescopic sight and through it to Lanyard's eye, shrunken by the reverse lens. It narrowed slightly, bracing for the recoil. Then it snapped open wide in surprise.

The report came after, fading as it walloped around among the hills. The rifle faltered. Hammett closed one fist tightly around the copper pipe and swept up his other hand, grasping the barrel and wrenching it out of the eel's grip, in the same moment hurling it away.

Lanyard, reeling from the impact of the distant bullet, disappeared. Hammett grasped the pipe in both hands again and closed the last three feet before the top in three seconds. His back was wet, his breathing sounding like steam exiting a ruptured boiler. He took hold of the iron rim that circled the top of the silo, raised his good foot, missed the rim with it, raised it again, hooked it with his heel, and pulled himself up and over.

Something flashed into his vision. He moved his head just as the eel's fist swept past his jaw and glanced off the top of his shoulder.

It was the wounded shoulder. He lost vision, and when it returned, he was lying on his back with the weight of the world on his chest and two hands closed around his throat. Something hot streamed under his collar and humid, whistling breath dampened his face. Lanyard's eyes bulged. His face, ordinary— invisible—in repose, was split from east to west by the rictus of his mouth and from north to south by a stream of red coming from a matted temple and the torn remains of one of his small, flush-mounted ears; the blood dripped from the corner of his jaw down inside his shirt and came out the cuff on that side where he was throttling Hammett. His hat was gone, his hair in his eyes.

Hammett couldn't get to the .38 in his belt; his assailant's weight was pressing too hard for him to work his weakening arm between their bodies. He groped in the pocket on his other side, felt something solid, and swung it in an upward arc, tearing the pocket and connecting with the center of Lanyard's head wound. Something collapsed beneath the brass knuckles; the gust of breath in Hammett's face robbed him of his own. Then the eel's eyes rolled over white. The grip loosened on Hammett's throat and he lay beneath Lanyard's lifeless weight.

———

How long they lay together couldn't be measured in terms of time.

When Hammett's heart rate approached normal, he heaved at the thing pinning him down, but it was like pushing at a sack of wet cement. He braced his hands and his good foot against the planks beneath him and tried to slide out from under. At first he was unsuccessful. He rested again, braced again, tried again. He gained an inch. Three more attempts, with rests in between, and he'd gone six. With one last lunge he shoved his body free, then hauled his leg and arm out into the open.

Sweet oxygen filled his lungs. He tasted it for a while, then dragged himself to the rim, grasped it, and hauled himself erect. Leaning with his hands on the rim and his back to the horizon he looked down at the man sprawled at his feet. He stared at him a long time. The stirring of his back was a fragile movement, the breathing shallow enough to be taken for the action of a breeze from outside. Unbelting the .38, Hammett knelt and placed his ear against the man's back. His heart beat. Rested. Beat.

Hammett stood, cocked the hammer, and took aim at a point between Lanyard's shoulder blades. Then he lowered the hammer gently, returned the weapon to his belt, and bent to grasp the man by his collar with both hands. His own back was drenched with his draining strength, but after a few tries he began to make progress, dragging the eel toward the silo's rim. Hauling him up and over took most of the rest of his stores. He had him draped over the top and was resting again before the final push when Siringo's voice called behind him.

"Don't bother, son. Can't you see he's dead?"

The young man bent again, listened. The beating had stopped.

For the second time in his adult life, Dashiell Hammett wept.

33

"You're all under arrest."

Becky London giggled, clapped a hand over her mouth.

Hammett grinned. It was the first flash of humor to appear on the girl's grave pretty face.

Siringo told him to keep still.

Hammett was straddling a chair in the cottage kitchen, stripped to the waist, gripping the back of the chair with both hands, as the old Pinkerton finished cleaning his wound with hydrogen peroxide. Hammett's skin jumped at the contact.

They had a clear view through the doorway into the dining room/parlor of Vernon Dillard and his men standing unarmed with their hands raised, staring at the weapons in the hands of the grim-faced ranch laborers, the shotgun Charmian held. The residents of Beauty Ranch had kept the posse at bay while Siringo climbed down from the concrete silo and up the wooden one to assist Hammett.

Dillard repeated his announcement.

"Did you bring that warrant?" Charmian asked.

"No, ma'am, I sure didn't. I don't need no scrap of paper to keep the peace in my county."

"The law says you do. It says also that a citizen has the right to defend herself on her own property with all force necessary against an armed intrusion."

"Those men in the kitchen don't live here. They ain't got the right to attack a sheriff and his deputized officers."

"They do, because I asked them to help. But the only attacking done here was by you and your men, including that creature of yours on the silo."

"He ain't my creature. I don't even know who he is."

"Then you're a fool as well as a liar. You brought him here, turned him loose on my property, and you claim he's a stranger. On whose authority did you take that chance?"

"You can't prove I did nothing of the kind."

"It's a small village. I imagine someone saw you both in the car."

"Anybody says he did's a damn liar."

Becky seemed to grow weary of the circling conversation. She came into the kitchen. "Is it bad?"

"It's never good when metal hits flesh." Siringo unwound two yards of gauze from the roll from the first-aid kit and tore it loose with his teeth; the ones up front were complete and sound. "It's just luck the man that shot him was using a pistol. It was near the end of its range and the slug only went in an inch: A rifle round would of gone straight through and come out the front. It's there in the basin if you like souvenirs."

She looked at the bloody lump of lead and shuddered. "No, thank you."

Hammett said, "Good. I'll hang it on my watch chain."

"You'll need it. Your bump of good fortune's big as mine, but I wouldn't trust it."

"I should be the one tending him," Becky said.

"All due respect, miss, you're a whiz with a blistered foot and a cracked head, but I was patching up gunshot wounds when your father was in knickers. I'm good for something, if not sharp-shooting. Good thing I tried for the back and not the head, or I'd of got sky. Mr. Hammett done the rest with his pocket jewelry."

"It was too good for him at that. I wish he'd kept breathing long enough to take the same trip he sent me on."

"That ain't Christian, boy."

"Daddy would approve," Becky said. "He believed in praying only to humanity."

Charmian's voice rose in the other room.

"I will offer you a bargain, Sheriff. Tell me who sent you and I'll promise not to prosecute."

"Nobody sent me. A complaint was made and I carried it out."

"Very well." She turned. "Becky, use the telephone and get Mr. Rance at the *Morning Call*. He was an admirer of your father's. I doubt even Mr. Clanahan's friends in Sacramento will interfere with the process of justice once the world's read about the Battle of Beauty Ranch."

Dillard's big face lost its high color, but only for a moment.

"You don't want to do that. There's a little matter of a murder committed."

She slid her gaze along the men of the posse, shifting their weight from foot to foot with their hands near the ceiling.

"You all saw what happened. Will you testify under oath that Mr. Siringo acted from any other motive than to defend his partner's life from a man who will certainly prove to have been implicated in murders of his own?"

To a man they all looked down at the floor.

"Mr. Siringo, what's the penalty for perjury in a homicide trial?"

"I can't answer for today, but in my time it was the rope, same as accomplice to murder."

"We'll err on the side of mercy and agree it's life imprisonment. Gentlemen, I ask you, is it worth it?"

"It wasn't murder. It was kill or see murder done."

The man who had raised his eyes to hers was the man in the tweed suit Siringo had sent scurrying back to the trees with one shot. His pugnacity seemed to have been spent in that failed attempt at glory.

"Becky, place that call."

"Hang on." Siringo had tied off the bandage binding the gauze to Hammett's shoulder. He stepped into the main room, looking up at the ceiling. There was a yawing noise just above the roof, close enough to vibrate the panes in the cottage windows.

Charmian said, "There's a private aerodrome just down the road. We're always being disturbed by amateur pilots pretending to be Eddie Rickenbacker. It upsets the hogs."

He went to the window and looked out. "You better hope this one's no tenderfoot. He's coming in for a landing, and them hills don't look any too accommodating."

Charmian leaned her shotgun in a corner beyond reach of the captives and joined him at the window, followed by Becky and Hammett, drawing on one of Jack London's shirts. It was too big in the collar and too short in the sleeves.

It was dusk and the biplane had its running lights on, but its pale fabric-covered wings and fuselage were visible in the rays of the setting sun. It flew east. It seemed to float entirely on the air, a fragile-looking thing of wood and canvas that resembled nothing so much as a box kite. The moaning sound of its engines seemed separate from the craft, as if added as an afterthought, in case it failed to stay aloft forever on nothing more substantial than warm air from the ground. It bore no markings.

It descended gradually, the wings dipping on the right side, then trading places with the left by way of some adjustment by the pilot. Just as the wheels seemed about to touch ground, its engines swelled and the nose pointed skyward, placing more space between it and the horizon. It shrank in the distance, then turned back westward, its nose flashing as it caught the sunlight. From that point on it seemed to grow steadily, its propellers roaring louder, its course stable, wobbling only when its wheels encountered a wave of heat escaping from the earth. They touched down, bounced, touched again and stayed. Siringo heard the hogs squealing and snuffling in the pens.

The plane continued directly toward the cottage, its engines slowing, until it turned in a lazy half-circle facing east again and then there was silence. The propellers slowed, seemed to rotate briefly in the opposite direction, and stopped.

The man in the front cockpit vaulted down to the ground easily and strode around the machine, working the tail rudder manually and kicking the tires. The man in the rear climbed out more awkwardly, found his land legs, and started toward the cottage, unstrapping his leather helmet, which didn't match his business suit. The last patch of scarlet sunlight flashed off the round lenses of his spectacles.

"Well, scald me live and call me pork," Siringo said. "I never saw such a one for gall since Billy Bonney."

"Who is it?" Charmian asked.

Hammett's teeth bared in a wolfish grin.

"It's himself. Joseph P. Kennedy, Senior."

34

Kennedy was smoothing the hair rumpled by the aviator's helmet when Charmian snatched open the door. She hadn't given him the chance to knock.

"Come in, Mr. Kennedy, and join your accomplices."

He smiled tentatively. The shotgun she was cradling inside her elbow appeared not to concern him.

"Have I the honor of addressing Mrs. London or Mrs. Shepard?"

"Mrs. London. I sent my sister-in-law away hours ago. I wanted to cut down on the casualties should things go badly."

"I'm pleased to make your acquaintance, although I won't accept the remark about accomplices. I am a law-abiding man."

"That you are a partner to murder and assault we shall discuss; but you are certainly a smuggler of illegal merchandise. Every bootlegger in California knows your name."

"I doubt every one. But thank you for giving me the benefit of the doubt as to the other."

She closed the door behind him and led him into the main room. Kennedy's smile crystalized when he saw the men standing with their weary arms raised inside a half-circle of men dressed as laborers. He looked from the assembly to the pile of confiscated weapons on the floor.

"You gentlemen have been busy, though I'll not say you worked. Where nothing has been accomplished, no work has been done."

"Will you tell these damn—" Dillard began.

"There are ladies present, Sheriff. I assume you *are* the local exemplar of the law?"

"I am; and who the he—heck are you?" Something in the quiet Irishman's demeanor seemed to quell his natural truculence.

"My name is Kennedy. Perhaps Mr. Clanahan mentioned me in passing."

"Oh." The big man seemed to shrink. "I'd be obliged if you'd ask these ladies to take away all this artillery and let us put down our hands. I can't feel mine no more."

Siringo spoke up. "You'll find two more rifles outside. Mr. Hammett dropped one belonging to London and another belonging to a man named Lanyard."

"Dropped them?" Kennedy looked at the young man seated in a rocking chair, a bamboo cane leaning nonchalantly against one knee and a stockinged foot resting on an ottoman. The smoke from his cigarette seemed to hang motionless in the air.

"I'm careless that way," Hammett said. "I also neglected to bring Lanyard down from the roof."

"I take it from your phrasing the man is dead."

Siringo said, "He was born dead. He just didn't acknowledge it till now."

"I hardly expect you to believe me, but I never heard the name until just now. I assume he's one of those unfortunate people Clanahan feels he needs to have around him in order to do business."

"I believe you," Siringo said. "You said you only bet when you hold the cards. That means you don't bluff."

Kennedy smiled at Becky. "Which daughter have I the privilege of meeting?"

"Becky. His youngest."

"Thank you, Mrs. London. Is the child mute?"

"I'm neither mute nor a child," Becky said. "My father taught me not to speak to strangers. Based on your performance here today, I find you stranger than most."

"Spoken like your father. I never met him, but I've studied his speeches in the Socialist cause. I think the Democratic Party would do well to adopt some of his better ideas, such as old-age pensions and medical assistance. I recognized you by the eyes and the frontal development."

"She's got a bump of intelligence for a fact," Siringo said. "Also one of obstinacy, which I don't regard as a failing, except in the case of Dillard. A man who don't know when he's beat can't ever expect to win."

"Mr. Siringo. I wish I'd known who you were when we met in the Shamrock Club; Mr. Hammett too. Since then I've had ample opportunity to study your careers. Would you agree with me that these men are now quite harmless, and may be excused?"

Charmian said, "The decision's mine, as the mistress of this house. If you're too impatient to wait for my decision—"

"I am not, and I apologize. I assumed these men of action were in command upon your approval. It's always a mistake to assume something just because it seems obvious. Certainly it's bad politics. I defer to your authority; although may I point out that these men may be relied upon never to return to this ranch without your invitation, and to take no further action in regard to this affair on pain of humiliation at the least?" The predator's eyes behind the mild spectacles were trained on Dillard throughout this speech. The sheriff fidgeted.

"And at the most?" she asked.

"Incarceration, and possibly although not probably the rope. I have some influence in this regard—should I feel to exercise it."

She looked to Siringo, then Hammett. They offered nothing in return.

"Very well," she said after a moment. "But their weapons remain here until I see fit to return them."

"Hold on," said Dillard.

Kennedy's eyes were on Charmian. "Agreed. You know where to find them should you need to," he added.

She looked from one face to the other, as if burning the features into her memory.

"It's a small village," she said. "And Jack has many friends."

"Sheriff, you may go. Take your dead with you."

Dillard lowered his arms and shook circulation back into his hands. "Clanahan won't like it."

"What Clanahan likes and doesn't like has never been part of the matter. He's shortsighted. He can't see beyond the end of this man Lanyard's rifle. My vision goes much farther, to places where even the threat of murder carries no weight. Do you understand?"

It was clear from the look on Vernon Dillard's face that he didn't and never would. It was just as clear that he feared the things he didn't know more than the things he did. He looked at his men, jerked his head toward the door, and led the way out. Hammett smirked, started to say something; but Siringo caught his eye and shook his head. A man stripped of all his authority was as dangerous as a yellow coyote trapped in a corner.

———

"I've heard wonderful things about your wine," Kennedy told Charmian, when the last motor had throbbed out of hearing, taking the eel's body with it. "I wonder if you might take pity on a man who's survived his first ride on an aeroplane. The year I was born, Boston was still celebrating the miracle of the horse-drawn trolley."

"You'll pardon me if I don't join you. Jack wouldn't approve of my drinking with a potential murderer."

"I hope to dissuade you of that opinion before this conversation is through."

"Can I get you gentlemen anything?" she asked the others.

"I wouldn't mind having some of that beer," Siringo said. "Shooting's thirsty work."

Hammett said, "Beer for me, too. And a ham sandwich, if it isn't too much trouble. Surviving's hungry work."

"What would you like, Becky? We have fresh buttermilk."

"Could I have a beer?"

Charmian frowned.

"Really, Charmian. It's illegal for us all; and I think I've earned it."

She nodded and left.

"Well, sir, what shall we talk about?" Kennedy sat in a rocker with his legs crossed, the crease in his trousers perfect, the aviator's helmet on the table at his elbow and a glass of Jack London Vineyards in his hand.

Siringo, to whom the question was addressed, looked at Charmian, a woman who asked no superfluous questions. She unlocked the drawer of one of the display cabinets, drew out Hammett's notes, and brought them to Siringo, who tilted his head toward Kennedy. She frowned, but did as directed.

Kennedy glanced at the top sheet and dropped the notes in his lap. "You know, I could prosecute you for theft."

"Seems you started something along them lines."

"Clanahan's a fool, and shortsighted besides. The first affliction is universal. The second is congenital. He'll finish out his political career in the penitentiary."

"Dead, more like," said Hammett. "It's a brave new world."

"I assumed he'd go through the proper channels. If he'd come here with a warrant, it would have saved everyone a world of trouble." He sipped at his cabernet, directed an appreciative expression at Charmian, who sat stone-faced in the rocker facing him. "I blame myself, of course. I'd be a poor politician if I did not. I expected too much of my associates when I should have dealt with the business directly.

"I knew nothing of this man Lanyard. I don't expect you to accept that, but it's the truth nonetheless. What are you asking for the original?"

"That's up to Mrs. and Miss London," Siringo said. "It's this spread we're sitting on that's at stake."

"They have nothing more to be concerned about in that regard. As of this moment, Beauty Ranch and *The Valley of the Moon* are immune to a transaction that should never have been undertaken in the first place."

"Becky?" Charmian looked at her stepdaughter, who hadn't yet touched her glass of beer. Siringo was certain she'd never held one before in her life.

"I don't know what to say."

"Not an admission confined to youth," Charmian said. "Mr. Siringo? Mr. Hammett?"

Hammett sipped beer. "I want to know what all this has to do with Teapot Dome; and with a ten-year-old kid in San Francisco who wants to be president."

Kennedy smiled at Siringo. "Well, sir?"

Siringo wrapped his hands around his glass of beer. The cold felt good. Not too long ago he hadn't counted on ever feeling anything again. "I want what Mr. Hammett wants. You can take the man out of Pinkerton, but you can't take the Pinkerton out of the man."

"Well put. I'm curious, also: Aren't we all? These amounts don't constitute evidence in any court. They could as well be suggested wagers, which although illegal in most states are hardly worth justice's time, had it any to squander. What I say from here on in must be regarded as confidential to these premises. Yes?" He looked to Charmian.

Siringo said, "I'll do the negotiating. I've had to deal with criminal enterprise in the past. So has Mr. Hammett, but he's less experienced. I'll let you know when we're wandering into dangerous territory for you."

"Fair enough. My people have done enough homework to assure me you're a man of your word, as am I, whatever else you may think of me. Ask your questions, and I'll let *you* know when we're wandering into dangerous territory: Your phrase, and I'd be a shanty-Irish idiot if I thought I could come up with a better one."

"Were you hoping to buy into this oil business?"

"Quite the contrary. It was—it's still—my hope that I can squash this scandal involving my political enemies before it reaches the press. It would be disastrous to my plans."

35

Charmian said, "I don't understand. The embarrassment would be to the Republican Party. You said you're a Democrat."

"I am, and when the timing is right, nothing would gratify me more than a scandal of these proportions shattering the opposition. Unfortunately, the public's memory is short. Within two presidential terms, unless my party succeeds in everything it attempts—which is as unlikely as it is unprecedented—some fair-haired fellow with the GOP will manage to charm and connive his way into office.

"Politicians' memories are made of sterner stuff," he went on. "If Teapot Dome breaks now, my esteemed opponents will be especially careful in their nominations: In their quest for a candidate who never did anything wrong, they'll probably propose a dodo who never did anything. That may work to our benefit, or it may not. Warren G. Harding is a fool of the first water, but the electorate fell for him because he takes a distinguished photograph. The upshot is, we won't see an opportunity this promising for generations."

Hammett inserted his grating chuckle into the conversation.

"I get it. You're interested in the next generation, not two or three down the road."

"Precisely. Too much foresight can be worse than none at all. My boy Joe is a level-headed youngster, whom I think will make a fine president in twenty-five years, reflecting well on our party, our family, our heritage, and our faith. I'm not so certain about little John; he shows signs of being covetous, which in maturity can take a lecherous turn. I expect to father more sons, but for all I know the next will be completely inadequate. A strain of moral cowardice runs through the Fitzgerald side of the family."

Siringo said, "You wanted to squash this bug and save it for later."

"Yes. You'd make a fine orator, Mr. Siringo. I admire your bluntness. I can see how you managed to impress Handy Muldoon."

"I hope I didn't get him in trouble. I never seen a better right cross, in or out of the ring."

"You needn't worry about that. The man is useful."

"You mean those bribes—" began Becky.

"Incentives. I apologize for interrupting, young lady, but I intended to pay all the principals and their instruments involved in the fraud to behave honorably instead. I don't see how anyone could interpret offering someone a reward to do good an act of bribery."

"Here's some more of that bluntness you like so much," Hammett said. "A man like Secretary Fall would take your dough and go on as usual. There will always be a Doheny to pay him to do bad, and a Fall to take the money."

Siringo looked at Charmian. "It's what I was telling you before. You can't feed a puma and turn it into a housecat."

"I concur." Kennedy sipped wine. "However, my investors agreed with me that if we divided their shares in the proper amounts and directed them enough places, the more cautious cats in the pack would restrain people like Fall, and possibly even alert Harding to the perils of weak leadership." He smiled without mirth. "It's a thin hope, I confess. Like you gentlemen I know that what my colleagues call a dishonest buck will always find a home. But not on this scale, and considering the odor it will leave if we fail, not soon enough for my plans. I intend to live long enough to see a Kennedy in the White House."

"With that notebook we could put one in the big house right now." Hammett drained his glass and thumped it down.

Kennedy stopped smiling, and it was as if no such expression had ever found a foothold on that stoic face.

"I misjudged Clanahan. I gave him sufficient money, and the promise of much more, to make force unnecessary. Instead of using it to grease the wheels, he paid an assassin to eliminate them entirely and kept the rest for himself, when he could have been vastly more wealthy if he'd done as I directed."

"He plays careful poker," Siringo said. "Too careful. He could have been secretary of the Treasury, but he went for table stakes."

"Not under any administration I supported. It would be disastrous to give him the key to the Bank of America. He's through. Tomorrow everyone in the state will read the details of his private affairs on the front page."

"What if he talks?" Siringo asked.

"He has no proof. As far as the world is concerned, we're casual acquaintances who met at the Harvard Club for a friendly game of poker."

Charmian said, "I don't believe you had nothing to do with the eel. You're a bootlegger, a base smuggler. 'Scratch a crook and see a liar,' Jack used to say."

"This morning I divested myself of all my interests in the liquor trade. The decision was a relief. I was never comfortable dealing with the class of person I was forced to in order to raise the funds I needed in order to raise more. I suppose you could make the case that even if I was ignorant of the path Clanahan chose I'm guilty of being an accessory to murder and attempted murder, but I doubt it would ever go to a jury. You've seen my list."

"Come this time tomorrow, they'll all be out on their ears," Hammett said. "Even if those *were* just wagers."

"That list would certainly bring down the Democratic Party, as well as its Tammany division. That would guarantee a second term for the most corrupt administration since Grant's. However, we can spare ourselves a great deal of misery. What will you accept for that notebook?" Kennedy reached inside his suit coat and brought out a gold fountain pen and a checkbook bound in green leather.

Charmian said, "I don't want your filthy money."

"Nor I," said Becky.

Kennedy's brows lifted above the rims of his glasses. He turned to the old Pinkerton. "Mr. Siringo?"

"Talk to Hammett. He's got possession. I only stole it."

"Mr. Hammett?"

Hammett stretched out his bad foot. The bandage Siringo had applied to his bullet wound made a white slash inside the open collar of Jack London's shirt, a heroic effect.

"How do I know once you get what you want you won't come after us?"

"I can't convince you I'm not the monster you think me, but you're an intelligent young man. Surely you can see what Clanahan would not: that even without evidence, the accusation alone of participation in this venture would exile me from politics forever."

"That's certain," Siringo said. "I got paid to bury a parcel of horseshit in my day; begging you ladies' pardon."

Hammett nodded.

"Money's not dirty," he said, "just some of the hands it passes through. But it can ruin a man with ambition. If I had money, I'd never write a word. But there's a matter of all those notes your people bought up when you wanted to swipe the ranch."

Kennedy laid the checkbook in his lap, reached inside another pocket, and brought out a fat wallet with a clasp. "Are you thinking of going into the wine business?"

"I'm strictly on the consumer end. Give it to Becky."

"One moment," said Charmian, as he was rising.

He waited.

"Am I correct in assuming you've abandoned your original plan to buy off all the people involved in the scandal?"

"You are. I am an investment counselor, and it's time I listened to my own counsel. There is a time to stay the course and a time to cut your losses, and the first rule of investment is never to use all your own money. This new plan is far less certain of success, but it falls within the means we have now that the vineyards have lost the appeal of secrecy."

She sprang out of her chair before Kennedy could get up. He handed her the wallet. "You'll find most of them there. Any others that are still outstanding would have no effect upon the disposition of the property. You're out of debt, Mrs. London; Miss London. Congratulations. I haven't done so well I don't recall the feeling."

Hammett said, "Now it's Siringo's turn. I wouldn't have the notebook if he didn't steal it."

Siringo rubbed his sore knee for a moment. Then a grin slid across his features. "What's a new roof cost?"

36

"Mr. Siringo—"

"I wisht you'd call me Charlie."

She shook her head with a smile, wrinkling her nose. "I'd rather keep this on the same basis where it started."

"What was you about to say, Mrs. London?"

"Is your leg up to a brief walk? I think Becky and Mr. Hammett would appreciate some privacy."

"He's getting married in June."

"It shows, though he doesn't seem to know it. She's quite capable of looking out for herself."

"I see that. There's nothing wrong with my eyes."

The moon was nearly full, washing *The Valley of the Moon* in silver light. They walked down the lane that led between the stable and the pigpens. Despite the competition from both buildings, the smell of Kennedy's engine exhaust was still strong ten minutes after he and his pilot had taken off, bound for San Francisco and the package waiting in General Delivery. All the hands were back at work at their various chores.

"I had 'em all wrong," Siringo said, watching them. "They're a good bunch of fellows."

"They haven't had so much excitement since we lost Jack."

She caught him when he stepped in a small depression, wrenching his knee. "Should we go back?"

"No, but I wouldn't mind a little support just in case."

"You're incorrigible, aren't you?"

"I wouldn't say that, but there was a time."

"You could have been rich, you know."

"I had my shot at pay dirt before. It ain't as much fun as you'd think. It was my bad roof got me into this business. It don't pay to lose sight of things."

"You're just too modest to say you don't agree with Mr. Hammett about dirty money."

"Not modest, just the opposite. A lot of folks think you're a fool when you're honest, so you learn not to advertise it."

"What do you think will happen now?"

"I got to decide betwixt tin and wood shingles, and you can afford to blow up that pile of firewood you call Wolf House. I reckon Becky'll marry someone who ain't afraid of willful women and Hammett'll write *Moby Dick*."

"I don't mean that. I mean Teapot Dome."

"Nothing can stop that, now. We're all going to get sick reading about it. Some of the small fry will lose their jobs, that's sure, and one or two big shots for show. It don't signify, because this time next year or the year after, another gang of bandits will be in the saddle. Kennedy wasn't lying about folks' short memories."

"Do you think he'll get his presidency?"

"He didn't strike me as the kind to give up riding the first time he got throwed."

"Me, neither. How can I ever thank you for what you've done?"

"You won't let me court you, so let's just forget it."

"I wish you'd known Jack. He'd have liked you."

"Maybe. I ain't a Socialist, though."

"I've a confession to make. I have only the vaguest idea what Socialism is all about."

"It's an *ism*. That's all I need to know to ride clear of it."

"Do you ever wonder what it all means?"

They were at the corral now. They leaned their elbows on the top rail and watched the new stable boy leading Washoe Ban around the track. A puff of breeze brought the sweet smell of grain from the silos and blew a lock of Charmian London's black hair across her cheek. She reached up to push it away. Siringo smiled at her.

"This here," he said. "This right here is what it means." He kissed her good-bye.

Becky asked Hammett how he was feeling.

"I've been thrown off a train and almost off a silo, shot, hit on the head, and forced to listen to a political speech. Under the circumstances I'm swell. How about you?"

"I'm short of breath and my heart is pounding. I haven't felt like this since my father was alive."

"Maybe you've got the Spanish flu."

"What are you doing?"

He got up from his chair, levering himself with his bamboo cane. "I'm getting saddle sore like Siringo." He spun the cane's crook. "This is a peachy thing to carry. I think I'll hang onto it after I heal."

"I've treated you very badly, I'm afraid."

"Not as bad as the eel. But you were kind of rough on me just because I saw a pretty girl I liked."

"I think you're going to give your wife a hard time."

"You don't know Jose. She's a rock."

"Don't count on that just because she looks like she is." Her lower lip trembled.

He leaned over her chair, took her chin between thumb and forefinger, and tilted up her face. "I hope you find what you're looking for."

"You, too. I suppose you think I want some version of my father."

He let go. "I've got the advantage there. I never knew mine."

"Neither did Daddy, really. His father never acknowledged him. But he survived. Will you?"

"I've had plenty of practice."

She rose, went up on her toes, and gave him a brief peck on the lips. Hers tasted of a single sip of beer.

"First kiss?" He gripped her upper arms.

She smiled at last.

"Wouldn't you like to know."

He grinned.

"You're good. You'll be okay once you climb out from under your old man's ghost."

"As will you, once you get over the conviction the world owes you something because of a little cough."

———

Charmian called for a taxi. Siringo turned to look through the rear window at the two women standing on the front porch of the cottage.

"They didn't wave," he said, turning back around.

"Good. I never saw the reason for it. We said our good-byes."

"You ain't a sentimental man, Hammett."

"Nuts to that. I'm a romantic. I've got a question."

"Some detective. I got hundreds."

"When you go under the blanket and change your name, how come you always keep Charlie?"

"It's just smart. You never know when an old pard might see you and sing it out when you're with folks who think you're somebody else. Also you answer to it quicker. They take it suspicious when you don't right away."

"That *is* smart."

Hammett rolled a cigarette, concentrating on the operation.

"My first name's Samuel, you know. My friends call me Sam."

"Bully for them."

"Maybe I'll use it in a story."

Siringo reached for his pipe, then remembered. He let his hands drop in his lap.

"My middle name's Angelo. I don't use it anyplace. I'm part Mexican."

"Which part?"

"The middle part. Wasn't you listening?"

They rode for a while in silence, miles of vines rolling past the window.

"You going to get that new roof or drink up what Kennedy paid you?" Hammett asked as they turned onto the main road, leaving Beauty Ranch behind.

"Come see me next year and we'll find out."

Hammett grinned.

"Charlie, are you inviting me to visit?"

"Don't call me Charlie, you bomb-throwing bastard."

––––––––

They sang, startling the driver:

> "Oh, see the train go 'round the bend,
>   Good-bye, my lover, good-bye;
>   She's loaded down with Pinkerton men,
>   Good-bye, my lover, good-bye."

HISTORICAL NOTE

The Teapot Dome scandal exploded during the election year of 1924, as a congressional investigation discovered that Mammoth Oil magnate Harry Sinclair had advanced $260,000 in Liberty Bonds and Edward F. Doheny of Pan-American Oil had advanced $100,000 in cash as "loans" to Interior Secretary Albert M. Fall in return for receiving access to the vast California and Wyoming oilfields originally intended for the U.S. Navy; Fall was revealed to have persuaded President Warren G. Harding to transfer ownership to the Department of the Interior.

Under oath, Doheny testified that he had indeed sent his son to deliver the cash in a "little black satchel" to Fall, and remarked that he saw nothing wrong in lending money for personal profit.

The investigation resulted in criminal trials. Fall was sentenced to a year in prison for accepting a bribe from Doheny, but Doheny was found not guilty of paying any bribes. Sinclair, too, was acquitted, but years later was jailed on one count of contempt of the Senate and one count of contempt of court for hiring a detective from the Burns Agency, a rival of Pinkerton, to follow the jury panel around in one of his trials.

Although Sinclair was found to have made massive contributions to the Harding campaign, the president himself was never subpoenaed; he died in 1923—in California—of reported apoplexy, and was succeeded in office by his vice president, Calvin Coolidge, in a providential move that may have been chiefly responsible for a Republican victory that November. Rumors still persist that Harding was poisoned, either by officials in his administration hoping to defuse Teapot Dome or by his wife, Florence, out of jealousy over her husband's longtime affair with Nan Britton, who claimed to have borne his illegitimate daughter. (Although there is no evidence to confirm it, the last theory sheds a sinister light on Florence's comment when told Harding had secured the Republic nomination in 1920: "I can see but one word written above his head if they make him president: 'Tragedy.'")

Whatever the circumstances of his death, Warren Gamaliel Harding remains the standard against which every succeeding president is measured. He is considered our worst and most ineffectual chief executive, and Teapot Dome our worst national scandal, although there have been several runners-up.

Joseph P. Kennedy, of course, lived—barely—to see his second son, John Fitzgerald Kennedy, become the first Roman Catholic president of the United States. (His first choice, Joseph P. Kennedy, Jr., was killed while serving with the armed forces during World War II.) Before that, the only serious Catholic contender, former Governor Al Smith of New York, was defeated in 1928 by Herbert Hoover, who lost his reelection bid to Franklin D. Roosevelt, under whom Joseph Kennedy served as ambassador to the Court of St. James. Although nothing but this work of fiction suggests the elder Kennedy tried to quell an oil scandal in which he had no part, his activities in the bootlegging trade during Prohibition are legendary, and it may be significant that after John was elected, Rose, Joseph's wife, was quoted as saying that she saw nothing wrong with the family having bought her son's election.

This is a work of fiction. Apart from partnering two men who probably never met, I've taken certain liberties with the order of events in 1921, moving up the Fatty Arbuckle scandal, the first rumblings of Teapot Dome, and Hammett's move to San Francisco prior to his June marriage by a matter of months. However, the particulars of the lives of the two principal characters were as reported: While Charles A. Siringo and Dashiell Hammett were political opposites, both men left the Pinkerton National Detective Agency because they became disenchanted with its bullying tactics. Throughout his adventurous and literary life, Siringo, who had witnessed the bloody Haymarket riot in Chicago firsthand in 1886, despised radicals of any kind. Hammett, who deplored his time as a strikebreaker for the Agency, invoked the Fifth Amendment more than eighty times during questioning by the House Un-American Activities Committee in 1951, refusing to divulge details about his connection with the Communist Party, and served six months in federal prison for contempt of Congress. Wherever one stands on these matters, both men were remarkable for the courage of their convictions.

I ask the reader to forgive my use of literary license and to accept the truth of the historical personalities herein—particularly Becky London, who was so very kind to me in her final years.

Glen Ellen, best known to readers as the *Valley of the Moon*, is still home to Beauty Ranch, Jack London's last home and final resting place at the end of his colorful life, social activism, and influential literary career. It's maintained for tourists by the California state parks system and the Jack London Foundation, founded by the late Russ Kingman, Jack's biographer, proprietor of the Jack London Bookstore, and landlord pro bono to Becky London in her energetic old age, and Kingman's late wife, Winnie.

Wyatt Earp, whose name is synonymous with the gunfighting

West, denied any intention of a career in law enforcement. He went from boomtown to boomtown hoping to get rich in the tradition of robber barons Cornelius Vanderbilt and John D. Rockefeller, and pinned on a star in order to carry a firearm to protect his interests. He died, deep in debt, in a rented bungalow in Los Angeles in 1929. His widow, Josephine Sarah Marcus Earp, spent the next fifteen years polishing his reputation.

Samuel Dashiell Hammett, the man who gave us such icons as Sam Spade, the Continental Op, and Nick and Nora Charles, served in the U.S. military in both world wars, beat tuberculosis, and lived to revolutionize the detective story. He died January 10, 1961, in New York City at the age of sixty-six.

Charles Angelo Siringo, the "cowboy detective," who befriended and hunted Billy the Kid, infiltrated Butch Cassidy's Wild Bunch, wrote and published seven books based on his experiences as a working cowboy and private investigator, and in his last years helped adapt his memoirs for the silent screen, died October 19, 1928, in Hollywood, California. He was seventy-two years old.

He never did fix his roof.

ABOUT THE AUTHOR

Loren D. Estleman has won Shamus Awards for detective fiction, Spur Awards for Western fiction, and Western Heritage Awards. The Western Writers of America recently conferred upon Estleman the Owen Wister Award for Lifetime Contribution to Western Literature. He lives with his wife, author Deborah Morgan, in Michigan.

Learn more at www.lorenestleman.com.